I'd left my purse in the car, but my keys were in my pocket and I took them out. I had a small canister of pepper spray on the ring. I'd never used it but hoped to God it worked.

I slipped into the hall that ran between the den and the staircase. When I looked up I could see feet through the spindles. A man's feet. In heavy black boots.

He came down another step and I eased in the same direction. I would wait for him to reach the foyer, and if he turned in my direction I'd zap him with the spray.

Then, all of a sudden, he came the rest of the way down the stairs.

I lunged around the banister ahead of him, squirting the stuff as I went.

"You dirty bugger!" It was my grandmother's voice on the opposite side of the stairs, and she was holding a hiker's pikestaff.

She looked at me. I stared at her. And the man on the stairs used that split second to run like hell for the door.

But not before I recognized him. . . .

Divorce Can Be Murder

Victoria Pade

A Dell Book

Published by
Dell Publishing
a division of
Random House, Inc.
1540 Broadway
New York, New York 10036

This novel is a work of fiction. Names, characters, places, and incidents either are the product of the author's imagination or are used fictitiously. Any resemblance to actual persons, living or dead, events, or locales is entirely coincidental.

ISBN: 0-440-22646-5

Printed in the United States of America

Published simultaneously in Canada

January 1999

10 9 8 7 6 5 4 3 2 1

WCD

To my Rose Nell

ACKNOWLEDGMENTS

Here comes the boring Academy Award speech that matters only to me and those mentioned.

Thanks to my grandfather Nick Marone, who bought me my first typewriter and whom I'll miss forever.

Thanks to Jim and Doris Pade for more things than I can count.

Thanks to Maryann Immordino for keeping the old memories alive and for just being Mo.

Thanks to Cori and Erin for keeping me in touch and making me proud.

Thanks to Jim King for answering my cop and procedural questions and for the manual; I'm keeping my fingers crossed that you'll see your own words in print soon.

Thanks to Maureen Walters and Susan St. James—wherever you are, Susan—for not giving up.

Thanks to Maggie Crawford for letting me have a shot at this.

And special thanks to Maggie Osborne for what-ifing this book with me, contributing to crucial parts of the story, as well as to the more noble character traits of Jimi. Not to mention thanks for being a good friend.

Chapter One

"KILL HIM! I could just kill him!"

"We don't get into that until the sixth night," I said.

I was glad I was driving to the evening's meeting—the third in a series of ten that make up the Hunter Divorce Adjustment Seminars—because my neighbor Linda Kraner had a blood-anger level, to coin a phrase, way above the limit.

Not that it shocked me. I'm a veteran of the divorce angst she was in the middle of. I'm also a veteran of the seminars we were on our way to on that balmy October evening.

Linda had paid to take the Hunter seminars. I was back by special request as a volunteer. I'm Jimi Plain. Short for Jaimes Plain, named after my father even though I was the firstborn daughter instead of the first-born son. My folks weren't sure there'd be a second child so the first got to be Dad's namesake no matter what sex. I've always wondered if my younger brother resented that but never asked.

I'm thirty-nine years old, eight years divorced, the mother of two daughters and the owner of a terrific schnauzer named Lucy. I'm a freelance technical writer by trade—pamphlets, catalogs, brochures, prospectuses, training manuals, a little ad copy here and there. Basically I'm a writer for hire.

"The money's gone! Nearly every penny of it!" Linda wailed loudly enough to rattle the windows of my station wagon. No small feat; the Subaru is pretty sturdy. But then, Linda is no small woman. At five feet ten inches she towers over me by a good six inches, and I have no doubt she tips the scales at 220, a full hundred pounds more than I weigh. She has coal-black hair, which she wears in a mid-length poodle perm, brown eyes, a baby doll mouth, and jowls that were jiggling with fury at that moment.

I knew she'd had plans to spend some time at a fat farm once the divorce was over and wondered if this new turn of events canceled that idea. Not that Linda gives the immediate impression of being fat. She's one of those large women who can carry it. Plus she dresses well and expensively and moves with the poise of a dancer. But since her husband left her for a reed-thin twenty-two-year-old four months ago, her weight has been bugging her.

I'm sorry for that. I like her the way she is. She might not be the same Linda in a size eight. This Linda is a warm, compassionate, generous woman and a true friend.

She's also a good neighbor. Though not for much longer.

But I didn't want to think about the current upheaval in my own life right then.

"Do you know what this means, Jimi?"

"Nothing good."

"No, nothing good!" She turned and looked at me quizzically, as if she'd just realized we were headed in the wrong direction. "Where are you going?"

"We have to pick up Audrey. She called and asked for a lift. Her car is in the shop."

"I knew that. I just forgot. I went with her to drop it off yesterday after my session with her."

"How's the therapy going?" I asked more to diffuse a little of Linda's anger than because I expected her to tell me what was happening in her counseling sessions.

"Good." She answered almost as if I'd confused her. "You were right: Talking to Audrey isn't like seeing any old shrink. It's like bitching to a friend. Wait till I tell her this newest twist."

"She doesn't know?"

"I just found out about it today when my lawyer called to tell me our financial statements didn't agree as to what our marital assets are."

"Then you might as well save your breath and tell us both at once."

"I just can't believe it. I just can't believe it," Linda said like a mantra as she drew into herself for the rest of the ride to Audrey's.

Audrey Martin is a licensed psychologist who also happens to be a Catholic nun. As a therapist she sees people privately and also runs the Hunter groups in the evenings.

I'm not sure where being a nun fits into everything she does or what it involves beyond confession on Saturday, mass on Sunday, and turning over most of her earnings to the church, but I guess it does.

I'd met her when I'd signed up for the seminars myself five and a half years ago. She'd asked me to be a volunteer when my ten weeks were up and I'd done it a few times. But eventually I'd had to bail out for the sake of my own sanity. I could take once-a-week emotional wringers for only so long.

We'd kept in touch, had dinner a couple of times a year, and she'd been a good sounding board for a rough patch I'd gone through with my younger daughter the summer before last.

Since she'd done that over dinners instead of officially, I'd felt that I'd sort of infringed on our friendship and figured I owed her one. So when she'd called to say she was in a bind for a volunteer for her Monday night group at my end of town, the suburbs northwest of Denver, I didn't feel right about refusing. Back to the once-a-week emotional wringers.

On the other hand, my going to the seminars gave Linda the impetus to join the group, so I was glad of that.

I pulled up in front of the tiny apartment Audrey rents in a single-story redbrick six-plex. She was out the door before I honked.

I come from a Catholic background, so I've known some nuns in my time, but none quite like Audrey. She's a fair-size woman herself—probably five feet nine—but carrying less weight than Linda, 165, maybe 170 pounds. She has salt-and-pepper hair, cut shorter than a lot of men wear theirs, but her features are delicate and feminine, pretty enough, even at sixty, that there's really nothing masculine about her. Except maybe her eyebrows, which tend to be bushy. But aren't prominent eyebrows fashionable these days?

She also doesn't dress like any nun I've ever known. As usual, tonight she had on blue jeans, a lightweight turtleneck sweater, and penny loafers. The only indication of her vocation was a nondescript cross that hung around her neck on a gold chain.

"Hello, hello," she said as she got in back. "I really appreciate this, Jimi, but the mechanic called not five minutes ago, and my car is finally ready. If you wouldn't mind swinging by there, I can pick it up now so you won't have to bring me home later."

"Sure. Where to?"

She gave me directions but still didn't sit back once she did, staying on the edge of her seat to keep her face between our headrests like an eager, energetic child.

"Is something the matter, Linda? You look upset," she asked.

"I'm penniless," Linda said in a voice as flat and defeated as any I'd ever heard her use.

"You received his financial statement," Audrey guessed.

"And there's nothing there. Nearly every cent is gone. All the savings, including the retirement funds, the certificates of deposit, the money markets, all five kids' college accounts, everything."

"Where did it all go?" This from me.

"When my lawyer called his lawyer, his lawyer said Steve had to draw from our personal accounts to get the store stocked and up to speed. Then business has been so bad that every month he's had to take a little more and a little more until that's it. Nearly three hundred thousand dollars, and there's less than four thousand left to our name."

"He didn't tell you he was doing this?" Me again.

"The lawyer said Steve said he didn't want to worry me. Besides, Steve handled all the money anyway; he didn't check with me when he needed to make a withdrawal. I was only in charge of the household allowance he gave me every month. He did everything else, and we didn't talk about it."

That kind of dependence and blind trust was scarier to me than a chain saw massacre movie. But maybe I was jaded.

"What about the store?" Audrey asked. "Won't you get something out of that?"

"Steve's closing it. He has to sell all the inventory to pay his suppliers what he can, and then he may have to file for bankruptcy. He just overextended himself. Tried to start out too big instead of gradually building. The whole thing was a huge bust."

Steve Kraner had been the CEO of a major furniture chain in Colorado and the surrounding states until the first of the year, when he'd quit to open his own competing store. How could a man do so well with someone else's nickel and so lousy with his own?

"There's still the house," I said, thinking of my situation. "Since Steve essentially took and lost everything else, surely you're entitled to all the equity. Your place is bigger than mine, and you've been in it longer; that should amount to—"

"He second-mortgaged it to the hilt to open the store in the first place."

Neither Audrey nor I said anything to that. What could we say? Linda was right. She had just been financially wiped out.

"No wonder Steve has gone off the deep end," Linda said then, as if it had just occurred to her. "Imagine watching his dream crumble around him and keeping it all to himself. All the pressure. All the worry. All the fear. He must have turned to *Nan* out of desperation."

Nan was Nan Arnot, the reed-thin twenty-two-year-old. Linda never said her name without making it sound as if the word tasted bad.

"That must be it," she went on. "*Nan* must have been a way to escape from it all. Coming home to me and the kids must have been just a horrible reminder of how he'd failed us. Knowing he'd have to tell us the truth sooner or later must have made it pure hell to walk through the front door every night. He had to find comfort somewhere."

I glanced at the front passenger seat and found Linda staring out the windshield as if she were having a vision.

I was not so ready to feel sorry for Steve Kraner. I could sympathize with a guy who'd chucked a great job to open his own business. A guy who'd worked his tail off and for some reason watched that business not turn into the success he'd expected it to be. A guy who'd slowly siphoned off his personal assets trying to save it.

But a guy who'd hired a bunch of teenagers to run the place while he spent his afternoons in a hotel room with his girlfriend? My sympathy was harder to come by than that.

Audrey's gaze met mine in the rearview mirror, and I could tell her heart wasn't breaking for good old Steve Kraner either.

"Imagine him having to use even the kids' money," Linda continued, oblivious of us. "He must have felt so awful."

As awful as she'd felt since he'd announced on her birthday that he was leaving her for another woman? As awful as she'd felt when he'd stabbed her with the I-never-really-loved-you knife? As awful as she'd felt being left high and dry with five kids and no means of supporting herself or them? As awful as she'd felt when he'd been more conscientious about taking his vacation to Acapulco last month than about sending his support checks?

Maybe. But I had some trouble believing it.

"Poor Steve," Linda said more to herself than to us. "I wonder what I can do to help him."

From wanting to kill him to wanting to kiss his boo-boo. Ah, divorce! Better than mania for causing mood swings.

Audrey patted Linda's shoulder. "For tonight why don't we keep the focus on you?"

Linda sat up straighter in her seat, and when I glanced over at her this time, her eyes were so bright she looked feverish. "Maybe I shouldn't go to the meeting tonight. Maybe I should go see poor Steve, tell him I know now what he's been going through. That it's all okay. That he doesn't need *Nan* for comfort anymore. That now that I know what's been troubling him we can work on it together. It could be like things were when we were first married. We didn't have a pot to pee in, but those days of struggling, when we only had each other, were the best ones of our life. It could be that way again—"

"Do you think you might be getting just a little ahead of yourself?" Audrey asked.

"I *know* that's what's been going on. I *know* that's what wrecked our marriage. It wasn't that he didn't love me. It wasn't even that he loved Nan. It was all the business and money problems and keeping it all to himself. But now that I know everything I'm the best person to help him through it. I can talk to my family, get us a loan to help out. I can take care of him—"

"Did you read the chapter for tonight, Linda?" Audrey asked gently.

"Yes, but—"

"Parent-child relationships," she reminded her.

"I know. And I saw when I read it how I'd been like a child in the marriage, looking for Steve to be the parent. But that's just the point: I'm ready to be the adult, to take care of him now that he needs it."

"What you're talking about is trying to parent him. About just switching roles. But even if that were possible, or even if that were what Steve wanted, it would still be a parent-child relationship. A successful marriage needs to be a joining of two adults."

"Which I'm ready to be. I'm ready to take on my part as an adult."

"No, you're talking about trying to rescue him as if he were a child in trouble." Audrey managed to say this so kindly that it didn't set Linda off the way it would have if I'd done it. Instead, my neighbor just sat there quietly, as if she were thinking about it.

I spotted the transmission repair shop and pulled into the lot. A teenage boy in mechanic's coveralls was hosing off Audrey's old Buick.

"They fix it and wash it too?" I asked to lighten the tone and change the subject if I could.

"I get preferential treatment. I taught the owner his catechism when he converted in order to marry in the Church."

Linda seemed to hear what we were saying on a time delay and glanced out the window as if just coming from a trance to stare at the kid squirting off a dusting of clay-colored dirt.

"Why don't you ride with me the rest of the way?" Audrey suggested to her. "Jimi won't mind, will you? And we can talk a little more."

"That's fine with me," I put in. "I'll just have to follow you because I didn't bring my map or the directions. I was counting on Linda's navigations to get to this guy's house."

"Okay," Linda said absently.

I had a strong feeling that what was still absorbing my neighbor's thoughts was this sudden new plan to get her husband back. Too bad we weren't headed for week four's seminar, the stages of grief. The pitfalls of calculating ways to get the spouse to come back were part of that night's discussion.

But maybe Audrey could get through to her on the way to tonight's meeting and do a little damage control.

Audrey got out and opened the passenger door for Linda. "We won't be a minute," she said to me.

I watched the two of them walk into the office. Audrey clamped her arm through Linda's and said something to make my neighbor laugh.

I just hoped Audrey could talk some sense into her too. But I was afraid that wasn't going to be so easy.

Chapter Two

AUDREY DROVE THAT old Buick like a bat out of hell. I had trouble keeping up with her, especially on the highway headed for Morrison. My Subaru is six years old and a luxury car to me—automatic transmission, power windows, air-conditioning, four-wheel drive—but as a result of all those extras dragging on the engine, it also has next to no power. Luckily there wasn't a lot of traffic headed for the foothills at six-thirty on a Monday evening, or I'd have lost them. Then I'd have been sunk.

The introductory meeting of the Hunter Divorce Adjustment Seminars is always held in the basement of a Wheat Ridge church. But from then on a different group member volunteers to host a meeting in his or her home each week. There's at least one member in every group who's willing to do it who lives in a place that's a real challenge to find. Tonight's was one of those.

Not only was the house on an isolated piece of property at the base of the mountains, but from the owner's directions there was a tricky-to-spot gravel road that was the only way to get to it. Miss that gravel road, and it was three miles before you could turn around and try again.

But Linda happened to know the owner of the house, Bruce Mann, the head of the tax department of one of Denver's biggest downtown banks. Years ago he'd gone to high school with Linda and her husband, Steve, and the Kraners had been to dinner at Bruce's house a couple of times since they'd reconnected with him at their high school reunion a year ago.

Linda had explained this to me on the way home from the first meeting. She'd been surprised to see Bruce there. Several months had passed since they'd last seen each other, so neither of them had known the other was getting divorced. But beyond being surprised to encounter each other in the same support group, neither seemed bothered by the other's presence in the group. In fact, they seemed to be commiserating with each other, both of them being dumpees.

Dumpees and dumpers. That was the topic of one of the early seminars.

Part group therapy, part enlightenment and education about the normal stages people go through when a marriage ends—that's what the Hunter group is all about.

The course of the meetings runs the same. The first two sessions discuss the emotional process of divorce, using a sort of twelve-step program. There's talk about accepting that the marriage is over and disentangling from it, what's normal to feel and how to ride the roller coaster of it all to emerge with your life and sanity intact and a better understanding of why the marriage has failed.

The third session puts everyone to work figuring out who were the dumpers and who were the dumpees. Healing is quicker for the dumpers, but having a few in every group is surprisingly helpful in seeing the other side of things and rehumanizing the ogres who've become most people's exes by then.

We were on our way to the fourth session, the parent-child structure of most marriages that failed. Or so contended the Hunter Divorce Adjustment Seminars.

My maiden voyage with the Hunter groups had been so long after the end of my own marriage that I'd gone in with a different perspective from the rest of the group. Most people were right in the middle of the process: separated, filing papers, getting the final decree, dealing with the open wound. I'd been trying to get a festered wound to heal.

I was still hurting two and a half years after the fact, and it concerned me. It seemed way too much time for that to be hanging around. A friend of the family had recommended the Hunter seminars, and that's how I'd hit on them.

Audrey must have realized I was struggling to keep up, because she slowed down, and I actually managed to close the distance between us to two car lengths.

We took an exit off the highway that put us onto a two-lane blacktop. Audrey slowed down a little more, so I was able to enjoy the scenery. By October the summer heat is usually over—thank God because I hate the heat—and turtleneck temperatures have set in. But the sun still shines nearly every day, the air is clear and sharp, and the leaves on the trees turn electric yellow.

I was born and raised in Colorado. I've never lived anywhere else. Ditto for both my parents and all four of my grandparents, although my folks travel so much since my dad's retirement that living here is really only a part-time thing for them now.

Still, we're a close family. Maybe that comes from the Italian blood on my mother's side. My father is Heinz variety—English, French, Irish, and German—and there's a difference between the way the Italian side pulls together and the way the other side does. For some reason the other side of the family seems to drift apart, not keeping in touch for months or years in spite of the fact that they all live in or around Denver too.

But even while my parents travel, I talk to them and my aunt and uncle (who travel with them) at least once a week on the phone, once a day when they're all in town.

I'm closer still to my only living grandparent, my grandmother. The Italian one. In fact, she and I are about to get a lot closer.

Up ahead Audrey was braking to a snail's pace, obviously searching for the turnoff to Bruce Mann's house. He wasn't kidding that it was hard to spot. It was barely a separation between the evergreen trees that covered the hillside. I could see Linda pointing to it or I would have missed it for sure. Bruce had promised to leave a flag of some sort at the turnoff to make it easier to spot, but apparently he'd forgotten.

Once we were on the gravel road it was a straight shot through dense forest, and Audrey hit the gas again, spewing a few rocks my way. But she and Linda appeared to be so deep in conversation that I knew she hadn't realized what she was doing. I just kept my distance again.

Bruce Mann's house was about three miles off the

road, set in a man-made clearing with its rear butting right against the hillside. Or so it appeared as I pulled up into the wide drive alongside the Buick. There were two cars already parked there: Bruce's Porsche and a tiny, battered Ford from which Janine Cummings was alighting.

Janine is over the crest of fifty but doesn't look it. Her blond hair is cut short and sporty, her face is barely lined, and what wrinkles there are are meticulously hidden under light makeup. There isn't an extra ounce of fat on her body, and she had on casual slacks and a blouse just snug enough to prove it.

She's a receptionist in a veterinarian's office, a fanatical environmentalist, and I had the impression she joined the group not so much to get herself through her divorce as to look for husband number two from among the freshly available. From the looks of her car she needed the second income. But then, didn't we all?

I have to say one thing for her, though: She's cheery for a woman ending a twenty-year marriage. I hope that cheeriness isn't burying what she's come to work through, but her good spirits did offer some relief to the usual tone of things.

I glanced from her to the Buick. Linda and Audrey were still deep in discussion and made no move to get out of the car. I was the only one of us to head for Janine, who was waiting for us but staring at the house.

"Nice place," I said when I reached her.

"Wow, I'll say," she answered like a kid who'd just walked through the gates of Disneyland for the first time.

The large two-story chalet came complete with three rough stone chimneys, a deck that looked as if it wrapped all the way around the place on the lower level, and a yawning veranda from the second floor.

The white wicker furniture on the veranda made it look like a picture postcard invitation to curl up with a cup of cappuccino after the last run down a ski slope.

Very impressive.

"It'd be worth the drive to live in a place like this," Janine said more to herself than to me. I had the impression she was talking about the drive to and from the vet's office in Broomfield, not Bruce's drive to and from downtown.

"How was your week?" I asked.

It took her a minute to peel her eyes away from the house and look at me. "Oh, it was okay. Nothing great, nothing awful. Not as bad as Bruce's."

The Hunter program asked each group member to do homework in the form of three phone calls between meetings, either because you're down in the dumps and need to reach out for help to raise your own spirits or to let three other people know you're thinking about them and wondering how they're doing.

As a volunteer, I wasn't required to do phone call homework. I made it a point, however, to check up on anyone who seemed particularly bummed out or upset and to touch base with whoever might be headed for a hurdle that week: a court appearance, a hassle with a lawyer or an ex, the first time a person was going to be without the kids, the first time he or she was going to have the kids, a move—things like that. But I didn't call just to say hi. Bruce Mann had seemed okay at the last meeting and had nothing coming up, so I hadn't checked on him.

"What happened to make Bruce's week bad?" I asked now.

"I guess his wife disappeared. He went to her place to pick up the kids for the weekend, and she was gone—lock, stock, and barrel. No forwarding address, no word to him, nothing."

"And the kids? Did she take them too?"

"She did. He was going to contact their school today to see if they had any idea what his wife was doing or where they went, but he was afraid it wouldn't matter. Apparently none of the kids' friends even knew they were going or anything."

"That's terrible."

"He was really crazed over it. I offered to fix him dinner last night, but he said he couldn't eat, he couldn't sleep. He didn't know what he was going to do if his ex or the kids didn't call or write to let him know where they are."

"Does he think that's a possibility?"

"I guess so. I guess his wife threatened to take the kids and go somewhere he'd never find them if he pulled something on her, but he said he's been absolutely straight with her, so she wouldn't do it."

"*If he pulled something on her?*" I asked. "Like what?"

"I wasn't sure what that meant either. He was bawling like a baby when he said it, and he kept on talking, wildlike, and I never had a chance to ask. I just listened mostly. I didn't know what to say."

"It's good he called you for some support, though."

"Oh, he didn't call me. I called Clifford Silver just for one of the check-ins, and he told me. Bruce had called him. So then I called Bruce right away. I called a couple of times Saturday and yesterday too."

"Well, however it happened, it's good he had someone to talk to." I glanced at the Buick and found Audrey patting Linda's shoulder again as Linda cried. They didn't look close to coming out yet, so I nodded toward the house. "We might as well go ahead in.

Linda's just had some bad news too. Audrey's talking to her about it now. They'll come in when they're ready. We can see how Bruce is."

The walk from the driveway to the house was a hike up fifteen cobbled steps amid landscaping that so artfully used the same columbines, wildflowers, and grass that grew naturally around the beds of the fir trees that it looked as if nature itself had designed it. Clearly, even though the house had been built in the middle of a forest, attention had been paid to not disturbing any more of it than was necessary.

I could see that Janine approved.

More steps took us up above garden-level basement windows to the wide wraparound deck of the first floor. The hollow sound of our steps seemed like announcement enough that we were there. I rang the doorbell anyway, just for good measure, while Janine took deep breaths of the pine-scented air.

I tried a few myself as we waited.

And waited.

No one came to the door.

Janine rang again. I cocked my head just enough to peek into the diamond-paned bay window without seeming to be actually peeping. There were no lights on; that was odd since dark was falling pretty rapidly by then. There were also no signs of life or of anyone coming to the door.

"Did Bruce remember he was hosting the group tonight?" I asked.

"I know he did. He mentioned it. That was another reason he didn't want to come to dinner at my place. He said he was going to clean to get ready for us. Do you suppose he got tied up looking for his wife and kids today?"

"I think he would have called somebody if he

needed to cancel. Besides, his car is here." I jabbed a thumb over my shoulder in the direction of the Porsche.

Janine rang the bell again and then knocked.

I did some more overt peeking, but still nothing inside budged.

"Maybe he's in the shower or on the phone or in the back of the house and can't hear the doorbell," I said. "You stay here in case he comes, and I'll go around to the other side of the house and see if he's there."

Janine agreed with yet another push of the bell. I headed around the deck.

The house was even bigger than I'd thought. I have a friend who's always talking about opening a bed-and-breakfast, and she came to mind as I realized just how big it was. It made me think of a quaint hostelry. It would have made a good one.

Along the way I glanced into the windows I passed—without pressing my nose to the glass the way I would have liked—but I didn't spot anything. I also craned my neck backward over the deck's carved railing to see if there was a light on in any of the windows upstairs, but they were all dark and blank too.

I was betting Bruce had come home from work, fallen asleep somewhere inside, and stress and exhaustion had taken over to stretch a short nap into a deep sleep. We probably just needed to stay with the doorbell until it managed to wake him up.

I headed for the sliding door that opened onto the deck, thinking I'd do a little pounding on it for added effect. My steps echoed through the quickly falling night, and I was about two of them away when I saw Bruce through the glass of the door.

He was home all right. And the nap he was taking had definitely stretched into a deep sleep. The deepest sleep.

He was dead.

Chapter Three

THERE WAS NO mistaking the fact that Bruce Mann was dead. He was lying on his kitchen floor not far from the glass sliding door. He looked like a great big rag doll flung in a fit of temper. His eyes were wide open, unblinking, glazed. His mouth was a gaping oval of disbelief. He was dressed the way my ex-husband used to be about midway through getting ready for work: white shirt and tie, but no pants or shoes or socks. Jockey shorts. And there were coal-black marks of some kind on his hands and feet.

It wasn't a pretty picture, and along with the shock wave that rippled through me when what I was looking at sank in came a sense of intrusion, as if I didn't have the right to see him that way.

I turned my head just as Audrey came around the corner of the house on the same path I'd taken.

"Any luck?"

I held a palm up to her like a school crossing guard to stop her from coming any nearer and seeing what I'd seen. "He's dead," I heard my voice say, feeling removed from myself, from the whole scene, as if it couldn't be real.

Audrey stepped closer anyway, glanced inside, then closed her eyes, made the sign of the cross, and said what I could only assume was a silent prayer.

I managed to get some juice to my legs and moved to the railing to lean against it and take a few deep breaths, though now it wasn't to enjoy the piney air; it was to get hold of myself. When I'd accomplished that—to some degree at least—I went around to the front of the house again and dialed 911 on the cellular phone my cousin and best friend had insisted I get for emergencies. Even though Bruce Mann was beyond an emergency.

Then I called that cousin. Danny Delvecchio. He and my grandmother were at my house, helping the girls pack boxes. He is also a Jefferson County Sheriff's Department homicide detective. But I wasn't thinking about that. I was only thinking that finding a dead body was more his territory than mine, and it would just make me feel better to have him there.

Within ten minutes a fire rescue truck came bounding up the gravel road, spewing rocks like bullets from the rear tires. The city of Golden police followed close behind about five minutes later, and I directed them all to the rear of the house.

Audrey, Janine, Linda, and I were ordered to stay at the foot of the driveway, and that's what we did, silently watching the two male and one female cops and four firefighters who ended up there.

Since none of us had a key to the house, the first order of business was to break the beautiful columbine-design stained glass window in the center top half of the front door. The fire department got that job, reached in, and unlocked the lock. Once it was accomplished, the rescue squad and four of the cops rushed inside as if there might be some hope for Bruce, leaving the youngest officer stationed on the porch.

Right about then the rest of the Hunter group began arriving.

Clifford Silver and Ron Arnot pulled up first, carpooling the way most of us did. Clifford—and it was Clifford, not Cliff or even Ford—taught at the Warren Tech Center, a trade school near Red Rocks Community College in Lakewood.

He was forty and slight, with dishwater-blond hair and a mustache that was hard to see unless you were up close. He had a deep baritone voice that offset what was otherwise an almost wimpish appearance, lending him some stature when he opened his mouth.

Ron Arnot was driving and parked his green pickup behind the cop cars that blocked the rest of us in. He worked in construction and was a good-looking twenty-seven-year-old. Blue eyes; long black hair he wore pulled back into a ponytail low on his nape; sharp, hawkish features; and the sort of deep tan that comes from working out in the sun.

He was having a tough time being part of the group. Exploring his feelings and analyzing what went wrong with his marriage were not his long suit. Besides, he believed he knew damn good and well what had gone wrong with his marriage: Linda's husband had stolen his twenty-two-year-old wife.

He and Linda's being in the same divorce group struck me as an unusual arrangement. Not that it was out of the ordinary for several people in any one group to know one another in some way or another. People tended to talk about the group, to recommend it to friends and relatives going through the same thing or who knew someone else who was, and the participants ended up forming a sort of chain-letter link. I'd just never been in a Hunter group that had both of the scorned spouses of an affair.

But in this case Linda had suggested it to Ron and given him the admission form. Neither of them seemed to be having any problems with the arrangement.

While we told Clifford and Ron what was going on, Gail Frankin showed up. She and Ron also knew each other from before the seminars, but I didn't know how.

Gail was our resident dumper. That had surprised me when I'd heard it. She was one of those quietly beautiful women, always well dressed, her brown shoulder-length hair perfectly blunt-cut, her makeup understated, her voice modulated. She seemed so nurturing with everyone else in the group that it was hard to accept that she'd left her husband because she couldn't deal with a future as his caregiver when she'd learned he had multiple sclerosis.

Ron took over the task of explaining things to Gail as Beverly Runyan arrived. She was the group member most difficult to like. There was a hard edge to her, as if her personality were as angular as her bony face. She had coarse black hair cut to chin length and close-set eyes that narrowed whenever someone said something she didn't agree with. That happened frequently. When it did, she had virtually no patience with it. And less tact.

She was attending the seminars reluctantly, only because her supervisor had insisted she get herself some help. Beverly was a nurse.

Even if it were the best of circumstances, I wouldn't have wanted to be under her care. I imagined that these days she was downright hazardous to her patients' health.

It was into this eclectic bunch of spectators that Danny arrived half an hour later. He was driving the truck he'd borrowed to help me move, and its rear end was loaded with boxes of my belongings and a few small pieces of furniture.

Danny Delvecchio is six feet four inches tall and weighs in at 230 pounds of hard-packed muscle carrying around a face that turns every woman's head in every room he walks into. The guy is gorgeous. Dark mink-colored hair, darker eyes, prominent cheekbones, a cleft in his chin, olive skin, and one of those noses that manage to be big but so well shaped it doesn't matter.

My grandmother on my mother's side and his grandmother on his father's side were two of nine sisters. He grew up in the house next door to my grandparents, and if he hadn't been my cousin, I probably would have had a major crush on him.

He's eight years older than I am, but even when we were kids and I'd followed him around like a shadow, he'd been good about it. He'd joked about my being his sidekick and given his friends the hard stare when they balked at having me around.

He'd also taught me to smoke cigarettes, drink beer, play poker, defend myself against the second-grade bully who'd tormented me and later against any date who might get out of line. As a result, I have a pretty fair right cross and a lethal knee.

The minute he got out of the truck he spotted me standing with the group and headed in our direction.

"Who's *that*?" Janine Cummings asked first.

"Dan Delvecchio. He's a cop." I wasn't sure why I'd added that except that it somehow seemed relevant and nobody could tell his occupation the way he was dressed in torn blue jeans and a gray sweatshirt.

Janine didn't seem to mind. The clothes or the cop part.

"You okay, Jimi?" he asked as he joined us, without wasting time on hellos.

"Yeah, I'm okay," I said. Then I introduced him to everyone. Janine was suddenly at my elbow, the only one of us to extend her hand and smile as if she were Cinderella at the ball. Sometimes that cheeriness got out of control.

Danny didn't seem to notice. He nodded toward the house. "What's happening?"

"Good question. Cops keep going in and coming out and going back in, but they still haven't turned on a light or told us anything. I think they're just in there playing with their flashlights."

I was being sarcastic, but Janine giggled, poked me in the ribs with her elbow, and said, "Oh, yoooo," as if I'd made an off-color party joke.

In the time I've been divorced I've run into a lot of women who turn into horrible imitations of Scarlett O'Hara at the first sight of a man, but it never fails to make me cringe for them. I wished she'd cut it out.

Again Danny seemed oblivious. "I'll go in and see what I can find out."

We all watched him walk up the steps from the driveway to the front porch. When he got there and was showing the young cop at the door his badge, Janine said, "Is he yours?"

"Danny is my cousin." And soon to be housemate—or actually renter—but I didn't offer that bit of information.

"Is he married?"

"Divorced. Three times. The hazards of the job." Along with lousy taste in women, but I'd never say that behind his back. I'd said it to his face a time or two, but that was different.

"How old is he?"

"Forty-seven." I didn't mean to snap at her, but that's how it came out. I just don't like being grilled about him as if I were presenting him for auction. No matter how many times it happens. Danny is a lot more than a side of Italian beef, and I find it as offensive for him to be treated like that as I would have for one of my daughters or any other woman to be referred to that way.

"Forty-seven is a little young for me," Janine was saying, "but if he doesn't mind, I don't."

I didn't stick around for more of that. I moved to Linda's side instead and asked how she was doing.

Right about then a public service van joined the increasingly long line of vehicles that stretched down the gravel road. It hadn't occurred to me that the reason the cops hadn't turned on a light inside the house was that there was no power, but it did then.

"Why are we waiting around here anyway?" said Beverly Runyan's caustic voice when yet another man had bypassed us and gone inside. "It isn't like Bruce is going to rise up and invite us in to talk about that parent-child crap after all. He probably dropped dead of a heart attack, and there's no reason for us to stay to watch him brought out in a body bag."

"She's got a point," Ron Arnot put in like her tough-guy backup.

"I don't think we'd better do anything until we're told to," Clifford said.

"Well, I can't go anywhere," Janine pointed out.

"My car is stuck in front of the police cars. And so are Jimi's and Audrey's."

"I think the best thing to do is to ask the officer at the door if there's any need for us to stay and, if not, to get someone to move the vehicles that are blocking the driveway." As usual Audrey's was the voice of reason.

"I'll do it," I said. Actually I was curious to have a look in the front window of the house to see what was going on in there since the place seemed to have swallowed Danny too.

The young cop up on the porch stood with his hands behind his back, his legs spread apart the same distance as the span of his shoulders, watching my approach with the benign expression of a Buckingham Palace guard. I relayed the group's desire to leave, but before he could answer, Danny came out. He took my arm and led me to the porch railing. "What's the matter?" he asked.

"The natives are getting restless. They'd all like to call it a night and get out of here."

"Can't do that. Statements are going to have to be taken from everybody."

"Statements? For what? We came here for a divorce seminar, found our host dead, end of story."

Danny's thick eyebrows collided over the bridge of his nose. "It's not that clear-cut, Jimi."

"Why not?"

"The cause of death was electrocution. But this was no household accident. The place was rigged. Looks like he was murdered."

Chapter Four

IT WAS AFTER eleven by the time Linda and I got the go-ahead to leave Bruce Mann's house. Danny was staying on, though I wasn't sure in what capacity or how formal his involvement was.

I knew that he mainly handled investigations in the mountain cities that didn't have either police forces or homicide squads of their own. I also knew that he could be asked in for assistance anywhere in the county if manpower was low, if more expertise was needed, or if a crime just couldn't be solved. And since he'd spent a few years as an LAPD detective and come back with commendations out the yin-yang, that happened pretty frequently.

Beyond Danny's résumé the only other thing I knew was that the Hunter group had been left cooling our heels—literally in the chill of the October evening air—

in the driveway until the public service worker had given the all-clear to turn the power back on.

Then we'd been allowed into the living room, from which one by one we'd been taken to the den and questioned about our relationships with and knowledge of Bruce Mann.

My interview had been pretty quick. I'd explained that before the seminars I'd never met Bruce. I'd heard Linda mention his name in passing when she and Steve had gone to dinner at his house. I knew Bruce had been in the process of getting divorced. I knew he was the dumpee. I didn't know why or any other details. I'd also described how I'd found his body.

The rest of the interviews had been of varying lengths, Linda's the longest because she'd actually known Bruce. Then we'd all been let go.

"I don't know why we had to stay and be asked all those questions," Linda complained on the way home. "Even if Bruce's death wasn't accidental, none of us could have had anything to do with it. What did the police think we could tell them?"

"Danny said it was just routine. Besides, you did know Bruce."

"Not that well. I've seen him only a handful of times since high school graduation. Including the group."

"That's still more than the rest of us. Did they ask you if you knew of anyone who might have wanted him dead?"

"They asked. But I couldn't tell them. Unless he did something bad to his wife and she got as mad as I was earlier."

That reminded me of how this evening had begun. I didn't want to get into Linda's financial problems again, but it did lead me to recall her staying in the car talking to Audrey while I'd chatted with Janine. I repeated to Linda what Janine had told me about Bruce.

"Do you have any idea what his wife could have meant by his 'pulling something' on her?"

"No. It doesn't make any sense to me. But maybe he 'pulled something' on his first wife when they got divorced and Melanie knew about it and didn't want him doing it to her."

"I didn't know this was Bruce's second marriage."

"His first was to his high school sweetheart, Cynthia Dooley. The four of us used to double-date."

"Did he do her dirt?"

"I couldn't tell you. Between graduation and that reunion last year Bruce could have been living on the moon for all I knew. We'd heard he and Cynthia got married, but other than that, zip. We were shocked out of our socks to hear they'd gotten divorced and she'd died."

"Died?"

"She was killed in a hit-and-run accident. I guess she'd been driving a horrible old junk heap of a car, it broke down late one night, and she was looking under the hood when somebody hit her and kept going. If they'd have stopped and called for help, she might have lived, but no one found her until morning, and she'd bled to death by then. I understand Bruce was pretty upset about it even though they were already divorced when it happened."

"Was the driver caught?"

"I don't think so, but I'm not sure. I talked to somebody else at the reunion who said that when it happened, Cynthia's sister was going around saying it was Bruce's fault. But there was no way that was true. He was home with Melanie at the time; they were about two weeks away from their own wedding. Or so I heard."

Melanie was the name of the wife who'd just dumped Bruce. I was familiar with it. I'd heard him say it often enough during the discussions.

"Was Melanie the reason Bruce got the first divorce?" I asked.

"I'm not sure about that either, but I wouldn't be surprised. She's younger than he is—was—by about a dozen years, and she's great-looking. She definitely qualifies as the trophy wife. And they got married really soon after his divorce. But I suppose it's possible he didn't start up with her until after he separated from Cynthia."

Linda didn't seem convinced. Neither was I.

We were home by then. I pulled into my driveway and stopped for Linda to get out. Her two-story house is just across the street, so she could walk over.

But neither of us budged. Our attention seemed to be riveted to the big For Sale sign on my lawn, complete with a Sold banner across the Realtor's name.

Linda opened the door but didn't get out. "So tomorrow's the big day."

"Yep. We're out of here. The new owners will be moving in on Wednesday."

"The closing went all right?"

"Fine."

"You doing okay with it?"

"Sure." Not great, but okay. I tried to think more about how nice it was to have a glimmer of the old, caring Linda who'd put my problems before her own until hers had gotten as big as or bigger than mine.

"That two miles seems like a long way away," she said.

"It isn't, though," I reassured her as if I were taking

it all in stride. "If one of us took up jogging or power walking, we wouldn't even need to drive the distance. Shannon and Joey will still be in the same school, so if you need me to pick Joey up or I need you for a ride for Shannon, we can go on doing that just the same. A lot will be just the same. It's not really a big deal."

But my moving wasn't as irrelevant to our friendship as I was trying to make it sound, and we both knew it. No more trotting across the street to borrow something or escape for an hour while still being able to watch whatever was going on at home. No more keeping an eye out for each other. No more impromptu begging to stop-me-before-I-scream-again at a kid trying to drive one of us over the edge. No more tea and sympathy at the drop of a hat. No more of a lot of things that proximity bred.

Change was in the air for both of us, and it's always hard to say where it will end.

"I'll miss you just the same." Linda reached over and gave me a hug.

"You won't even know I'm gone."

"Yes, I will," she said in a voice that cracked. Then she squeezed a little tighter, let go, said good night, and got out as if I hadn't seen her cry before.

It was better, though. I didn't want to start up myself.

Ours was a pretty safe neighborhood, but still I watched her until she was inside. Then, once her front door closed behind her, I looked up at my own place, and my mind wandered home for real. At least to what was home for one more night.

If I hadn't been sure of it before, divorce had taught me that almost everything has a good side and a bad side. This move was no exception.

Eight years ago the court had ordered my ex-husband to pay child support until both kids were twenty-one. At first he'd paid every month, in full, even if it had been late more often than not. Then it got to be so late that he'd skip a month. Then he'd pay less than he was supposed to. Then skip more months and pay only about thirty cents on the dollar. And so on until he'd moved. To Minneapolis. To Miami. To Dallas. To Detroit. To Las Vegas, where he is now.

Good-bye, support money.

Collecting it from someone out of state is difficult. Collecting it from someone who decides to start moving from one state to another every time the whim strikes is worse.

Over the last three years I've gotten as good at tracking him as any private eye specializing in missing persons. But the bottom line is that it takes a lot of effort and energy for very little return. In short, he'd move, I'd find him, whatever state he was in would agree to garnish his wages, but before it'd get a chance, he'd take off again, and the money would stop.

I'm a tenacious person. But enough is enough. I'd finally given up the ghost.

The problem is that without support money I'm going under.

Freelance tech writing does not make millionaires, and teenagers are expensive. Something had to go: the house or the kids. And since I was counting on at least one of the kids to tie my shoes in my old age, that left the house.

I finally quit sitting there like an idiot and pulled into the garage. But as I pushed the button to close the door, I had a serious twinge about leaving this place. It wasn't that I was in love with the moderate-size three-bedroom ranch-style house. But I'd lived in it for fifteen years, and there was a lot about it that I'd gotten just right.

It was also my refuge from people, kids notwithstanding. I have a bit of a reclusive streak and need to hide out now and then. But that was going to be pretty tough to pull off in the living arrangement I was about to embark on.

When I put the house on the market, it had sold within a month. Thanks to all those years of building equity and a huge rise in the cost of housing in Colorado, I'd made a nice profit. That was the good side of that deal.

The bad side was that when it sold, I didn't know where I was going to find a place to rent that would allow two kids and a dog and would be cheaper than my house payment so it wouldn't suck up the money I'd made.

That was when my grandmother had approached me with her offer: She'd sell me her house for a flat 50 percent of my equity. I'd own it free and clear and still come out with the other half of the money for a nest egg. I'd have a place to move us all to, extra income immediately from the basement apartment my cousin Danny rents, and more income later if I wanted to move myself out of the attic and take over the second floor when the girls left home.

This was not a deal I could refuse. It was the answer to my current problems and security for the future.

It was also communal living with Danny and my grandmother. I was a little worried about that.

I turned off the car and went into the house to be greeted by my miniature schnauzer, Lucy, as if my homecoming were a joyous event. Unconditional, devoted love. Never underestimate it. Sloppy kisses and all.

My daughters were in the kitchen just beyond the laundry room I'd stepped into. They were sitting on the floor because the table and chairs had been sold with most of our other furniture.

Chloe and Shannon Fiarelli.

Chloe—the elder at nineteen—was eating a slice of cold pizza. Shannon was dining on what she considered a balanced meal: maraschino cherries and dill pickles. She's seventeen.

They both benefited from their father's gene pool. Tall, thin, and long-legged. Shannon has a slightly bigger chest, which she never fails to mention in goading Chloe.

Chloe could also thank dear old Dad for her tawny skin and coffee-colored hair that curls just enough to look the way an expensive perm ought to. She wears it very long and full, and it is definitely her crowning glory, framing a face with delicate features and great big brown eyes.

Shannon, on the other hand, had been born a blond. She'd recently abolished it with mahogany dye and a stripe of coal black right in front.

Strangely enough, I liked it, but I'd never tell her that and ruin her rebellion. The black stripe could go, but the rich darkness of the hair color made her pale skin look luminous. It also offset her nearly black eyes.

The girls resembled each other only vaguely, but neither one failed to draw admiring glances from men of all ages when we walked through the mall. And I'd more than once had to do some fancy driving to dodge a man or a bunch of boys in another car who'd spotted them and decided to follow us home.

I guess next time that happened I'd just lead them into the hands of Detective Danny Delvecchio and really spoil their fun.

"How was your meeting?" Chloe asked.

"And why did you call Danny to come?" Shannon added.

I didn't want to tell them the truth. They had enough on their minds at the moment without hearing that their dear old mom had found a dead man a few hours earlier. So I said, "There was a problem, and we didn't end up having the meeting. Did you guys and Gramma do all right on your own?"

"Sure. Then, when we got tired, we took her home," Chloe volunteered.

"When *you* got tired, not when *she* got tired?"

"She could have gone on all night," Chloe said. "I think she's really anxious to have us move in with her."

"She's had a bad two years." Since my grandfather's death.

"Uncle Dad called," Shannon offered, adopting my name for her father.

It seemed like an accurate title. He had been the sperm donor, so that earned him the dad part. But the role he'd chosen to play in their lives was more like a not very attentive, long-distance uncle. Besides, it was better than referring to him as Deadbeat.

"Did he call while Gramma was still here or after you guys had taken her home?"

"While she was here," Shannon said with malicious delight.

"Yeah, and real loud she said why'd he bother calling when he couldn't bother to be a father any other way," Chloe said. "I was so embarrassed."

"Gramma's right," Shannon pointed out.

"I don't care. She didn't need to say it so he could hear," Chloe shouted, instantly defensive. "And I'm tired of making excuses to him about why you won't get on the phone. I told him you were here, and then, when it was your turn to talk to him, you were nowhere around."

"I went to make sure Danny had left the gate closed so Lucy wouldn't get out."

"Oh, yeah, like it needed to be done right that minute."

"I don't care if you make excuses for me or not. Just tell him I don't want to talk to him. Don't blame me because you try to protect him and I won't kiss his ass the way you do."

"Keep it clean." That was me.

"Well, that's what she does," Shannon insisted. "She talks to him the way she'd talk to a guy—all sweet and sickening—like he's some jerk she's trying to get to ask her out. Then she gets pissed at me if I do talk to him and don't play that game, or pissed if I don't talk at all."

"I'm not sickeningly sweet. Just because I don't see any reason to pick fights and be a bitch like you are—"

"I'm not a bitch. I'm just honest."

Brutally, as a rule.

"Honest? Oh, please. You look for anything to get mad at him about."

"I don't have to look very far."

"You just like being mean."

"That's right, I do. I'll tell you how mean I can be—"

And they were off. . . .

I tuned it out. My daughters could argue about nothing quicker, louder, and more heatedly than any two people I've ever known.

I poured myself a glass of soda water, squirted a wedge of lime into it, and slid down the wall to sit with my back against it. Lucy climbed onto my lap. She hates it when the girls fight.

I wondered how my grandmother and Danny were going to like it.

But then, I'd been wondering about a lot of things since agreeing to this move.

It had been a long time since my grandmother had had kids living in her house. Let alone teenagers. I wondered how she'd like it.

I wondered how I was going to like parenting under her constant scrutiny. Great-grandmothers are supposed to be indulgent and understanding after all. But mothers have to be the heavies to do their job. I wondered how it was going to mix under the same roof.

I wondered how the girls would adapt to a seventy-two-year-old's ways. Not to mention having a cop keeping yet another eye on them.

I wondered how both my grandmother and Danny were going to like living in a PMS palace twice a month.

I wondered if Lucy would stay out of the garden or if she'd pee on the zucchini.

And I wondered if my grandmother would ever get used to the way things really were with Uncle Dad and stop getting upset over it. Or if she'd at least not say anything about it to the girls. The way I'd asked her.

Ah, life's adventures.

Chapter Five

DANNY SHOWED UP at my house the next morning before the movers did. He came bearing cheese Danish and two cups of convenience store coffee. The coffees were for him. The only kind I drink is the sissy stuff that's really hot chocolate with a shot of instant coffee thrown in as a technicality.

He'd taken the day off to help us move and looked as if he should have been sleeping instead.

"You must have stayed at Bruce Mann's house a long time after I left," I said as we ate sitting Indian fashion on the kitchen floor.

"Until three this morning." He took a drink of coffee and stared into the cup for a minute. "I talked to the coroner a little while ago. He said Bruce Mann definitely died from electrocution. His hands and feet were charred."

"I saw the discolorations on them. I wondered what they were."

"We were pretty sure anyway. The vent in front of the sliding doors was the kind with a heater connected to the underside. The repairman from public service found the ground wire for it disconnected and a hot one hooked to the metal trough down below the grate. It was an accident waiting to happen. Apparently the victim stepped on the grate, grabbed the metal handle of the door to open it and 'That's all,' she wrote: He got to be the conductor. The breaker was tripped by the jolt, and the electricity went off. The clocks stopped at five forty-seven. Makes setting the time of death convenient for the coroner; he just had to determine whether the guy had been dead one hour or thirteen. He'd been dead one."

So Bruce had probably just come home and was in the middle of changing his clothes, instead of being in the process of getting ready to go to work the way I'd thought.

"Isn't there any chance it was a faulty connection or that the wires just came loose somehow?"

Danny shook his head while he chewed a bite of Danish. "The hot wire was pulled from the source and skinned, then purposely brought into contact with the trough and secured there with electrical tape so it wouldn't budge. And the ground wire was cut off clean as a whistle. This was no fluke."

"Was any place else in the house rigged?"

"Nope. Only that back door. And it could have been done just about anytime. The electrician said the victim could have stepped on that register a million times and never had a hair singed if he were wearing leather-soled shoes when he did."

"So it's hard to know when the killer set it up."

"Which makes it harder still to pinpoint who the killer is."

"Someone with access to the house."

"Maybe. Or maybe not. We found a window in the basement broken out. We'll check glass companies for work orders to fix it. If we find one, it could narrow down a time frame. But there wasn't anything in that basement, which means the victim had virtually no reason to go down there. And the window is so far back under the deck that the shadows would have made it nearly invisible from outside unless he actually got under there for some reason. Could be he never knew it was busted out."

"Do you have any suspects at all?"

He shrugged in a way that could have meant that he did and didn't want to say or that he didn't, then said, "Tell me what you know about Beverly Runyan."

That took me by surprise. "You're kidding, right? She's a member of the Hunter group. She just met the guy four weeks ago the same way I did."

"Things can happen in four weeks, Jimi."

"Things like getting to hate somebody enough to kill them?"

Danny shrugged again. "What do you know about her?"

"I'll tell you all I know about both Beverly Runyan and Bruce Mann. They're going through nasty divorces. Bruce was a nice, brainy Ivy League tax accountant. Beverly is a nurse who's proud of being from what she calls the wrong side of the tracks; that was how she introduced herself to us the first night, wearing it like a badge of honor. So if you tell me she felt there was a social gap between herself and the rest of us, I'll agree with you. Tell me she didn't like any of us because of it, and I'll agree with that too. But tell me she killed

Bruce, and I'd have to see some pretty convincing evidence."

"We found her birth control pills under his bed."

I admit that took me a minute to digest. Maybe it was easier to believe she'd killed him than slept with him.

"It looked like maybe they'd fallen out of her purse," Danny said.

"Did you ask her about it?"

"We didn't find them until after you'd all gone home for the night. In her interview she claimed she knew him only in conjunction with the seminar."

"I would have bet money on it. Do you suppose they knew each other before or just started something up through the group?"

"You tell me."

I thought about it. Thought about the meetings, about the way Beverly and Bruce had acted. "I don't know. If they knew each other from before, there wasn't a mention of it or a sign that they did. But I suppose they could have hidden it. Or I guess something could have just clicked between them and they could have been discreet about it."

"Love at first sight?"

"Audrey always makes a point at the introductory meeting of warning against any kind of romantic involvements between group members, at least during the course of the seminars. Usually it doesn't matter because everybody is involved in their own misery and is eyeing the opposite sex as the enemy anyway. But this time around there's Janine Cummings; she's definitely the exception to that rule. And if there's one exception, I suppose there could be others. But Beverly and Bruce? That's hard to imagine."

"She's a tough cookie. Not who I'd have picked myself."

"Was there somebody you *would* pick?" I asked, spurred by a particular note in his tone of voice.

"Not Janine Cummings. She comes on way too strong."

"She'll be disappointed. That leaves Audrey or Gail Frankin. You have a thing for nuns?"

"I don't have a thing for anybody."

"But Gail Frankin spurred your interest."

"Gail Frankin is not too hard on the eyes. What do you know about her?"

"In terms of being a murder suspect and knowing Bruce? Or in terms of date material?"

"Either. Or both."

"Come on, we can't all be suspects. What about the rest of the people in Bruce's life? Like his ex-wife, for instance. Did Janine tell you what happened this weekend on that score?"

"She was more interested in asking questions than in answering them. But apparently she called the department at the crack of dawn and left me a message that she just remembered something I should know. I'll bet she wants to tell me over dinner or drinks or something more cozy than the murder victim's house. What do you think?"

"I think if her response to you last night was any indication, she's in hot pursuit." And I was the last person who had any business expecting Danny to have patience with her since I hadn't had any. But I still felt inclined to try to temper his assessment of her. "She's a decent enough person. She works long hours for little pay. Worries about the environment. I just think she's one of those women who can't fathom themselves without a man. Makes her desperate."

"How desperate?"

"Would you quit with the suspicions of everybody? She's looking for a new husband. Why would she kill one of her prospects?"

Danny's only answer was to raise his eyebrows at me. "So what did Janine tell you about Mann's ex-wife?"

I repeated the story and watched Danny make a mental note of it all. But I still didn't like how sharply focused he was on the Hunter group. He hadn't given me any good reason for it, so I felt inclined to broaden his field of vision.

"Did the subject of Bruce Mann's first wife come up when you interviewed Linda, by any chance?"

"It didn't come up in any of the interviews."

"We were just talking about things on the way home, and she told me about it. I guess the first wife was killed in a hit-and-run accident just after the divorce and his sister-in-law went around saying it was his fault."

"Why?"

"Linda didn't know. She said it wasn't as if Bruce could have been the driver, because he was at home with the soon-to-be second wife when it happened."

"Was the driver found?"

"Linda didn't know that either."

"How about the name of the first wife?"

"Cynthia."

"And the sister-in-law?"

"Linda didn't say."

The doorbell rang just then, and as I went to let the movers in, I could tell Danny was thinking in a direction other than my divorce group.

Mission accomplished.

I just hoped I hadn't put him onto a track that

would be painful to the family of the late Cynthia Mann for no good reason.

The point of hiring professional movers was to get everything out in one load. By noon that's just what they'd done. Then Danny, Chloe, and Shannon took Lucy and led the way to my grandmother's house while I stayed behind to clean.

Vacuuming doesn't usually make me nostalgic. But that last one did. I kept having flashbacks. Of Chloe trying to roller-skate across the carpet in the dining room. Of Shannon at about eighteen months pressing her nose to the glass in the back door, her pants at half crack. Of Chloe sleepwalking after her first dental appointment to stand in front of me, head back, mouth open, until I told her she could close up and go back to bed. Of Shannon charging down the hall in her She-Ra getup to save civilization from the evil Skeletor.

Christmas mornings were all jammed into one image as I vacuumed the corner where the tree always went. I even had some good memories of being alone with Uncle Dad, sitting in front of a fire in the fireplace on cold winter evenings. Friday night pizzas on the coffee table in the living room. Sex here and there.

Not that the memories were all good. That house was also where my marriage had fallen apart, and I could see myself hugging my then husband in the entryway the day he left me. That was a weird picture, hugging the SOB before he went off to live with his girlfriend. But I was trying to be a good sport, and I hadn't known what else to do. A handshake had seemed silly. Or maybe that hug had just been a last-ditch effort to hang on.

Hey, maybe keeping this house in the first place had been.

But it was gone now, and the sooner I was too, the better.

I locked the back door; did a slow tour to check cupboards, drawers, closets, nooks and crannies to make sure nothing had been left behind; turned the thermostat down; pulled the shades. And that was that.

"Wish me luck, house," I said.

Then I took the keys off my ring, set them on the kitchen counter, and left.

Linda had been wrong. My grandmother's place wasn't only two miles away; it was more like five. As I headed there, it suddenly seemed an even greater distance than that.

I drove directly east, out of my subdivision, passed some more expensive houses, which had been built in the last year, passed a shopette with a great little sandwich shop called Ala Carte, into an area of much older houses.

My grandmother's neighborhood—my neighborhood now—is made up of houses that were built separately by each owner on half-acre lots about fifty years ago. They're all set fairly far apart, sitting in the middle of their own tiny kingdoms of widespread lawns.

The love of my grandfather's life had been his yard, and even now, two years after his death, the grass still had the precise, manicured look he'd cultivated. That was thanks to Danny, who maintained it along with that of the house next door. He owned that one but rented it out because the two-story three-thousand-square-foot colonial was too big for him alone.

My grandmother's house was no slouch either. A

triple-tiered wedding cake of red brick with a huge front porch behind three identical archways, another balcony at the second floor, and dormer windows jutting out from all four directions of the attic level. It was big, classic, and solid. The place would probably stand for another hundred years. Or at least long enough for me to sell it for a song to *my* divorced grandchild.

Since my grandfather's death my grandmother had been rattling around in it. I'd known she felt a little lost, but it was Danny who had realized just how lonely she was. I think my grandmother had been more candid with him than with me, wanting to spare me her grief. A year ago he'd come up with the plan to lease his own place and move into the basement apartment in my grandmother's house.

He got home-cooked meals whenever he wanted them, and my grandmother got someone to cook for plus a little company. But not so much company that it had helped round out her life again. The girls were right: She was eager to have us there too to do that.

Frankly, in spite of the drawbacks I was worried about, there was another part of me that was glad to be with her. My grandfather's passing had reminded me that my time with my grandmother was limited.

The moving van was backed into the drive when I got there. The truck Danny had borrowed and Chloe's car were at the curb. But there were no signs of life.

I didn't doubt that everyone was inside, the movers included, with my grandmother feeding them lunch. The movers were in for a treat.

I parked behind Chloe's old blue Toyota and got out. But for a minute I leaned against the car and took a look at the place, trying to let it sink in that it was mine now.

The ground floor of the house is the main living

space. There's a big country kitchen, a formal dining room, a living room, a den, the master bedroom, and one bath. That had always been and would go on being my grandmother's domain.

The second level has two bedrooms and another bath. Chloe and Shannon were taking that over, even though they'd both put in a bid for the attic.

But the attic, like the basement, is a small but complete apartment with inside access to the rest of the house as well as a separate outside entrance up stairs in back. There was no way I was going to let either of my teenage daughters have the kind of freedom that arrangement could afford. So the attic was mine.

Besides, it's a space big enough for my bedroom furniture and my office. Also, along with having its own bathroom, it has a miniature kitchen, so I can hole up there when I need to. I was counting on its being my salvation when communal living got to me.

I took the vacuum cleaner and the bucket of cleaning supplies out of the car, crossed my grandfather's lawn, and went in.

"Is that the last of my little dollies?" my grandmother called from the kitchen.

I heard a lilt in her voice that hadn't been there in a while, and it helped throw a dustcover over my uncertainties about this move.

"It's me," I called back as I set down what was in my hands.

The kitchen was full of people. Danny, the two burly movers, and my daughters were sitting around the Formica table on one side of the breakfast bar that cut the space in half. My grandmother was on the business side of it, making a sandwich.

Not an ordinary sandwich. Nothing my grandmother makes in the way of food is ordinary. At that moment she was piling fried capacolla and smoked provolone cheese onto thick slices of home-baked bread and topping it with chopped black olives, roasted red peppers, and sautéed onions that she'd marinated in olive oil and a vinegar she makes herself when her wine goes bad.

"Sit, Jimi. I'll have this ready in a minute, and you can eat too."

"You sit, Gram, and finish your lunch. I can make my own sandwich. Remember what I told you about waiting on us."

She waved me away and didn't concede her spot at the breakfast bar, so I ended up just standing at her side while she made my lunch and ignored my request for only half a sandwich.

The girls and Danny didn't have any problems with their weight, but if I didn't watch it, my grandmother would have me fattened up in no time.

My grandmother is Rose Nell Marconi. Everyone calls her Nell.

We're a family with a history of early pregnancies. Not before marriage, but early nonetheless. I had Chloe when I was just shy of twenty. My mother had me at eighteen. My grandmother had her at seventeen. Add it all up, and the sum total makes my grandmother seventy-two. Even though she hasn't admitted to anything more than thirty-nine since she actually was.

She's about an inch over five feet tall and has a pillowy body maintained by a strict regimen of vitamins and very mild exercise with Jack La Lanne, her secret heartthrob.

Her face is a bit doughy, her nose on the large side, and she keeps her bubble of hair a dark black to hide the gray. Whenever I see a repeat of an old *Bewitched* with Marion Lorne as Aunt Clara, I think of my grandmother.

She has the character's sweetness about her too. When it comes to everything except my ex-husband. She loves weddings. Doesn't mind a funeral as long as it isn't for anyone too close. Is crazy for babies and kids. And has a sparkle in her hazel eyes that, although it had been dimmed since my grandfather's passing, was back now.

She leaned close to my ear and said, "I saved you a little bite of eggplant from last night too."

"This is only lunch, Gram," I whispered back. "I can't eat that much."

But again she waved away my comment, took the full plate, and sat me down with everybody else.

I looked at what she had heaped in front of me, thought maybe I could grow fond of good old Jack La Lanne too, and dug in.

"Our phones work," Shannon informed me then.

There were already two lines coming into the house—my grandmother's and Danny's—but I'd had two new ones added. On the second floor for the girls and in the attic for myself, although I knew that Chloe would occupy the second-floor phone almost every minute she was home and Shannon would end up using mine more than I would.

"You had a call," she added.

Our numbers from the old place had stayed the same, so that was no surprise.

"I was up there to talk to Derrick because Chloe had to be the first one to use our phone, and when I hung up, it rang again and I answered it."

"Who was it?"

"Some woman. I wrote her name on the side of one of the boxes because I couldn't find a piece of paper.

Or a pencil either, so I used the polish I was painting my nails with."

"You were supposed to be getting things set up in your room, not talking on the phone and doing your nails."

"Yeah, right. Like that's more important."

"Do you remember what the woman's name was?"

"Paul Bunyan or something."

"Paul Bunyan was not a woman."

"Yeah, yeah, I know. But it was like that Bunyan part."

"Runyan? Beverly Runyan?"

"Yeah, I think that's it. She said to call her back later. She's not very nice."

I didn't say anything. Instead, I took a bite of my sandwich and caught a glimpse of Danny out of the corner of my eye. His interest was piqued, I could tell.

But then, so was mine.

Chapter Six

I CALLED BEVERLY Runyan twice that afternoon and again that evening. I didn't reach her, so my curiosity kept me company while I helped the girls set up their beds and then did my own.

I still couldn't get hold of her the next morning, but by then her answering machine was on, so I left a message.

After one day of ditching classes to move, both girls were back in school. With Danny gone to work, my grandmother and I were alone in the house. She'd asked me at breakfast if I wanted her help unpacking boxes, but when I told her no, that I didn't want any of us to disrupt her schedule or add more work for her, she'd accepted it pretty easily.

Every time I'd taken trash or empty boxes downstairs and peeked in on her, she was busy with her ironing or her exercises or her cooking. I was glad to see she intended to go about her days as if I weren't there at all. That way I knew I wasn't bothering her, and I hoped it would also mean that once I had my computer set up and was working again I could do that without interruption too.

We did have lunch together, though. Nothing too elaborate, just a homemade minestrone soup and what was left of the Italian bread with a pungent Swiss cheese and slices of plum tomatoes slipped under the broiler for a few minutes.

"You don't have to eat lunch with me every day if you don't want to, Jimi," she said at the start of the meal. "If you aren't hungry when I am or you want to stay working or eat at your desk or just be by yourself, I'll understand."

But when I thought about it, I realized I liked the idea of her and me having a quiet lunch alone together most days and told her so.

The doorbell rang as we were cleaning up, and I went to answer it. I was expecting the cable TV installer but found Audrey on the porch instead, carrying a basketful of housewarming goodies.

"This is a nice surprise," I said as I let her in.

"Happy home," she answered, handing me the basket. "How's it going?"

I'd talked to her about my concerns in making this move and appreciated that she'd remembered and cared enough to check in on me. "So far, so good. Come and meet my grandmother."

I led the way to the kitchen and introduced them. My grandmother is an old-school Catholic who still doesn't eat meat on Fridays, and I could tell she was slightly shocked by Audrey's faded blue jeans and sweater. But Gramma recovered quickly and offered her some of the coffee she'd just made.

"What a beautiful home this is," Audrey said as my grandmother poured coffee and I emptied the basket of a bottle of wine, crackers, cheeses, and a tiny chocolate torte.

"It's Jimi's house now, you know," Gramma answered.

"She told me what you were doing for her and her girls. She's lucky to have someone who cares so much about her."

My grandmother waved away that notion. "I'm lucky to have Jimi and the girls. They keep me young."

Gramma brought two cups of coffee to the table where Audrey and I sat. "Do you have family, Sister?"

"I have a niece in Santa Fe. She's twenty-four and getting married at Christmastime. I'm giving the bride away, if you can imagine that."

"Where are her parents?" I asked, opening the torte and cutting us all a piece.

"My sister and brother-in-law both died in a car accident several years ago," Audrey answered as she sweetened her coffee. "I'd just come back from Africa a few months before. We were barely getting reacquainted and boom! They were gone."

"Africa?" my grandmother said. "You were in Africa?"

"For fifteen years."

"What did you do there?" Gramma again. I'd heard this part but waited while Audrey filled her in.

"The church has several missions going strong. We worked with native tribes, brought them religion, helped teach them to modernize their lives, their medical practices."

"Like the Peace Corps."

"Pretty much, yes. It was very rewarding, but the church decided fifteen years was long enough and brought me home. I wasn't sure what I was going to do when I got here. Teach, maybe. Then I inherited my niece Carin and started feeling a yearning to work with families. That's how I got into counseling."

"I wondered why a nun was doing that divorce business," Gramma said.

"The church recognizes family therapy, and these days you can't do family therapy without a big portion of it including divorce. Like it or not."

"I didn't know you'd raised your niece," I said, coming full circle back to the part that was new to me.

"We weren't together long before she went off to college. I don't think you could say I raised her really."

"The church let you have her with you?" Gramma again.

"It isn't common practice, that's for sure. But Carin had only three semesters left of high school, and because she didn't have any other family, it was considered a special circumstance, and I was allowed to take her in."

"Not into the apartment you're in now?" I'd seen Audrey's place. It had one bedroom, and the whole thing was so tiny it seemed to be built for munchkins.

She laughed. "It was definitely close quarters. We took turns sleeping on the couch and made do. So believe me I know all about the adjustments that have to be made when you start sharing living space even with people you love."

"More coffee, Sister?" my grandmother asked as if she wanted to change the subject.

"No, thanks. I can stay only a few more minutes." Audrey homed in on me then. "I also wanted to know how you were doing after Monday night. I'm checking with everyone, but since you found the body, I wanted to make especially sure you're okay."

"Found the body?" Gramma repeated, alarmed. "What body? Is that why you called Danny to come to your group? Because you found some body?"

Audrey's bushy eyebrows arched. "Oh-oh. Did I say something I shouldn't have?"

"No, it's all right. I wasn't keeping it a secret." Although I hadn't been any more eager to tell my grandmother than to tell my daughters. But I did then, briefly. "One of our members died, and I found him" was all I said before addressing Audrey's concern. "I'm doing all right with it. Whenever the image of Bruce lying there pops into my mind, I push it out again."

"Danny does homicide," Gramma said into that. "Is this a murder? Did somebody in your divorce group kill somebody? Is that what you're saying? Aay, what kind of group is this anyway?"

"No, nobody in the group killed anybody," I was quick to assure my grandmother. "Danny is looking into Bruce's death, but the group isn't involved."

"Except that we found him the other night. Unfortunately. Our folks have enough on their minds right now without something like this happening. Poor Jimi, I roped you into volunteering, and you definitely got more than you bargained for, didn't you? I'm feeling very bad about that."

"Don't. It isn't your fault."

"It's just a terrible, terrible thing."

My grandmother asked a few more questions about Bruce, most of which I tried to answer in a way that downplayed the suspicious circumstances of his death. But she's a hard woman to fool. Audrey added her assurances that I was safe in continuing on with the group, and we finally seemed to convince Gramma.

Then Audrey stood to go. She clasped Gramma's hand for a small squeeze. "It was nice to meet you,

Mrs. Marconi. I think very highly of your granddaughter."

"She likes you too. Now, if only you could persuade her to go back to confession and mass. You know she hasn't done that since she was a girl."

Now we were into territory I really didn't want to talk about.

"I guess we'll have to work on her, won't we?" Audrey said, giving me a wink.

I hoped the wink meant she was only joking.

Gramma said her good-byes from the sink as she rinsed the coffeepot, and I walked Audrey to the front door.

"We've rescheduled this week's meeting for tomorrow night at Clifford's house. Will you be able to make it?" she said on the way.

"Tomorrow is Thursday? I can't think of anything I have to do, so sure, that's fine."

"I'm glad. I don't know how much of the material we'll get to, but I thought it might help everyone to be together, maybe talk over our feelings about Bruce and his death."

"That sounds like a good idea," I said.

All the while wondering what Beverly Runyan would have to say. And if she'd be any more forthcoming with us than she had been with the police.

I finally heard from Beverly at nine that night. I had my answering machine hooked up by then—I'm big on call screening—but when she identified herself, I did a wild crawl out from under my desk, where I was sorting computer wires.

"I'm here!" I said just as she was about to give the

last digit of her phone number. "Beverly? Hi. I'm glad we finally connected."

"Hello," she said as if she were reluctant to talk to me at all and was doing it only at my insistence.

Maybe she'd forgotten that she'd been the one to call me. "How are you?" I asked.

"I'm okay. Tired. I just got off a ten-hour shift on delivery. Last night or tonight must be a full moon. Women were popping right and left." Her tone said it was damned inconvenient of them.

I waited for her to tell me why she'd called in the first place, but she didn't offer that information. I decided to prompt her. "My daughter said you left a message that you wanted to talk to me."

"Yeah, I did. About that cop friend of yours who was at Bruce's house Monday night."

"Detective Delvecchio. He's my cousin." I wondered if she was after Danny as a replacement lover or if his being a cop was the point.

"Does he give you any inside information?"

"I'm not sure what you mean."

"Cops have been trying to get to me since yesterday morning. Calling here. Calling at work. Showing up when I was in the delivery room. Do you know why?"

"Haven't you talked to them?"

"I'm busy. Besides, I'd like to know what they want before I waste my time with them. I thought you might be able to fill me in."

"I'm afraid not."

"You don't know or you won't say?"

"Is there something you don't want to get into with the police?"

She gave a snorting chuckle. "You know I was sleeping with Bruce, don't you?"

"I'd heard," I admitted, hoping she'd think the information had come from a source other than Danny. "How about you?"

"How about me what?"

"Were you sleeping with him too?"

"Me? No."

"Yeah, well, don't act so surprised. I don't know who told you about him and me, or if they admitted to it themselves, but they probably were too. He was spreading himself around pretty good."

Bruce as the Santa Claus of sex?

"I didn't know."

"About anybody but me."

"Are you sure there *was* anybody but you?" I asked.

"Real sure. He was a big bragger."

I left a silence, hoping she might brag a little herself. Not about what she'd done with Bruce, but about who his other partners were.

But Beverly seemed to know how curious I was and took some pleasure in leaving me wondering. "I'm not spreading tales. At least not unless I have to in order to save my own ass."

"If you know something about Bruce's murder or who might have wanted him dead—"

"I don't know nothin' about nothin'. Unless I need to."

"Were you involved with Bruce before the group started?"

"I met him the first night just like everybody else."

"And you were attracted to each other that fast?"

"Yeah, that fast," she said facetiously.

"It must have been hard for you to know he wasn't faithful."

"It wasn't like we were engaged, so don't go making it into something it wasn't. We had sex, pure and simple. I think he was slumming. He said he got off on my 'rough roots.' For me? Hey, he had the equipment, that's all I cared about. What he did with it the rest of the time was his business."

Wasn't that romantic?

"Did that cop friend of yours find anything of mine at the house?" she asked then.

"Like what?"

"God, I hate it when people try to play coy. You're not very good at it. Here's what I'm after. I spent Sunday night with Bruce, got up at four in the morning for a five A.M. shift. When I went to take my birth control pill Monday night before bed, I couldn't find the compact they're in. Last I'd seen it was at Bruce's, which makes me think I left it there. Did your cop friend find it? Is that why the pricks keep calling? Because I may have screwed him but I didn't kill him."

"Why tell me? Why not just take one of the calls and tell the police?"

"I'd just like to know what they're after before I get into it."

"The truth?"

"Ha-ha."

"Seems like the best route to me. I thought Bruce was upset over his wife's disappearing with their kids and wanted to be alone Sunday?"

"He was upset. But Sunday was my night, and I wasn't letting him off the hook. I told him I could take his mind off his problems, and I did."

I pictured her breathing on her nails and shining them against her lapel.

"You know, maybe you and I could make a trade," she said then.

"A trade?"

"Your information for mine. I could give you some

names of Bruce's other playmates and even some details if you wanted them, and you could tell me what you know about the cop stuff."

I wondered if there really were other playmates or if she'd just been baiting me so she'd have something to bargain with. It didn't matter. "I don't have anything to tell you, Beverly. But if I were you, I'd answer the next call from the police and see what they want. Having sex with Bruce and leaving your pills there isn't a crime."

"Except I know cops and they like to clear things up fast and look like hotshots. If that means pinning it on the handiest sucker, they're okay with that. Innocent or not."

"I can tell you one thing: Danny is a fair man. If you haven't done anything wrong, you don't have anything to worry about from him."

"*If* I haven't done anything wrong." She mocked my words and made it sound as though I'd put suspicion in them when I hadn't.

"I don't know what else to say to you, Beverly."

"And you've been such a big help."

I didn't answer her sarcasm. "Has anyone called to tell you about the meeting tomorrow night at Clifford's house?"

"Little Cliffie himself."

"Then I guess I'll see you there."

She gave another of those snorting chuckles and slammed the phone down, leaving me alone with yet more curiosity. This time about who else might have been sleeping with Bruce. Busy guy.

Chapter Seven

It was Linda's turn to drive to Thursday night's meeting. When she got to the house, she came in to check out my new digs, say a few words to my grandmother and the kids, and then we left. The whole time she seemed to have trouble concentrating.

As she pulled the silver minivan away from the curb, I found out where her mind was.

"Are you going to the funeral tomorrow?" she asked.

"I thought I would. Are you?"

"Absolutely. Can we go together?"

"Sure."

"Then afterward I need you to do me a favor."

"What?"

"I know Steve will be there, but probably *Nan* will be too; she's like his shadow. I've been trying to talk to him since Monday night after you dropped me off, only

I can't get him to see me or return my calls; *she* probably won't let him. So I thought I'd get to him at the funeral."

"Are you sure that's a good idea?"

"Absolutely."

I glanced over at her, not liking the urgent undertone to her voice. Same old Linda: Her hair was poodle perfect; she had on a white blouse that nearly gleamed and navy blue slacks with creases sharp enough to slice bread, meaning that as always she looked more put together than I did, in my usual jeans and turtleneck.

But her eyes were a little too wide, a little too bright, as she stared out the windshield at the road and a sunset the color of rainbow sherbet minus the green.

"What I want you do to," she went on, "is to distract *Nan* so I can get Steve alone."

"So you can talk about the financial statements?" I asked, hoping that for Linda's sake she intended to demand an accounting of where all that money had gone.

"Sure. I know he's just embarrassed to face me, and that's why he's making himself unavailable, but as soon as I tell him I understand everything now and that we can work it all out together if he just comes home, it'll be okay."

So much for hoping. "Have you talked any more about this with Audrey?"

"Every day this week. She wanted me to come in for an extra session, and she's phoned at least once a day. I'm really surprised at her. I tell her what I'm going to do and what I'm sure will happen when I do it, and instead of supporting me, she keeps trying to get me to wait. She wants me to talk to my lawyer about what can be done to recover my share of what Steve lost first. She keeps saying something about protecting myself."

"That all seems reasonable to me."

"Well, it doesn't to me. It doesn't even make sense. She's the one who wanted me to go ahead with the financial statements the way the lawyers said, and then, when I do it and find out the whole reason Steve left me is fixable, she's pushing for me to do things that'll just shove him further away. You'd think she'd understand more than she does, but maybe this is where her being a nun gets in the way. I mean, how much can she really know about saving marriages, when she's never even had one? And wouldn't you think she'd be cheering over something that could avoid a divorce, being Catholic and all?"

What I thought was that Linda was the one who wasn't making sense. Divorce insanity. It happens to the best of us. "Has Audrey said why she isn't more supportive of what you're planning?" Like because Linda was fooling herself completely.

"She just keeps saying she wants me to protect myself. That protecting myself is not adversarial."

"And you don't think that's true?"

"I don't *need* to protect myself. Not from Steve. He's my *husband*. I know him. I know the kind of person he is. And now that I also know what's been happening, what he's been going through, we can turn everything around. I've even talked to my family about a loan to keep the store open. I just need to get to him so I can tell him."

Then what? Did she honestly think he'd throw his arms around her, thank God everything was finally out in the open, tell Nan it had been swell, and move back with Linda? Could she delude herself enough to believe that, or had she just not thought beyond the fantasy?

"I know how much you have riding on this, Linda,

but I think Audrey's right: Protecting yourself can't do any harm. Just in case."

"Of course it can. What do you think trying to recover my share of what he lost means? It means the lawyer will do something to attach Steve's future earnings. How is *that* going to show him I'm a hundred percent sympathetic to him, that I only want to help, that I can forgive him for it all, even for turning to that little tramp? It would only make him more upset and stressed, and what's he going to do about it? He's going to be pushed all the more into *Nan's* arms to escape. No way."

Linda was hell-bent, and nothing was going to stop her. Hey, maybe she was right. Maybe Steve would be overjoyed by her generosity, move back in, there'd be one less divorce in the world, and they'd live happily ever after.

And maybe my grandmother would become Mrs. Jack La Lanne.

But if Linda talked to Steve at the funeral and it didn't work out the way she wanted, at least then she might take Audrey's advice and ask her lawyer to put some more productive wheels into motion.

Only before that had any chance of happening, she was probably in for a very rude awakening, and if neither Audrey nor I could prevent it, I could at least be nearby to pick up the pieces.

"So will you mount a distraction if I need one?" Linda asked.

I sighed. "I'll do what I can."

Clifford's house wasn't far from mine. Just north on Wadsworth to Eighty-second Avenue, a few blocks from the high school where Chloe had graduated the year before last and that Shannon now attended as a senior.

Clifford's place was a large beige brick trilevel over which he and his ex-wife had battled mercilessly. She'd lost and out of spite had withheld the garage door opener. It was a matter awaiting a court hearing. By the time they were finished, that thirty-dollar remote was going to cost them both a couple of grand.

Like I said, divorce insanity.

I could tell by the cars parked out front that Linda and I were the last to arrive. We rang the doorbell and heard a "Come in" through the screen. Then a "We're downstairs" that drew us to a family room there.

Hellos made the rounds as Linda and I sat on the floor against one wall because all chairs and the sofa were occupied.

I'd done these groups often enough to have learned that the homes of members told their own stories. There were the tiny, bare apartments of those starting over from scratch, some dreary and dismal, others with a sense of rebirth.

There were homes where nothing seemed to have been disturbed, as if the departing spouse had just evaporated. I always wondered whether the departing spouse hadn't wanted reminders of their life together or if the remaining one wouldn't let go of anything. Once you got to know the person in the group you could usually tell which had been the case.

There were also homes that had a pared-down look with furniture rearranged so that it was impossible to do more than guess at the sites of the extractions. At least I hoped that was the case, because that was what I'd done.

Then there were homes with uncamouflaged shadows on the walls where pictures had been, unsteamed indentations in the carpet from tables or chairs or sofas that used to be there, all left like pockmarks.

Clifford's house was of the last variety. Bruce's had been undisturbed. Except of course for his body lying on the kitchen floor.

"We've decided to do the seminar first and talk about other things later. Is that agreeable to you too?" Audrey asked, aiming her question at Linda because as a volunteer I was not a participant in the group but essentially Audrey's assistant, there for moral support and as an example of the fact that divorce really could be survived.

"That's fine," Linda answered a little belatedly and again as if she were only half paying attention.

I saw Audrey frown just a tad and knew she probably realized where Linda's thoughts were. But then she began talking about the chapter that had been assigned in the workbook, and the evening got under way.

This particular chapter was the one we'd been scheduled to do the night of Bruce's death, parent-child relationships. I'd come into my first Hunter group convinced that in my own marriage I had been the parent. I'd complained often enough during its thirteen-year run that I felt more like my husband's mother than his wife. And that for me, it was a major turnoff.

What had been harder to come to grips with when I'd reached this meeting in my original group was that in some ways I'd played the child too. I'd been very dependent. That was part of why it had been so tough to get over the breakup.

It's funny, though. My husband's taking off had forced me to grow up in a way I don't know that I ever would have been able to do had he stayed. The good and the bad again. Only it had been a long, hard road to accepting that the bad had been *in* the marriage I'd thought was okay and that the good had come from all that damn pain of breaking it apart.

The group was pretty subdued tonight. Not many complaints surfaced about their most recent divorce injustices when Audrey ended her talk and left us to discuss the chapter and air gripes. So we ended the work portion at about the time we usually have our mid-meeting break.

Janine Cummings had volunteered to bring the snack, but not many of her bran muffins disappeared from the plate. We all did take coffee and tea with us, though, as we settled back in that downstairs family room in a semicircle around Audrey while she addressed Bruce's premature demise.

"A lot of things have happened in the course of my Hunter groups," she said, "but this is the first time death has touched one. I don't want any of you to be surprised if it brings up more feelings, more issues, than you might expect."

There were murmurings among the group to confirm it, but when no one offered more than that, Audrey went on.

"Think of it this way," she said. "If you had a bad cold and then got a case of stomach flu on top of it, that stomach flu would hit you even harder than it usually might and all the cold symptoms would be worse too. Divorce is an ending to a part of your life, and it leaves a lot of questions about where the rest of your life is going. It's normal to start to worry that you might spend it alone. That you might die alone. The death of someone we all knew and identified with—even if for only a short time—may make all those questions seem more frightening. But remember, you aren't alone. You can reach out to each other. And there can be a full, rich future even after divorce."

"Unless somebody decides to off you too," Beverly muttered loud enough for us all to hear.

"I don't believe Bruce's death had anything to do with any of us or anything to do with the group," Audrey said patiently. Then, as if she wanted to keep Beverly from saying any more, she went on. "I think that rather than dwell on the way Bruce died we should remember him for what we knew of him. He was a well-respected man. A father who loved his children and wanted the best for them. A member of the group who was generous with the time and attention he was willing to spend with his fellow members."

I didn't think Audrey knew just how generous he'd been. I certainly hadn't. Now I couldn't help wondering about the full extent of his generosity.

"Unless anyone wants to add a kind word," she concluded, "I'd like us all to spend a moment of silence and offer a prayer or a good thought for him."

But into that silence came one of those involuntary gulping, herky-jerky breaths of someone crying very hard and trying to hide it.

Everyone looked to see who had made the sound and discovered it was Clifford. Sitting on an ottoman, he was hunched over, elbows to knees like *The Thinker*, only his face was buried in his hands and he was sobbing so fiercely his shoulders shook.

Gail Frankin was sitting on the floor beside him, and she got up on her knees to stretch an arm across his back, patting his shoulder.

So much pain.

But then apparently Clifford and Bruce had become friends if Clifford was whom Bruce had called for support when he'd learned his wife had disappeared with his kids the way Janine had said. It made sense. Of the three men in the group, Clifford and Bruce were closer in age and experience than either of them was to Ron Arnot. Clearly they'd seemed to identify with each other's problems.

Now Bruce was dead, and poor Clifford had that to deal with on top of everything else.

It wasn't unusual for a group member or two to break down during the course of a meeting, but it was never easy to witness, and often it set off a chain reaction. This was no different.

I blinked back some telltale wetness and glanced around the circle. Audrey's expression was sympathetic. Tears were running down Linda's face. Ron was sniffling as if he'd prefer everyone to think he had allergies. Janine was blotting running mascara and looked as if she wanted to go to Clifford, though this time in the spirit of aid and comfort.

Only Beverly Runyan was unmoved. In fact, I wasn't sure what she was. Disgusted, if anything. She stared at Clifford the way people stare at exhibits in museums, only her expression said the exhibit wasn't all it was cracked up to be.

I wondered if she was really that cold a fish.

She looked up just then, caught me watching her, and we had a few seconds' worth of staredown. She blinked first. Then she nodded toward Clifford, gave me a nasty-looking grin, and arched one eyebrow.

I got the message.

Chapter Eight

THE NEXT DAY dawned without any remorse for the loss of Bruce Mann. The sun was high and bright, heating the air to a balmy autumn warmth, and there wasn't a hint of a breeze to ruffle anyone's feathers.

The memorial service was at eleven at Crown Hill mortuary at Twenty-sixth and Wadsworth, with the interment to follow immediately at the cemetery across the street. Linda and I left at ten-thirty, and neither of us had much to say on the way.

I don't know the origins of Crown Hill, but it looks like a mansion out of an F. Scott Fitzgerald novel. It's a multilevel stately white manor house complete with marble lions guarding either side of the front entrance and a long latticed arbor walkway with Doric columns separating the rear parking lot from the street.

Just inside the door were two well-tailored gentlemen in dark suits and white shirts, the human versions of the lions outside. They directed us to the main chapel for the service and prevented anyone from wandering astray.

If the number of mourners was any indication, Bruce Mann was either very well liked or from a huge family. The large room was packed.

It was done in royal blue carpet and pearly white walls with white chairs lined up in rows directly in front and to either side of a mahogany dais.

Bruce's silver coffin was between the first row and the dais, and I was glad to see it was closed. Attending his funeral was activating my vivid memories of finding him lying on his kitchen floor. I was fighting them, but I don't know how successful I'd have been if I'd had to see him again.

By the time Linda and I filed in, all the chairs were taken and people had filled the side aisles, leaving us to find space at the rear perimeter.

I scanned the crowd for signs of the Hunter group and spotted Audrey and Clifford sitting together about four rows directly ahead of us. I didn't know for sure, but I was betting it was by Audrey's design that they were together. It was like her to pick out the one person in the group most disturbed by Bruce's death and make sure she was there for him.

Clifford seemed fidgety. Or maybe I was imagining it. I'd been imagining a lot about Clifford since that look Beverly had shot me the night before. But no matter how insinuating that grin and nod had been, I knew that it was possible the insinuation coming from Beverly was more malicious mischief than revelation. At least that was what I hoped.

Nearer to the front of the chapel were Ron and Janine. I hadn't expected Ron to come. As we'd left the previous evening's meeting, we'd all talked about who could and couldn't make the funeral. Ron and Beverly both had been unsure if they could get off work. But Beverly was there too. Sitting alone near a side door as if she might want to make a quick getaway.

Standing to my right, Linda was checking out the other attendees as if she were searching for a felon. I knew when she'd located her soon-to-be ex-husband because I felt her take a step forward as if she were going to go to him right then and there. Apparently that was how eager she was.

She didn't, though. She stiffened up and stayed put.

I followed the direction of her gaze and discovered Steve near the middle of the left-hand section of chairs. His arm was around the back of Nan Arnot's shoulders.

I recognized her from a picture Linda had shown me of her, taken at an amusement park where Steve and Nan had entertained Linda's kids at the end of their summer vacation. The kids had come home with snapshots to remember all the fun they'd had. Self-torture had driven Linda to sneak one out of her son's room so she could see her rival, and she'd brought it over to show me too.

I'd assured her she was better-looking. I don't think it had helped, even though it was almost true. Nan was a lot younger, thinner, and firmer, but there was something classless about her that made me expect to see her chomping gum even as she sat there in her impeccable tan suit and cream silk blouse, with her caramel-colored hair in shoulder-length curls.

Then I noticed who was sitting beside Nan Arnot and did a double take. It was Gail Frankin.

Sure, the seating could have been coincidental, but the fact that there was a resemblance between the two women cut down on the odds and caused me to stare.

It wasn't that they looked enough alike or that I was familiar enough with either of their faces that it would have struck me before, but with them side by side it struck me then. There were similarities in the high cheekbones, the straight, thin noses, and the dark eyes.

I wondered if I could be imagining that too. Only the longer I studied them, the surer I became that I wasn't. And the more curious I got.

I was aware that Gail and Ron had known each other before the Hunter group, but no one had ever said anything about its being through Steve's mistress. Were they sisters? If they were related, shouldn't Gail have addressed it early on so that if Linda had been uncomfortable with it, one of them could have changed groups?

Finding out at this point that there was a connection between Gail and the other woman could be a can of worms. It was one thing for Linda to have taken Ron under her wing, to commiserate with her counterpart. But to be rubbing elbows with someone who could be expected to be in Nan's corner? I didn't know how Linda would feel about that.

Neither did Gail, to judge by the nervous looks she was casting our way.

Whether Linda noticed anything or not was hard to say, but I didn't think she did. She was like a racehorse waiting for the gate to open. Her sights were set on the finish line: Steve. For the first time since she'd hatched this plan I was glad for it. She had enough on her plate at that moment without adding the potential complication of having laid bare her soul in front of someone who could have sympathies with her enemy.

The memorial service began with the minister's introducing himself and saying a few words about Bruce. Then he turned the dais over to eulogies.

These things always go pretty much the same way. someone read a poem Bruce had liked. Others talked about what a good guy he was and how much he'd be missed.

When the eulogies came to a close, the minister took over again. He said a few prayers interspersed with hymns sung by a strong tenor.

It was a nice service. But my feet hurt like hell. I apologized mentally to Bruce for wanting things to hurry up and end, but I couldn't help it. I'm not used to pointy-toed shoes, let alone to standing in them for any amount of time.

Maybe he was listening, because about then the minister concluded the memorial, and we all drove to the cemetery across the street for the interment.

I took off my shoes for the ride to the graveside and rearranged that little seam of agony that cheap nylons have instead of reinforced toes. I never know what to do with that thing, and no matter where I put it, it bothers me. But moving it helped, and I exited the car in better shape than I'd left the mortuary.

Linda and I were already there when Bruce's widow and two kids were escorted to the site of his final resting place. I hadn't been able to see anything but the back of her head from my vantage point at the memorial service, but now I got a glimpse of her face.

Danny had told me that the story of Bruce's murder on the news had made the wife resurface, but not until I got a look at her did I have any idea that I knew her.

My mother had worked in the grade school not far from my folks' house for twenty-nine years, first as a teacher's aide and then as the library assistant. Not long before she'd retired, the librarian had been assigned a young and particularly tense and timid student teacher named Melanie Weider. My mother had felt sorry for her and started bringing her home after school to soothe her nerves and boost her confidence.

Melanie Weider was now Melanie Mann.

Small world.

I wasn't sure if she'd remember me. I'd met her a few times at my parents' home, and she'd come to Christmas dinner at my place that year because she hadn't been able to afford to go back to Nebraska, where her own family lived. But it had been a long time ago.

She didn't glance up from the coffin as the minister said the Lord's Prayer. She just kept staring at it, holding the hands of her two small kids. They all three looked as dazed and confused as they did grief-stricken.

I wondered what I would have felt had my husband died in the middle of the divorce proceedings. There were a lot of times I'd wanted to kill him myself, and I know there would have been a part of me that would have been relieved to have had all the misery he'd caused me cut short. Relief might not have been the biggest part of my feelings, but it would have been there. Probably bringing with it some guilt for feeling that way and making a whole stew of conflicting emotions.

Then I remembered what Bruce had said to Janine the night before he died about his wife's warning to him. *Pulling something*. What did that mean?

I still hadn't come up with any possible explanations when the interment drew to a close with the casket's being lowered into the ground.

The minister said a few final words and threw the first handful of dirt into the hole. Then he announced that Mrs. Mann would be accepting visitors at her apartment in Lakewood and gave the address. And that was that.

Someone led Melanie back to the waiting limousine before anybody could get to her. A lot of the mourners followed, going to their own cars, and a lot more began to greet one another as if a ban of silence and solemnity had been lifted. Life goes on.

Linda grabbed my arm and said, "We have to get to him before he leaves." *He* of course was Steve, the husband she was plotting to snatch back from under the nose of Nan Arnot.

I could tell just from the bits and pieces of conversations I caught on my way through the crowd that everyone was talking about Bruce's being murdered. But Linda and I were moving too fast to garner anything really interesting.

Then there we were, insinuating ourselves into the threesome made up of Steve, Nan Arnot, and Gail Frankin.

Even then I don't think the oddity of Gail's being with Steve and Nan clicked in Linda's mind. There was too much urgency in her intent to get Steve off by himself.

"I need to talk to you," she said to him, letting go of my arm to grab his.

Steve was three inches shorter than Linda and at least an inch under what I guessed to be Nan's five eight. He had oily brown hair and a pug-dog kind of face with a fatty nose and overly large pores. I'd never known him to be anything but bland. Not particularly personable or witty or funny or intelligent, even on those few occasions when I'd been alone with him.

It had forever amazed me that he was as successful in business as he was. But then, there must have been something I was missing, because not only had he done very well for himself—at least before venturing out on his own—but he also had two women hot for him. Go figure.

He looked at Nan as he spoke to Linda. "We have to be going. We have an appointment."

"It'll have to wait," Linda decreed, and pulled him several feet away.

Nan semiturned to follow them, and I took my cue.

"Hi. I'm Jimi Plain, Linda and Steve's neighbor on Miller Street," I said, holding out my hand to her.

Close up I noticed that she had quite a few lines under her eyes for someone not terribly much older than Chloe. Maybe her conscience kept her up nights.

She seemed unsure about whether to talk to me or run along at Steve's heels like a lapdog but finally showed some manners and shook my outstretched hand.

"I'm Nan Arnot," she muttered, keeping Steve and Linda in her sight.

I held on to her hand, covering it with my other one as if she were dear to me while I said hello to Gail. Really I just wanted to make sure Nan didn't escape while I did.

Gail returned my greeting with a smile that looked pained. She seemed edgy and kept darting glances from me to Nan to Steve and Linda.

I gave a little tug on Nan's hand as I released it to pull her attention in. "Am I imagining it or do you two look a little alike?"

"We're cousins," Nan answered when Gail didn't. "Her father and my mother are brother and sister."

"I see. What a surprise. And what a coincidence! Does Linda know?" I asked Gail.

"No. I didn't want her to," Gail said quietly, looking Linda's way again.

"Ron probably told her," Nan said peevishly.

"I asked him not to."

I was surprised at the venom in Gail's voice. It wasn't like Gail.

Or maybe it was because it didn't seem to faze Nan. In fact, I wasn't sure she'd even caught it. Instead, she sighed like someone kept too long in a doctor's waiting room. "We really need to get out of here," she said, pushing back the cuff of her silk blouse to check a silver wristwatch for the time. "We have lunch plans."

The watch was my second shock of the day. Another thing I recognized. It was an ornate antique silver with opals on either side of the face. It was also a gift Steve had given Linda a few years back for their wedding anniversary. I didn't know she'd returned it to him.

That shock was my diversion's undoing, though, because before I knew what was happening and without so much as a good-bye or a happy-to-have-met-you, Nan Arnot made a beeline for Linda and Steve.

"Oh-oh. I wasn't supposed to let that happen."

"You couldn't have stopped it," Gail told me. "Nan would have just bulldozed you if you'd have tried."

We both watched as the younger woman cuddled up to Steve's side and snaked an arm around his waist. Linda was talking fast and furiously, and after a bare glance at Nan she seemed to opt for ignoring her.

Steve, on the other hand, smiled at Nan and gave the impression that he'd tuned Linda out.

"You know," Gail said then, bringing me back around to her, "I was hoping Linda would never have to find out I had any connection with Nan. She's not my favorite relative."

"Why is that?"

"I've just never been able to stand her. Even before

she tried to get my husband to sleep with her when she was all of seventeen."

"No, I don't suppose that would endear her to you. I take it she likes married men."

"What she likes is to do her nails, watch daytime talk shows, and shop. Ron would have been all right if he could've afforded to give her that sort of idle life. As it was—" Gail nodded toward Steve and arched a telling eyebrow.

If that was true—and I had no reason to doubt it—I wondered how Steve's being broke now affected the relationship. Nan still looked enamored of him.

Just then Steve shouted, "No, Linda! Get it through your head. It's over." And my former neighbor started to cry.

"Poor Linda." This from Gail. "I don't know about her husband, but I know Nan should be shot for what she's done to Ron. She's never thought of anyone but herself as long as I've known her, and I doubt if it even makes her skip a beat to know she's devastated two perfectly nice people, torn apart a family, and hurt five kids."

"Steve isn't innocent," I pointed out. "How did the two of them meet? Do you know? I've never heard."

"I'm not sure. Through Bruce somehow, I think."

"Through Bruce? Nan knew Bruce too?"

"I'm not sure how well, but I think she met Bruce before she met Steve. Bruce came into a beauty shop where she did manicures until not long ago."

I did know that Steve had his nails done. I never understood why he'd go into a beauty salon for that but not have his hair at least washed while he was there. "Maybe Bruce recommended Nan as a manicurist."

"Maybe. But it seemed as if she and Bruce knew

each other better than that. Or maybe that only happened since she and Steve got together because they spent so much time with Bruce."

"They did?"

"It sure seemed like it. I was at a baby shower with her a month or so ago, and she talked as much about Bruce as she did about Steve. Bruce and his wife had just split up, and she made a bad joke about starting a divorce club, there were so many of us: her and Steve, Ron, me, Bruce. I said Ron and I were about to join one, the Hunter group, and that it was no joke. She ended up asking me for information about it to give to Bruce."

"So you knew Bruce too before the seminar started?"

"No. Nan had just talked about him. She said Bruce was helping them out."

"With what?"

She shrugged. "Nan didn't say, and I didn't ask. I never prolong our conversations. I always just want them to end. But since Bruce was a tax accountant, maybe it had something to do with taxes."

I supposed that made sense. Given Steve's other money problems, he was probably in trouble with the IRS and needed a good accountant.

"Please! You have to listen to me!" Linda's voice carried to us that time. "You can't just throw away eighteen years. *Eighteen years*, Steve! Don't they mean anything to you? Don't *I* mean anything to you?"

Gail and I turned to see Steve and Nan walking away from Linda as she tried to catch the tail of Steve's suit coat and nearly fell on her face. It wasn't a pretty sight.

"Oh, God," Gail said again. "Poor Linda."

Poor Linda was right.

For a minute I thought she was going to collapse on the cemetery lawn. But she seemed to pull herself together somewhat at the last minute and ended up just watching Steve and Nan cozy their way to the parking lot.

Still, I could see her whole body shaking and knew she was crying as hard as Clifford had the night before.

I wanted to pick up a rock and throw it at Steve.

Instead, I went to Linda. To pick up the pieces.

Chapter Nine

"MAKE YOUR HANDS do like a chicken beak: clack, clack, clack, clack. Make your arms do like wings: flap, flap, flap, flap. Squat a little and wiggle your butt good: one, two, three, four. Clap your hands: clap, clap, clap, clap. We do three more like that. Then we link together and turn—two times this way. Change arms—two times the other way. And that's the chicken dance."

Saturday night with my grandmother.

After a dinner of to-die-for puttanesca over angel hair pasta, she'd decided Chloe and Shannon needed to know how to do the chicken dance for all the Italian weddings they'd go to in their lives. I don't know about anybody else's family, but in ours the chicken dance is tradition.

The old walnut coffee table was pushed into the hallway to clear the living-room floor, and there she was, singing "doodle-doodle-doodle-do" and dancing that nutty dance until her cheeks were the color of the fresh tomatoes she'd squeezed for the sauce.

She'd unfastened the bottom three buttons of her shapeless shift of a dress, her favorite yellow one, and pushed her nylons and her garters down around her ankles. She'd even kicked off her pink bootie slippers, keeping her feet about eighteen inches apart so she could do the squat and wiggle for the best effect. And as always, as soon as supper was over, she'd taken out her lower denture plate.

But she had us all—the girls and me—laughing and dancing until none of us could breathe anymore and I tripped and tumbled over the arm of the tweedy recliner that had been my grandfather's chair but that Gramma had taken over now.

The living room would never make the cover of *House Beautiful.* Or an inside spot either, unless it was the "before" picture for a makeover. Besides the recliner there was my grandmother's couch, brown around the base and up the Cleopatra's barge arms, with all the cushions a white background around orange and brown flowers quilted into the centers. She had a console TV, where one of our VCRs was plugged in, and two tan brocade wing chairs below an enormous mirror.

Added to that was our navy blue plaid sofa in front of the big picture window, and what we had was plenty of seating in a decorator's nightmare.

"I know what we should do," Shannon said from her spot draped over both arms of one of the brocades. "We should go rent wedding movies and stay up all night watching them. Chloe and me and Gramma could go get them and Mom could make brownies while we're gone and we could get popcorn and show Gramma how to work the microwave when we pop it."

"Did you see *Four Weddings and a Funeral,* Gramma?" Chloe asked.

"Ooh, what kind of movie is about weddings and funerals too?"

"It's good. It's not sad," Shannon said. "And we could get *Betsy's Wedding,* and *Father of the Bride* with Steve Martin, and what else, Mom?"

"*Honeymoon in Vegas?*"

"No, I didn't like that one. Well, maybe, so Gramma could see the parachuting Elvises. Can we do it?"

"I want to," Chloe said.

"Please?" Shannon added.

"You stay up all night and watch those things?" my grandmother asked Shannon.

"And then sleep until noon. You can do it. You went to church already. We'll all put on our pajamas and lie around and eat a lot of bad stuff and drink pop, and it's really cool."

"Aay, I'm an old lady."

"You can go to bed if you get too tired," Chloe said.

"Please? It could be a celebration for our coming to live with you." Shannon again, without a single sign that she hadn't wanted to move here in the first place and had not made the decision easy for me.

"You let them do this?" Gramma asked me.

"Sure. But you don't have to do it too if you don't want to."

"But it would be fun," Chloe said.

It took my grandmother a full ten seconds to consider it. "Let me put my teeth back in and pull up my stockings. I can get a few things at the store while we're out."

• • •

I'm not a great cook, but chocolate and I get along pretty well. I have two recipe boxes. One for all things chocolate and one for everything else. But brownies I can make from memory. Dense, dark, rich ones that are fudgy on the inside and crusty on top.

The main kitchen cupboards were crammed to the gills with my grandmother's pots, pans, and cooking gear, so I had mine upstairs, overflowing from the tiny apartment cupboards in my current quarters. But I didn't want to bake the brownies in the minioven up there, so I brought my things downstairs.

I was just setting everything on the table when Danny came through the door that separated the kitchen from the back entrance that led down to his apartment.

"I heard a bunch of noise up here just before I got in the shower. Thought I'd come and see what was going on," he said as he closed the door after himself.

There's a big pane of glass in the top half of the old scarred cherry wood door, and if it isn't closed, it has a tendency to get hit and the glass to break. So we keep it shut even when Danny's with us and doesn't have the need for the privacy it allows him.

Danny had on a pair of gray sweatpants, a white undershirt, and tube socks. His hair gave testament to his just having had a shower, because it was still damp and slicked back.

"Gramma was teaching the girls to dance."

"The chicken dance, I'll bet. Or was it the polka?"

"I don't think even she could get the girls to polka."

"Where's everybody now?"

"Gone to rent wedding movies and buy popcorn. You're welcome to join us. The girls are planning an all-nighter. They're probably the only ones who'll make it, but they'll keep the sound down when the rest of us peter out."

"Hell, I'm just glad not to come in here at seven-thirty and find Nellie asleep already because she didn't have anything better to do. Then she'd wake up at two A.M. and pace until it was time to make breakfast. I guarantee the hum of the girls' watching TV won't be as tough to sleep through as that."

"I didn't know that was what she'd been doing."

"Not every night. But more often than not." He poked his dimpled chin toward me. "What are you making?"

"Brownies."

"With walnuts? Or pecans? Or coconut? Or chocolate chips? Or peanut butter? Or those little chocolate mints? Or cream cheese?"

He knew my repertoire. "Half with nuts . . ." I looked to see what I had in the freezer. "Pecans. And half plain. In case anybody wants to put—"

"Ice cream and hot fudge on top," he finished.

"And bananas."

"You guys'll make me fat." He sat at the kitchen table and put his feet up on the chair across from him. "I found out about the hit-and-run of Bruce Mann's first wife."

"Interesting stuff?"

"Not about the accident. Her car broke down. She got out, lifted the hood, was looking under it. It was late, dark. Driver probably didn't see her until he was right up on her."

"Was the driver found?"

"No. There weren't any witnesses. No one ever stepped forward and admitted anything. Canvassing body shops didn't pay off. Nothing much to go on: blue car, going fast."

"So somebody lives with it on their conscience."

"Victim's sister thought it should be on Bruce Mann's conscience, even though he wasn't the driver."

"You talked to her?"

"By phone. She lives in Montana now."

"How does she figure it was Bruce's fault?" I asked.

"Said if it weren't for him, her sister would have been driving a decent car that wouldn't have broken down. Seems he did something funny with all their money and assets just before they got divorced, made it so she came out without a penny."

I didn't like the familiar ring of that. "What do you mean, he did something funny?"

"Seems that when it came time to divide things up, damn near everything had been used to pay off loans—loans for his college, loans for starting up a private accounting firm of his own, loans for a down payment on the house, loans to meet the mortgage when times were tough. Trouble was, the wife never knew there *were* any loans; he handled all the money, being the accountant in the family, and didn't tell her. And all the loans just happened to be to his family and friends. Then once the divorce was final, seems like he got a whole lot of money reloaned to him that put him on sweet street again while she was left with nothing."

"Creative divorce accounting? Hiding money so the spouse can't have it?"

"That's what the sister thinks. But no one could ever prove anything. Mann had the IOUs, duly signed and dated. They looked legit to the court."

"But they weren't?"

"Like I said, no way to prove it. He had the paperwork. Friends and family confirmed it. Court ruled in his favor."

"Maybe the sister killed him for revenge."

"She has an alibi: She's been in a rehab center for too long to be considered seriously. Even for a murder that could have been set up a while ago. But she hated Bruce Mann all right. I made her day by telling her he was dead." Danny dipped a finger in the batter and tasted it. "I hear your friend Linda had some financial surprises from her husband recently too."

He made that sound nonchalant. As if it would fool me.

I thought of asking where he'd heard about Linda's money woes but knew better than to waste my breath. Danny always seemed to have eyes and ears everywhere. I suppose it's what makes him a good cop. Besides, Linda's most recent problems were hardly a secret. She'd even told my grandmother about them when she'd picked me up Thursday night.

"You think it's a coincidence that your friend's situation sounds something like this stuff about Bruce Mann?"

"I don't know. What do you think?"

Danny did one of his eyebrow shrugs.

"I know it hasn't even occurred to Linda that the whole thing isn't on the up-and-up," I told him. "She believes the poverty story a hundred percent. She's even trying to borrow money to bail Steve out and get him back. And their assets didn't disappear so he could pay loans. He lost it all trying to start his own business on too large a scale and compete with people he couldn't compete with."

"Doesn't matter where he says it went so long as he can get it back once the coast is clear."

As I poured the batter into the pan, Danny got up. "Keep it all under your hat for now," he said. "You tell her, she tells her lawyer or him, and he gets tipped off. Better for things to stay the way they are while we do some quiet looking into. That way she may not end up fighting a losing battle after the fact the way Mann's first wife did."

"Sure."

I headed for the oven with the pan of brownie batter.

"Think I'll take a rain check on your movies," Danny said.

"How come? Not enough car chases and things blowing up in wedding flicks?"

"I have a football game on tape. I've been covering my ears all day so I wouldn't know who won. I'd better watch it before it gets ruined for me. But I wouldn't turn up my nose at some brownies and popcorn when they're ready."

"I'll send them down."

He went back to the landing door.

I slid the brownies onto the oven rack.

"Hey, Jimi?"

I looked over my shoulder.

"It's good you're here."

Chapter Ten

I PHONED MELANIE MANN around eleven Sunday morning after conning the mortuary where Bruce's memorial service had been held into giving me the number of where she was staying. She not only remembered my mother—as was understandable—but me as well. She also wasn't too unenthusiastic about my coming by at around one to visit her, ostensibly to pay my respects.

Gramma and I had lasted through two of Saturday night's wedding movies and then gone to bed, but Chloe and Shannon had stayed up for the others, so they were still asleep at noon. That left Gramma and me alone for lunch. I told her where I was going while we ate toasted cheese sandwiches.

"I remember her," she said. "She was at your house one Christmas. She loved my pizzelles, that girl. She went out and bought herself a pizzelle iron and came over so I could teach her how to make them."

I'd forgotten that. But then, that particular response to Gramma's pizzelles wasn't unusual. Her wafer-thin wafflelike cookies are full of anise and always make a big hit.

"But she's not Catholic." My grandmother went on. "So she didn't know how to say a Hail Mary to time them. I had to teach her that too. I told her she could just count how long it took me to say it, but she thought maybe praying over the iron had something to do with how good they come out, so she wanted to learn it."

If my grandmother ever writes a cookbook, it will have to be full of things like prayers and other odd instructions, because anything she makes seems to have a little glitch to it, whether it is timing things with Hail Marys or full rosaries—that's for a cake she makes—or sidebars to directions, like: "one cup ricotta cheese (I ate some)."

Still, it's surprising how well the methods work, even when someone else uses them. I never make her Easter pizza without measuring a pound of ricotta and eating a spoonful or so of it before mixing it with the eggs and sausage to put into the bread dough, and it always turns out great.

"Maybe I'll take a ride over with you to see her," Gramma said. "And bring her some pizzelles."

I was glad for the company but wondered if I should confess that I was going with ulterior motives. I decided against it. Gramma is nobody's fool. She'd figure out what I was doing when I did it. "Sure, if you want to."

"Just let me put my good dress on."

• • •

Melanie and the kids were staying with a friend at one of a gazillion apartments in a complex of gray wood five-story buildings just south of Sixth Avenue off Union Boulevard. The friend was taking the kids to the zoo. Melanie would be alone.

I wondered if the friend was male or female. She hadn't said.

I pushed the button on the mailbox for Apartment 503, identified myself when she answered, and grabbed the glass security door to open it when she beeped us in.

Gramma and I shared the elevator up with a woman who I at first thought was a man because her features were coarse and she'd buzz-cut all her hair off. But when she set her laundry basket full of clean clothes on the elevator floor and straightened up, an ample chest came with her.

Actually, if she'd put on a little makeup to soften the features, she wouldn't have looked half bad. She had a beautifully shaped head. And I envied the easy care of that buzz cut.

"Just out of curiosity, how often do you need to shave your head to keep it like that?" I asked her.

"About once a week. Twice if I have a date."

"Can you do it yourself or do you have to have somebody else do it?"

"I do it myself. I use one of those men's shavers that are supposed to leave stubble."

Ah, the *Miami Vice* look. First men's faces, now women's heads. Frankly, I liked the look on women's heads better than I had on men's faces. I wondered if whoever marketed that shaver had somehow secretly instigated this fashion statement to keep sales going.

"You have to have a young face for it," my grandmother said. "If I did it, my double chin would show up more. I'd look like Ed Asner on that Lou Grant program."

The other woman laughed at that as she got off on the fourth floor, and we rode on alone to the fifth.

We found 503 without any problem, and Melanie didn't leave us waiting when I knocked.

Time had matured her face from cute to pretty: an oval of clear skin, full cheeks, a turned-up nose, and pale green eyes all surrounded by short moppet-styled dark brown hair. She had on a teal-colored tunic over matching leggings, and it set off her eyes to good effect. Still, she looked really tired, and I felt a twinge of guilt for coming to pick her brain at a time like this.

But when she asked us in, I went anyway, conveying my sympathy as I did.

She thanked me but was more interested in letting my grandmother know how good it was to see her again.

I handed Melanie the brownies I'd brought. She took them, and Gramma's pizzelles, and nodded toward an early American sofa a few feet inside the doorway. "Sit down. Can I get you both some coffee or tea or soda?"

We declined the drinks but went into the living room.

The apartment was a mélange. Besides the couch with its eagle-patterned upholstery and ruffled skirt, there were modern track lights, a chrome-and-leather director's chair, an antique steamer trunk for a coffee table, a big television, and a state-of-the-art stereo system.

Maybe she'd moved in with her grandmother too.

At any rate, it was neat, clean, and comfortable, and Melanie seemed at home.

"How's your mother?" she asked me when Gramma and I were sitting on the sofa and she'd settled into the director's chair.

"She's great. She and my father are in Marrakesh right now. It's a mystery trip through a travel club they belong to. But I know if she were here, she would have wanted to see you, so I thought I'd come instead."

"Is she still working?"

"No, she retired about a year ago."

Melanie smiled weakly. "She's the only grandmother I know who has a tattoo."

A butterfly on her hand, acquired long before it was popular.

"She isn't much like anyone expects a grandmother to be," I said.

"How about you? You teaching still?" Gramma asked Melanie.

"I'm on the substitute list. Bruce didn't want me doing anything more than that. I wasn't sure whether I'd need to go back full-time once the divorce was final." She finished that more dejectedly than she'd begun it, frowning as if it confused her somehow. "We had a court date set for next month."

"I'd heard that," I said.

"Oh, I forgot. You knew Bruce too, from that divorce group he was going to. I imagine you've heard a lot of things," she said, hitting *divorce group* with some resentment, as if the seminars were the same kind of social club as my folks' travel group.

"Usually people talk about big hurdles like court dates, but the Hunter meetings are really just a way of taking a look at why relationships fail and what part we all played in it. They aren't spouse bashing, if that's what you're thinking."

Apparently she was, because she said defensively to my grandmother, "I didn't want to divorce him, you know. But he just couldn't seem to be faithful. And I couldn't take any more of the things he did . . . the things he wanted me to do."

Her full cheeks turned red, and my imagination went into overdrive. Had the more worldly Beverly been a better match for him?

"I don't know why I expected Bruce not to cheat on me when he used me to cheat on his first wife." Melanie went on as though my grandmother's presence had sparked some need for confession. "Not that I knew it at the time. He didn't tell me he was married until just before he was all set to leave her."

"Oh, these men. What's the matter with them?" Gramma said, a refrain I'd heard often in reference to Uncle Dad.

"How did you meet Bruce?" I asked, hoping to get into what I needed to talk about with Melanie.

"I went to him to have my taxes done the year I finally got a full-time teaching job. I'd passed his office every day on my way to school the first semester, so I just thought why not make it easy on myself and go right there."

"Ooh, and he told you he was single?" This from my grandmother.

"Well, no, he didn't exactly say that. But he didn't say he was married either. And he didn't wear a wedding ring. Then, too, he was the most attentive man I'd ever met. He called me all the time and spent almost every night and most of every weekend with me. He didn't *seem* married." She gave a humorless chuckle. "He didn't *seem* like anything he was."

It wasn't much of a lead-in, but I had to take it because I was afraid I wouldn't get another one, and I wanted to let Melanie off the hook as soon as I could. "Did Bruce do any other type of accounting, other than taxes, by any chance? Maybe just for friends?"

The chuckle again. "He did a lot of things."

"How about for Steve Kraner? Did he do other things for him?"

"Why do you ask?"

"Oh, just some rumors I've been hearing. And Linda Kraner recently learned that everything she thought she and Steve had in the bank is gone."

"That girl is losing the shirt off her back," my grandmother added.

"I wondered if Bruce had been helping Steve deal with some financial problems or maybe IRS hassles that might have come with them or—"

Melanie cut me off. "So that's what the after-dinner chats in the den were about. I didn't think he'd do it again."

"Help someone with their IRS hassles?"

She shook her head, but it seemed more to herself than to me. "I thought it was funny that we had to start seeing more of Steve, and I couldn't figure out why I was always getting stuck with that girlfriend of his while the men went into another room."

"What were they doing?"

Again, she chuckled mirthlessly to herself. "I'm only guessing, but Bruce knew how one spouse could cheat the other out of their half of the money and assets that should be divided when they got divorced. He did it to his first wife. I was afraid he would do it to me. That's why I made sure my leaving him was such a surprise and why I got a court date as soon as I could, before he had a chance to pull any of his tricks."

But now that Bruce was dead Melanie didn't have to worry about that, I couldn't help thinking. She got everything. Free and clear and without any hassle . . .

My grandmother made a disapproving clicking sound with her tongue. "You think he would help that man do something to hide money from Linda?"

"I don't know. I don't even know exactly what it was Bruce did. It was only after his first wife died and his ex–sister-in-law started accusing him of things that I learned he'd done something before their divorce to turn things his way. He didn't admit or deny anything to me; he just said he'd made sure he got everything he had coming."

"He didn't take care of his wife when he left her?" Gramma said, outraged.

"I guess not. I was never in on the particulars."

"But you think he might have helped Steve Kraner hide money and assets from Linda?" I asked.

"I don't know anything for sure. I do know that he used to brag to people getting divorced that he could show them how to come out of it smelling like a rose. But I hadn't heard him say that since his boss took him seriously a few years ago."

"Did he do something then?"

"I think so. He wouldn't talk about it except to say he was sorry he'd shot off his mouth because he was uncomfortable getting into Mr. Humberger's personal life. Then I'm pretty sure whatever it was he was doing for Mr. Humberger turned sour."

"How so?" Me again.

"I couldn't tell you. I was away, visiting my family in Nebraska. Bruce called. He was upset, but he wouldn't talk about why. Something at work was all he'd say. Then the next day he called again and said he'd accepted a job in Chicago; he'd been offered it a few weeks before, but the money wasn't good enough for us to move. He acted as if they'd made him a better offer because when I asked why he was taking it after all, he said there were a whole lot of dollar-sign reasons for us to get out of this town. I think too that whatever was going on with his boss was getting too heavy, and he needed to get himself out of it. The only way he could do it was to leave."

"So you've been in Chicago?" Gramma asked.

"Until last year. But we didn't like it there, and when we came here for Bruce's reunion, he talked to some people he'd known before at CSB. The timing was just right because they needed somebody who could run the tax department as a one-man operation. Bruce ended up talking them into hiring him back. I was so glad. Seven years in Chicago were enough for me."

I was afraid we were getting off the track I wanted us on. "But you don't know what it was he was doing in his boss's divorce?"

"No. Bruce was a very secretive man. All that attentiveness when we first met? Well, I found out as time went by that he used that as a distraction. I'd ask him something, and he'd start acting as if anything going on with him was boring, as if he were more interested in me. He never would get around to giving me an answer. The deal with his boss was that way. Except one time when he got furious with me over it."

"Ooh, these men."

"What made him mad about it?"

"I came across a file one day while I was dusting his den. It had his boss's name on it, Bob Humberger. That seemed strange to me. Bruce had files all over the place for people he did taxes for on the side, but his boss could do his own taxes."

"Did you look in the file?" I would have.

"No, I didn't. But it got me curious, and I asked him about it at dinner that night. He got really mad and accused me of snooping through his things."

"Was there a file for Steve Kraner?"

"There'd be a tax file—I know he did the Kraners' taxes this year—but I don't know if it would have anything else in it."

"Where did he keep files like that?"

"At the house. In the den."

We talked for a while longer about what would happen to the house now. Melanie hadn't been back there yet and wasn't eager to go. She thought she'd wait until the following week, when her sister could be with her to deal with the contents at least, and after that she just didn't know.

The whole time she was talking about it, all I could think about was Bruce's files, just sitting in that house waiting to be found.

Chapter Eleven

THE SKY WAS such a clear blue it shimmered. The air was a dry fifty-nine degrees, and the Broncos were playing a two o'clock game, so there wasn't a lot of traffic; a fair share of Coloradoans are fanatical about the football team. I couldn't think of a better time for a drive to Morrison. Except having my grandmother along for what I had in mind was not a good idea.

I soft-pedaled it. "I think I'll take you home, Gram, and then go out to Bruce Mann's house, see if anyone's there, if I can have a look at the file on Steve Kraner or maybe get it for Linda."

"Who would be there? Melanie is at that apartment."

"You never know."

"I better go with you."

"Didn't you want to make soup?" I reminded her.

"I can do that in ten minutes in the pressure cooker. I better go with you."

I could tell she knew I was up to something. I considered just skipping it and waiting until I could slip out by myself later. But I felt a sense of urgency to get to that house.

If Steve were swindling Linda out of her half of the money and assets from their marriage and Bruce had had a file to document it, it would be in Steve's best interest to get rid of it. And precious time had already been lost.

"I think I ought to go alone." I tried one more time with my grandmother.

"It's okay. I like taking a little ride on Sundays."

I looked over at her, sitting there in my passenger seat just the way she would have been on a Sunday drive with my grandfather, and decided she'd better know what she was getting into. "If there's nobody there, I'm going to go in anyway."

"How will you do that?"

"I don't know. Break a window if I have to."

"You could go to jail."

"I don't think it's likely that anyone will know I'm there—the house sits back from the road—but it would be better if you aren't with me just in case."

"You shouldn't do this."

"But I'm going to. So will you let me take you home first?"

She frowned at me and shook her head. "If you're going, I'm going too."

And that was that.

• • •

Without anyone to follow I missed the gravel road turnoff to Bruce's house. I realized it only when Red Rocks Amphitheater came into view.

If I had to miss the turn and go out of our way, that was a nice side trip because it's a pretty spectacular sight. Tall, jagged mounds of sandstone turned a deep burnt umber because the iron deposits in them rust.

The theater itself is barely discernible in the distance. In fact, only the tiered seats can be seen: curved rows easing up into a cove of red rock backdrops that tower 440 feet high and bounce sound to form near-perfect acoustics. Hearing a concert there is not like hearing one anywhere else. The backless bench seating is hard on the buns, but it's worth it if you like your music pure.

Had I not been preoccupied by what I intended to do, I might have parked so my grandmother and I could enjoy the view of the sun-drenched pillars of titian stone. As it was, I made a U from the soft shoulder of the road and stirred up a cloud of dust to get back to where I needed to be instead.

I drove more alertly on the return trip, locating the turnoff I needed on my second try. Gramma wasn't saying much, so my tires on the gravel road seemed thunderous.

Or maybe it was just that my senses were suddenly more attuned to everything. Tension, pure and simple. This would be my first-ever stab at breaking and entering. Into a crime scene no less.

Not that that was going to stop me. It just made me uneasy.

When I reached the house, I pulled all the way up to the garage next to Bruce's Porsche, where Janine's old Ford had been last Monday night, and stopped the engine.

By the time I'd done that, my grandmother had spotted the yellow crime scene tape strung across the front door of the house and liked what I was going to do even less than she had before.

"Ooh, Jimi, you better not go in there."

"It's okay. I'm sure the police have already taken out everything they need or want. What I'm looking for is important only to Linda. You can stay in the car; it'll take me just a minute."

I didn't wait for her to agree or disagree but got out, facing the house to size it up and decide on a front entry or a rear one.

A rear one meant retracing the steps that had led me to discovering Bruce's body, and that didn't thrill me. Might as well try the front first.

The stained glass window inside the door that the fire department had broken to get in was boarded up so securely, I could tell as I headed for it that it wasn't going to allow me easy access. The coroner's investigator had done a good job in patching up the damage. But then, that's the coroner's investigator's job. Contrary to the title, the person holding that position isn't really an investigator at all. He or she is responsible for securing the crime scene and making sure everything is kept intact until the authorities locate next of kin and can turn things over to them.

But as I got closer, I realized that behind the yellow banner of crime scene tape, the door itself was slightly ajar. Maybe the coroner's investigator hadn't done such a bang-up job after all. Or maybe the fire department had broken the lock along with the window, and this was the best that could be done.

Acting like a visitor seemed a good cover in case someone was inside to witness my unlawful entry, although without any cars but mine and Bruce's in the driveway, I didn't know how anybody else could be there. Or why. Still, I pushed open the door and called inside, "Hello? Is anybody here?"

No answer. The coast was clear. I ducked under the tape and entered unlawfully.

In spite of the bright sunshine beyond the trees, the tall pines and spruce cast deep shadows that left the inside of the house dim. I could have used a light, but given the method of Bruce's murder, I wasn't crazy about getting near anything electrical in that place. Leather shoes or not.

I waited for my eyes to adjust and then took a look around to get my bearings. I was standing in the large tiled entryway beside a hall tree with an umbrella loop that held antique walking sticks instead of umbrellas.

Directly in front of me were stairs to the second floor, polished hardwood between two oak banisters with thick spindles a foot apart and round knobs the size of Florida grapefruits atop the newels.

I don't know why I felt inclined to have a look around before I went into the den. Maybe just to be sure I really was alone. But I followed the inclination and took a right into the formal living room in which the Hunter group had finally been allowed that night.

It was decorated in lodge furniture, just as I remembered from hours of sitting there waiting my turn to talk to the police. Two heavy pine-based sofas and two chairs with loose seat cushions and pillows formed a square in the center of the room around a coffee table that matched the slat design of the wood-frame seating. To me it looked like a cage. There was also a stone fireplace in front of which lay a bearskin rug.

Probably more than baby pictures got taken on that thing.

I went through a huge archway into the dining

room. There were two sideboards, a table that easily accommodated the eight chairs around it without a leaf, and a tall curio stand that held small statues of birds, the kind you find ads for in magazines that are supposed to be limited editions you pay for in three easy installments before you automatically receive the next one to do the same with until you have the complete collection and have spent more money than you thought. Bruce had the complete collection.

I didn't go into the kitchen from there but only glanced through the doorway. Oak cupboards. Fancy appliances. A copper cache rack over a butcher-block island. White tiled walls with a few squares dotting it that had blue delft pictures hand-painted on them.

I hoped there were no files kept in there because just peeking into it was enough for me to have a flashback of finding Bruce, and if I didn't have to go all the way into it, I preferred not to.

I went back through the dining and living rooms to the foyer again and looked up the stairs, but the thought of the bedrooms and Bruce and Beverly wasn't much of an improvement over the flashback. If I didn't have to go up there either, it was okay with me.

So much for doing a thorough enough search to make sure I really was alone. Except that the longer I was there, the more convinced I was that it was true and the more confident I felt.

I crossed the entranceway in the direction of the den where the police had interviewed each of us the night of the murder. It was the only room on that side of the staircase, and a narrow hall separated them.

I went to the end of the hall first and opened the door that was there, discovering a laundry room with yet another door that led to the kitchen, forming a complete circle around the stairs.

If Shannon had lived there, she'd have had Lucy chasing her around and around until I screamed for mercy.

I closed the doors the way I'd found them and went to the den. It was a classic study: paneled walls lined with bookshelves, leather couch, leather wing chairs, a large mahogany barrister's desk, and a three-drawer matching filing cabinet behind the huge bank president's chair.

I didn't waste any time before going to the filing cabinet, but I was disheartened to find it unlocked. That seemed to indicate that nothing worthwhile was inside. I looked anyway.

In the top drawer I discovered that Bruce didn't use plain manila folders. He used colored ones. Bright yellow, hot pink, neon orange, deep purple, powder blue, black. They all had names typed on labels attached to the flaps, and they were alphabetized, all the way from Ames to Yeager.

I checked three times between Jorgenson, Logan, and Louden, but there was no Kraner. Then I started at the beginning and went through file by file in case it was out of order. It wasn't. It wasn't there.

I pulled a couple of the files anyway and opened them to see what was inside, trying to figure out if each color meant something. If it did, I couldn't figure out what. I found basically the same thing in each one: copies of tax returns and notes from Bruce to himself about depreciations and deductions. Very dry stuff. No wonder he needed some spice in his private life.

Still, the lack of even a tax file for the Kraners was curious. Did the police have it or did Steve? Or maybe Bruce had kept only the innocuous ones in the filing cabinet and the Kraners' was somewhere less obvious.

Like the second and third drawers?

Nope.

The second held Bruce and Melanie's private files: records of investments, stocks and bonds, insurance policies, annuities, and college funds for their kids. I did a quick skip through it all in case the Kraner file was among them, but it wasn't.

That left the bottom drawer. I bent over to open it, but a creak from directly overhead made me jump about a foot.

Okay, so maybe I wasn't as confident as I'd thought.

I stopped cold and listened for more sounds, but nothing came, and I reminded myself I was alone. All houses creak. Especially when you're by yourself in them. It even spooks my dog when she and I are the only two at home in the evenings and I don't have the TV or stereo on. She'll drive me crazy barking off and on at nothing the whole time.

Still, my grandmother was waiting in the car, and I had no desire to drag this out, so I opened the last file drawer in a hurry.

It was filled with supplies—reams of computer paper, boxes of pens and pencils, printer cartridges, packages of unused manila folders, and old, unused tax forms. But there were no hidden files.

I closed it and heard another creak from upstairs.

Again I listened for more and felt my heart race.

Again nothing else came.

This house was really settling.

I turned to the desk, more determined to make quick work of the search even though I knew it was dumb that I was being rushed by my own imagination.

The desk drawers weren't locked either, and I was beginning to wonder if Bruce had anything at all to hide.

There were four drawers—two on each side of the

kneehole—and none of them contained anything but run-of-the-mill stuff. I checked the sides, underneath, and back of each one in case anything was taped to them but found zilch.

Then I sat in the big tufted leather chair, opened the small center drawer, and learned that Bruce Mann unbent paper clips; used his pencils down to the nub; liked pink Post-Its, yellow legal pads, and Godiva chocolates—there was one of the distinctive gold foil boxes on the left-hand side. A half pound.

I fought the urge to snitch a piece, seeing as how they're some of my favorites too, and instead took the box and legal pads out of the drawer to see if they'd been concealing anything. Zilch one more time.

I replaced everything, did the fast hand sweep along the sides, bottom, and back of that drawer too, and pushed it closed.

A new creak came so close to that that I thought it might have just been a drawer noise. Until right away another one sounded, and I knew better.

I also knew it wasn't coming from directly overhead anymore. It was closer to the top of the stairs.

Houses didn't settle in a path to the stairs.

I tried to convince myself again that I was alone because there weren't any other cars outside, but I had less success by then. Especially when I heard another sound, a quiet scraping that I couldn't identify but that was definitely not a sound produced by a shifting foundation. Also, it hadn't seemed to come from as far away as upstairs but more likely not too distant from the den.

An active imagination can be a dangerous thing. Odds were I'd step outside that room and find absolutely nothing. But in my mind I pictured myself having interrupted a couple of thieves burgling the place and I was really in for it. And so was my poor grandmother, waiting in the car like a sitting duck. We could end up as cheap thrills for a gang of creeps here in the secluded house where no one would ever guess we'd be.

I decided that rather than investigate the sounds the best thing I could do was climb out a window, run for the station wagon, and get us out of there.

I stood up from the chair very slowly so I wouldn't make any noise.

As I did, a glint of something gold on the desktop caught my eye, just a corner poking from beneath the blotter that had moved slightly out of place when I'd piled the drawer contents on it. Reflex curiosity made me slip it out, but it was really nothing. Just a Godiva gift card. I wondered who thought highly enough of Bruce to send him expensive candy, but with my grandmother's safety on my mind I couldn't spend the time to read the card. Instead, I stuck it in my jeans pocket at the same time I turned toward the single heavily draped window a few feet to the right of the desk.

I split the curtains and carefully unlatched the lock that secured the center pane. But before I began to slide it up, I realized I could see my car from the window. My grandmother was not in it.

My first thought was that she'd followed me inside and that that accounted for the creaks.

But the glimmer of relief this brought was short-lived. I knew my grandmother. If she had followed me inside, she'd have just called for me until she found me.

I broke into a cold sweat when a new image formed in my mind: Gramma somewhere beyond the den, being held at knife- or gunpoint while the creeps looked for me.

The window escape plan died with that, and I headed for the door.

I'd left my purse in the car, but my keys were in my pocket, and I took them out. I had a small canister of pepper spray on the ring. I'd never used it but hoped to God it worked.

Two more steps groaned as I slipped into the hall that ran between the den and the staircase. I was grateful for the shadow of the narrow space.

When I looked up, I could see feet through the spindles. A man's feet. In heavy black boots. I could also see the ankles of black leather pants.

He came down another step, and I eased in the same direction, hoping for a glimpse of whatever or whoever had caused the scraping sound before this guy reached the bottom.

I could see the entryway and the front door and slightly into the living room, but there was nothing and no one in sight. Not knowing if somebody was waiting on the other side of the staircase was a risk, but I decided I had to deal with the most immediate threat, and that was the leather-clad man on the steps. I'd wait for him to reach the foyer, and if he turned in my direction, I'd zap him with the spray. If he went the other way, maybe I'd follow him and hope he led me to my grandmother.

He stopped before he reached the bottom step, and I flattened against the walled base of the staircase while he glanced over it on my side. I didn't know if he'd seen me, but if he had, I was ready for him.

Then all of a sudden he came the rest of the way down at a faster clip.

It made me think he'd spotted me, so I lunged around the banister ahead of him, squirting the stuff as I went. At the same time, something swooshed through the air and landed a dull thwack against his breastbone that threw him back onto his rear end on the second step.

"You dirty bugger!" It was my grandmother's voice on the opposite side of the stairs, and she was holding a hiker's pikestaff that I'd seen with the canes in the umbrella loop of the hall tree, wielding it like a baseball bat.

She looked up at me, I stared at her, and the man on the stairs used that split second to run like hell for the door.

But not before I recognized him.

Chapter Twelve

I'D TAKEN A WEEK off to do the move and get us all settled into Gramma's house. But Monday was my day to get back to the computer.

I spent from eight o'clock that morning working on the Kiwanis newsletter, my current project. Before I knew it, it was dinnertime, and after a quick bowl of beef stew spiked with burgundy I had to leave the dinner dishes to my grandmother and the girls so I could get to the Hunter seminar on time. But just as I headed for the front door, Gramma came out of the kitchen to catch me.

She handed me a small pouch made from a piece of an old flowered pillowslip. "Here, you give this to Linda. Tell her to carry it around with her in the daytime and put it under her pillow when she sleeps."

I opened the tiny sack at the drawstring top and peeked inside. It contained trinkets that looked as if they'd come out of a gum machine: a fist carved from turquoise, three beads, a polished black stone, a kidney bean, a flattened coin, a religious medal, and what my grandmother called a moloyk. It looked like a brass tooth with two long roots or, probably more likely, like the sign she made with her hand: She held her two middle fingers into her palm with her thumb and extended her index and little fingers like horns. I'd seen her do it over babies, some who'd had something bad said about them, others who'd had too many good things said.

I don't have any idea where she gets these things, but it isn't from a gum machine. She's superstitious and seems to have an endless secret source for charms and amulets. She's always sewing up these little pouches and filling them with some conglomeration of fetishes that only she understands the purpose of.

"What's this one for, Gram?"

"It'll take away the evil eye that's on her. It's like what I gave you before. She's got too much bad luck now, that girl. This will help."

Hey, I hoped something would. "She's liable to think we're nuts, you know."

"That's okay. Tell her to keep them with her anyway. She'll see."

How could you argue with that? I closed the pouch, said I might be late, and left.

Ten minutes later I pulled up in front of Linda's house. I forced myself not to look at my old house for fear of getting really bummed out. I was grateful that Linda didn't keep me waiting, and one glance at her was plenty distracting all on its own.

I'd never seen her step out of her house without perfect hair, makeup, and clothes. Meticulous, vigilant grooming was her way of compensating for her size.

But as she came nearer to the car, I saw that she hadn't bothered with any makeup at all, her hair was a tad on the oily side, and she was wearing a pair of soiled chinos and an old T-shirt I'd seen Steve mow the lawn in. Plus her face was a mottled red and her eyes were swollen as if she'd missed more than one night's sleep.

God, I felt even worse for not having made the effort to see her when I couldn't reach her by phone after the funeral on Friday.

"Hi," I said as she got in the car.

She forced a smile that disappeared within a nanosecond and muttered a soft-voiced "Hi" of her own.

Then she just sat there.

"Don't you want to put on your seat belt?" I asked.

"Oh. Sure," she said as if she were humoring me.

I waited while she buckled up and then asked, "How was your weekend?"

That was all it took for her to deflate. Her shoulders hunched; her head sank. "Horrible."

"Were you sick?" She looked so bad I thought it was possible that some physical malady had struck her too.

"No. Unless you count the emotional stomach flu you said you went through when you got divorced."

In the Hunter seminars Audrey referred to the emotional craziness as a spiral with ever-widening circles that take you farther and farther away from the pain in the center while still periodically brushing against it to remind you it's there.

In my experience that analogy was too clean. I'd had weekends like the one Linda seemed to have just endured. Other times too, when the anguish mounted like nausea and I felt so lousy I wanted to be put out of my misery.

It was usually followed by a sort of exhausted relief,

a peace that would give me a glimmer of a possibility that I'd be okay, the way you feel after you've barfed up your guts and straightened from the toilet bowl nausea free. Until the next wave hits.

But Linda didn't look as if she'd done any barfing or found any relief at all. She also didn't look as if her spiral had curved away from the center of the pain.

"I tried to get hold of you, but your line was always busy."

"I had it off the hook."

"It's not good to cut yourself off like that. You should have called or come by," I said.

"I wasn't fit for company. I felt too shitty."

"But talking might have helped. Or we could have gone out, gotten your mind off things."

"Nothing would have helped."

"Were the kids home?"

"No." Her voice quivered. "They were with Steve and *Nan* at the Broadmoor in Colorado Springs."

That raised my eyebrows. The Broadmoor is a high-ticket resort. Not a place someone in financial ruin goes, let alone with his girlfriend and five kids. "Wow."

Linda started to cry.

I felt like shit for her. And I didn't know what to say. I handed her the pillowslip pouch. "This is from my grandmother. They're good luck charms. She believes they'll take away the evil eye." I said that with a bit of humor in my voice, hoping to lighten things up a little. Besides, how else could you give a person a thing like that?

Linda took it but didn't even look inside the sack. She just cried harder.

I pulled away from the curb and headed for Broomfield and Janine Cummings's apartment, where that night's meeting was being held.

"How could he do this, Jimi?" Linda said out of the blue then. How could he take so many years together and just trash them? The marriage may not have been perfect, but it wasn't awful either. If he was so unhappy, wouldn't there have been signs? Because so help me God, there weren't. It was just a regular marriage. We liked the same things, the same people. We did things together. We agreed most of the time. We thought alike. We were friends. He'd even say I was his best friend, and I always thought he was mine. . . ." Her voice trailed off on a sob.

"I know, Linda."

"It was the same with you, wasn't it? So how do they just throw it all away one day? And then once they do, once they've gotten just what they want—some nymphet and only playing at being a father on weekends that suit them—how come he treats me like I'm all of a sudden some monster? Why am I the bad guy, like he hates me? Like I did something terrible to him instead of the other way around?"

I'd asked myself similar questions but never found the answers. "I understand, Linda," I said. "I really do. He's like a stranger. He's doing things you never in a million years thought he'd do."

"Yes!" she said as if I were a psychic who'd just made an accurate call.

"I can't tell you why or how it happens. Or if this person he is now was always there under the surface and he hid it really well or if he just changed into it. What I can tell you is that there's nothing you can do about it. That the only thing you can do is concentrate on yourself and your kids and going on in the best way you can."

"Maybe he'll change back."

"Who knows? If he does and you still want him,

great. But there's nothing you can do to make it happen. And whether he does or not, you need to do what's best for you. You need to work on that, think about that. That's how you get to feeling like you have a little control back; it's how you finally start to get over things. To get strong again."

"But if I don't keep trying with him, he'll just go on with *Nan*. He'll forget about me."

"Has anything you've tried so far helped?"

She blew her nose. "I wish I were dead."

"It gets better. It really does. I know you feel so lousy now that it doesn't seem like it possibly can, but I swear to you it does."

"Time heals all wounds," she said facetiously.

"It's true. As a matter of fact I realized how true it is just about two weeks ago myself. You know that little park near the grocery store? Well, one day Uncle Dad took me there for a walk. I went thinking we were going to patch things up, and instead he started to tell me a lot of things I didn't want to hear. For so long I couldn't drive by that park without reliving the whole thing. My stomach would clench; I'd feel exactly the way I'd felt that day; I'd be totally wiped out. It just flattened me. Every time. It was so bad I started cussing him out every time I had to drive by there, like a chant to try to ward it off—"

"What did you say?"

I wasn't too sure I should let her in on that part. But one look at her, and I figured I'd better pull out all the stops. "I'd say 'you cock-sucking, mother-fucking, son-of-a-bitching, butt-reaming asshole.' "

That made her crack a smile even as she stared over at me in shock. "Jimi!"

I laughed. "I told you it was terrible." And probably not what Audrey had had in mind when she'd asked me to be a Hunter group volunteer. So much for being a shining example. But you have to work with what you've got.

"Anyway, the point is, one day a month or so ago I drove past that park, and I remembered this stuff I'm telling you. But it had been so long since I'd even noticed the place or thought about any of it or felt so much as a twinge that it seemed it had never happened. Even the memory didn't spark anything in me. So I promise you, you will feel better. And if you want to borrow my chant in the meantime, feel free. Just don't say it out loud if the kids are within earshot."

She blew her nose again, but this one sounded as if it had some finality to it. When I glanced over at her again, I saw that she'd stopped crying. And she was checking her bare wrist.

"God, I miss my watch. What time is it?" she asked, sounding as if the exhaustion had finally hit.

The image of the watch on Nan Arnot's wrist at the funeral flashed through my mind. "Twenty to seven," I said, pointing to the dashboard clock she'd apparently not noticed.

"Do you think we can spare a few minutes to stop at a gas station so I can splash some water on my face before we get to the meeting?"

"Sure." It was on the tip of my tongue to ask about her watch, but I was too afraid I'd be bringing up something painful.

Then she said, "Did I tell you what happened to it?"

"To what?"

"My watch. It broke last month, and since Steve was still actually speaking to me and pretending he was going to be a model ex-husband then, he offered to take it in to be repaired."

"And you haven't gotten it back yet?"

"No, and I never will. It was at the jeweler's when the place got robbed, and it was part of what was taken. I was sick about it. The store's insurance wouldn't replace it because Steve had lost the claim ticket and they wouldn't take the jeweler's word for it that it had been there. I'm just out one watch. Maybe it was an omen. Out one anniversary watch. Out one husband."

And Nan Arnot had inherited them both. What kind of person made up a stupid story like that so he could take his wife's anniversary gift and give it to his girlfriend? And what kind of girlfriend took it?

"It just seems like we've been under a black cloud for so long now," Linda said as I pulled into a gas station just off the turnpike on the outer edge of Broomfield.

"Could be worse."

"I don't know how."

"The IRS could be auditing you." I looked at her out of the corner of my eye. "The IRS isn't auditing you, is it?"

"No, of course not. We never had any tax problems."

So no tax reason for Steve to have been seeing a lot of Bruce.

I didn't say any more about it as I parked near the ladies' room.

"I'll just be a second," Linda said as she got out.

"I'll be here." Chanting my dirty little ditty about her ex now instead of mine.

Chapter Thirteen

THAT EVENING'S SEMINAR was the no-pain, no-gainer; growth and development coming from the agony of divorce; drawing into a shell, emerging from it a new person.

I knew going in that I would be preoccupied. Not because the subject was boring but because the closer I got to Janine's place, the more Sunday's encounter at Bruce's house was on my mind.

Her apartment was above the vet's office where she was the receptionist, a two-story blond brick cube of a building on the corner of a suburban street. The only parking was at the curb.

Spare and brown was my initial impression of the apartment itself when we went in off a wooden landing that topped wooden steps from the rear of the building. The place had a faint odor of animal lingering beneath a citrusy air freshener that no doubt came from a nonaerosol can.

Janine's living room was large. All the walls were paneled in walnut the color of strong coffee, and the unrelenting darkness was broken on only one wall with three rows of gold marbled mirror tiles about two feet apart. There was also a single bedroom, a closet-size bathroom, and a kitchen that was really just a narrow hallway with cupboards and ancient appliances along one side.

She'd done well by the place, though, with a tan couch that boasted loose pillow cushions; two overstuffed chairs, again in tan, only with a tiny duck-foot print of green running through it; and enough well-placed lamps to chase away the dreariness of the paneling—wasted energy be damned.

I was a lot less interested in her decor, however, than I was in scanning the room for one particular group member. When I spotted him, I was a little surprised that he was there. But then, I'd had the guts to show up and face him, so why shouldn't he have the guts to show up and face me?

All through the first half of the meeting I kept an eye on him, wondering if we were just going to pretend yesterday hadn't happened. Maybe. Because he made a point of never so much as casting a glance my way, as if there were just an empty chair where I sat.

I debated about whether to play along and keep my distance but decided against it. Curiosity again. And a sense of obligation to ask if my grandmother and I had hurt him.

The coffee break was the logical time to approach him, but he was really intent on avoiding me. Every time I took a step in his direction he escaped to the bathroom or took cover with other group members.

Then the break ended, we went back to discussions, and I'd missed my chance.

Luckily for me, Audrey took Linda aside at the end of the evening to ask how she was doing, so I was free to nab him just as he was making a hasty retreat to his car.

"Clifford!"

He shot me a glance over his shoulder without stopping, and I wondered if he was actually going to make a run for it. But I was determined and not so far behind him that he could unlock his car door and get in before I caught up with him. As it was, I stood in the street while he stood in the lee of the open door as if he needed the protection. But then after yesterday he was probably afraid for his physical well-being. Who could blame him?

On the other hand, it struck me as odd that this man who was nearly cowering alongside his Ford Fairlane had just the day before been decked out in an all-black leather ensemble, riding a Harley-Davidson he'd stashed in the woods around Bruce Mann's house.

"I wanted to know if you're all right," I said, cutting to the chase. Or actually, at the end of the chase he'd led me on.

"I'm fine."

"You scared the bejesus out of my grandmother and me yesterday. She saw you look out the upstairs window while she was waiting in the car for me, and the way you were dressed, well, she thought you were dangerous. I heard sounds in the house, and when I realized my grandmother wasn't in the car where she was supposed to be, I got spooked too. I'm sorry for the pepper spray and her hitting you."

"Sure."

"She can pack quite a wallop, but she didn't do any lasting damage, did she?"

"No."

Wasn't this enlightening? Maybe if I gave a little, I'd get a little. "You must have been as surprised to see us as we were to find you there. I was looking for a tax file for a friend."

"Your police friend from that first night?"

Sounded good. Why ruin it with the truth? And why not press the advantage of his thinking I had some official capacity? "What were you after?"

"Who said I was after anything?"

"Just a hunch. Not a lot of reasons to be up in a dead man's bedroom." I hadn't intended for that to be a shot, but something about it made him flinch just the same.

"Did you tell the police I was there?" he asked.

"I haven't talked to Danny since yesterday." True.

"But you will." He sounded defeated, as if the jig were up.

I didn't say anything one way or another.

"I wasn't doing anything wrong."

"You were an unauthorized trespasser on the scene of a crime." Like I wasn't. "Why?"

He hesitated. "I was making sure there was nothing lying around that could be misleading if the police found it."

"In the bedroom."

He let his head fall back so his nose pointed to the sky. "Oh, God."

"What could the police find in Bruce's bedroom that might be misleading?"

"Not necessarily in his bedroom. Anywhere."

"Okay. What could the police find anywhere in Bruce's house that might be misleading?"

More hesitation. "Probably nothing." Pause. "Or maybe just a picture," he nearly whispered.

A friendly photo of fishing buddies? "What kind of picture?"

"Oh, God."

I'd seen Clifford's divorce angst. Heard him complain about his ex and the injustices he was suffering. But this was different. There was no martyrdom to it. It was just deep-down despair.

"Were you involved with Bruce?" I asked quietly.

"I'm not a homosexual. I was married. I have kids."

I just waited.

"A couple of weeks ago that bastard tried to seduce me. A night on the town, that's what he said. Two unattached men, a whole city full of beautiful women for us to choose from. Let the exes see that somebody else wanted us."

"But it didn't work out that way?"

"No. We just got drunk. *I* got drunk. Maybe he wasn't as drunk as I thought. He was driving, but my car was at his place. When we got back there, it was three in the morning. He said why didn't I just stay in the guest room, no sense going home. It wasn't as if I had someone to answer to. I said okay and about passed out the minute I got my clothes off. Next thing I knew, I woke up with him . . . with me—"

He cleared his throat, but it almost seemed as if he'd gagged, and I thought he might lose it right there.

He didn't, but it seemed to take some effort not to. "I was so plastered . . . plastered out of my mind. Oh, God. Then he shows me this camera he has set up. In a damn fern. It takes pictures automatically, on a timer, and he'd had it going."

Clifford grabbed his forehead with one hand and squeezed hard enough that I could see his knuckles turn white even though the only illumination came from a streetlight down half a block and the dome light inside his car. But he didn't say anything else.

I didn't think he had to. At least not about what had happened that night.

"And you were afraid the pictures might have been in Bruce's house for the police to find?"

"One picture. There was only one picture that came out."

"How come?"

"I don't know. Something went wrong. But there was the one, and that was enough. I guess it was pretty explicit."

"You guess?"

"He didn't show it to me. He only told me about it. I don't think I could have looked at it anyway. And I know I couldn't stand it if anyone else saw it. He said nobody ever would. That I could have it. I'd just have to pay for it with more nights with him."

Nice. "But you never actually saw the picture itself?"

"No. But he had it. I could tell he did."

Maybe he did. Maybe he didn't. What I was reasonably sure of was that if Bruce had been bluffing, Clifford would have never seen through it.

I suddenly flashed on Beverly's smirk over Clifford's head at the last meeting, and my skin crawled. Was this what Bruce had bragged to her about? Or had he shown her the picture to prove something was going on between him and Clifford?

Just then Linda called my name and interrupted my thoughts. She was standing by my station wagon, which was parked closer to the vet's office, and she waved when I spotted her.

"I don't know who killed him," Clifford said, apparently too lost in his own problems to hear her, "but nobody deserved to die more than Bruce Mann did."

"I wouldn't repeat that to anyone if I were you."

The loathing that had been in his tone turned to supplication. "If you find out the police have the picture, will you tell me?"

"If the police have it, they'll show up with it to ask you questions. You won't need me to tell you."

"Oh, God." He got into his car all of a sudden and pulled the door closed as if it rendered him invisible. I was pretty sure he wished something could. Then he started the engine, cast me a sidelong glance, and pulled away from the curb.

I felt bad for him. Whatever had happened between them, Bruce had preyed on him at a time when he was vulnerable. And then blackmailed him. Really nice.

I was getting to like Bruce Mann less and less.

"Jimi!"

Linda's voice jolted me out of my thoughts, and I realized I was still standing in the middle of the street looking after a car that wasn't there anymore.

I got back on the sidewalk and went down to my own car, where she was waiting.

"Do you care if Audrey takes me home?"

It took me a minute to switch mental gears. "No. That's fine. Why?"

Linda closed her eyes wearily and gave a limp shrug. "I seem to be her number one priority these days. She thinks we should talk."

"She's worried about you."

"I know."

"We all care."

"Everybody cares except the person who should. But if you don't mind driving back alone, I guess I will take her up on her offer."

"Sure, no problem."

"I'll see you later then."

"I'll call you tomorrow, but if you need anything before that—"

"It's okay," she said. "Good night."

I watched her as she walked away, for some reason hearing again her earlier comment about how she wished she were dead and suddenly wondering if she was more seriously depressed than I'd realized.

And if I should tell Audrey about it.

But surely if Linda were suicidal, Audrey, of all people, would spot it.

Still, I just stood there and kept an eye on my friend, feeling a little like the mother of a kindergartner wanting to make sure my kid got all the way to the teacher.

She didn't make it. Audrey had gone back up to Janine's apartment and Linda had almost reached the building when Gail Frankin intercepted her.

That seemed good enough. And I could hardly stand there and watch them talk, so I unlocked my door and got in.

A nice quiet ride home alone with a Hal Ketchum tape in the deck was not an unappealing thought by then.

As I put on my seat belt, I hit the rearview mirror and had to readjust it. The perfect position put Linda and Gail directly in my line of vision again. Just as Gail slipped Linda something.

Granted the light wasn't great, and neither was my view, but I could have sworn that what Gail gave Linda was a file folder. A hot-pink one. The kind I'd seen at Bruce Mann's house the day before.

Chapter Fourteen

I HAD A FEW days to think about whether to tell Danny about Clifford and Bruce. My grandmother saw Danny early in the mornings before I was even up to get the girls off to school, but he was working late every night, and I didn't hear him come home until I was already in bed watching TV.

Not that I couldn't have gone down then or made an effort to see him in the mornings. But I considered it an omen that our paths weren't crossing naturally and held on to my information instead.

But by Thursday I had to make a decision. He'd told my grandmother he'd be home for dinner that night.

As I did some laundry late in the afternoon, I was hoping he already knew that something had been going on between Bruce and Clifford. It wasn't that I felt any need to protect Clifford. I just didn't want to be the one to cast suspicion on him. If Danny had dug up information—or in this case a photograph—that was one thing. It was his job. But if he hadn't and the only thing that turned the focus of his investigation onto Clifford was what I told him, that was something else again.

Still, as I went through pockets before stuffing jeans into the washing machine, I finally resolved that I had to fill Danny in if he didn't already know. Just about the time I decided that, I reached into the pocket of the jeans I'd been wearing on Sunday and found the Godiva gift card I'd lifted from Bruce's desk blotter.

I'd completely forgotten about it. That wasn't surprising with the whole Clifford thing on my mind along with Linda and the file folder Gail had handed her when no one else was around, on top of needing to work on the Kiwanis newsletter.

I opened the little gold card.

The first thing to catch my attention was a lipstick mouthprint in the lower-right-hand corner. It wasn't perfectly shaped as if it had been computer-generated. It was someone's attempt at the real thing.

Then I read the inscription written diagonally from the top-left-hand corner in flowery script: "To my BIG BAD Brucie Bear, I can't wait to be your gold, gold Goldilocks every single night!!! Love licks, Nan"

Oh, my.

By six-thirty the girls, my grandmother, and I all were waiting for Danny. Gramma's buttermilk batter–fried chicken was crisping in her favorite electric roaster with herbed potatoes. An endive salad was ready for dressing in the refrigerator, and there was a pan of green beans simmering in olive oil and garlic on the stove.

The table was set, and Shannon was teaching Gramma and Chloe card games. They'd moved on from Egyptian Ratshit to one called Bullshit. It wasn't a particularly good game; the fun in it seemed to be mainly shouting "bullshit" for no real reason. I opted for calling Linda rather than participate.

I'd been checking in with my former neighbor every day. More than once a day actually, coming up with excuses to stop by her house on my way to or from anywhere I went and phoning in between the visits. I was worried about her. She wasn't the Linda I'd known for fifteen years. Also, the idea of her doing herself harm kept cropping up again and again in my head.

Since Monday night she still hadn't curled or combed her hair or bothered with makeup or good clothes. In fact, most days she wasn't even getting out of bed. And talking to her was like talking to somebody on another planet: She was remote, removed from everything going on around her. And very calm. Very quiet.

Too calm and definitely too quiet.

I'd read that sometimes a peacefulness settles in on people who've made a decision to kill themselves, and I was worried that was what this was. I'd called Audrey about it the night before, and she hadn't eased my mind any. She was as worried about Linda as I was and was keeping close tabs on her too.

Part of the result of all this was that I also hadn't been able to get Linda to tell me what Gail Frankin had given her Monday night even when I'd asked outright. She'd lied outright, barely managing to mutter something about leaving her workbook behind. But I'd seen the workbook in her other hand.

The phone rang and rang. Linda finally answered with a "hello" that sounded dull and uninterested just as I was about to hang up and do a quick trip over there to make sure she'd actually rallied enough to go out and wasn't lying on the floor of her garage sucking exhaust fumes.

"It's just me," I said.

"Hi, Jimi."

"Wondered what you were up to."

"Fixing dinner."

"What are you having?" I knew I sounded like a nosy mother-in-law, but that's the breaks. I could hardly call and say I was just checking to see if I should send the rescue squad over.

"Macaroni and cheese. It's all I had on hand. Luckily the kids like it."

"Didn't you do your grocery shopping?"

"No, I didn't really do much of anything today."

That probably meant she'd stayed in bed again. I'd stopped by after taking Shannon to school and found Linda lying amid sour sheets, refusing to get up and have coffee even if I made it. I'd been afraid that was where she'd spent the whole day.

"What are you doing tonight? Why don't we take a walk in an hour or so? I'll drive over and we can—"

"No, thanks. I think Audrey is coming here later. Paying a house call, I suppose. She's hovering and driving me crazy."

There was a message for me in that, but I ignored it.

"I called to ask you a question. Do you happen to know if Bruce Mann knew Nan Arnot?"

"You ask the weirdest things. Why?"

"Danny was just wondering, and I thought you might have some idea." Lies, lies, lies.

She sighed as if I were forcing her to use energy she

didn't have. "As a matter of fact Bruce met her not long ago. He ran into her and Steve at a restaurant and told me at group the next night."

"Did he like her?"

"Like her? I don't know. He said she seemed shallow. A real space cadet. But who knows? Men don't seem to care much about that, do they?"

Apparently some of them didn't.

"I have to go, Jimi. Something just crashed upstairs."

"Okay. Tell Audrey I said hello."

Linda just hung up.

Danny came in apologizing for being late and sniffing the air like a starving basset hound. He had on khaki slacks, a brown sport coat, a white shirt, and a cocoa-colored tie with yellow dots. The tie's knot was loosened, and his collar button was undone, but all he did to get more comfortable than that was to take off his jacket and hang it over the knob of the cherry wood door before he washed his hands.

My grandmother and I set out the food while Shannon put away her cards and Chloe poured drinks for everyone. Then we sat down at the kitchen table the way any nuclear family might have.

I'd made a black bottom rum pie for dessert, and between the girls and my grandmother there was no shortage of chatter up to and including that. I was glad to see it, though. The girls were laughing and telling us about their day in a way they hadn't done much of when the three of us had been alone; those meals had been more gripe sessions or fights than anything.

My grandmother seemed to be in her glory even with all the noise of two teenagers competing against each other to be the center of attention. Her cheeks were pink, her eyes had their old sparkle, and she was throwing her two cents' worth in here and there.

The phone rang in the middle of Chloe's tale of how the table washer in the student union had tried to pick her up at lunch. The girls' phone is cordless, a boon to a teenager's life but no doubt something contributing to statistics on lower physical fitness because they weren't constantly running to answer it and instead could keep it with them at all times. Even at the dinner table, where it was at the moment.

Shannon answered it in spite of Chloe's certainty that it was for her.

"A collect call from who?" Shannon said after her initial hello. Then she rolled her eyes, copped her best disgusted attitude, and said to me, "It's Uncle Dad. Calling collect. I don't want to talk to him. Can I just say no, we won't accept it?"

"Calling collect?" Gramma shouted. "Why's he calling collect? You mean he can't even pay for his own phone calls?"

Chloe grabbed the phone out of Shannon's hands. "I want to talk to him, to tell him about college. Can we pay, just this once? He's always having to."

Not true. He usually called from work on the WATS line there, which also happened to be the only number the girls had if they needed or wanted to get hold of him. He wouldn't give them his home number for some reason no one knew.

"That dirty bastard." Gramma again.

"Please?" Chloe said after a cringe as if my grandmother's words had slapped her.

"Mom shouldn't have to pay for him to call," Shannon said.

"Just this once. Maybe something's wrong and that's why he's doing it."

Chloe was on the verge of panic at just the thought of it, panic being something she's easily pushed to. I knew there was nothing wrong. My grandmother was on target: He was just being a bastard and trying to see if he could get away with one more shenanigan.

But if I didn't let Chloe talk to him, she was going to spend the whole night fretting.

"Well, I'm not talking to him no matter who pays," Shannon announced, suddenly leaving the table and the kitchen for upstairs.

"Please, Mom?"

My turn to roll my eyes. "You know there's nothing wrong with him, Chloe."

"We *don't* know that. Please! If it's just one of his tricks, I'll never ask you to do it again."

I did one of those I-give-in-against-my-will sighs that are on page 302 of the mother's manual. "I suppose. But make it quick. And this is a once-in-a-lifetime deal. Never again."

"He doesn't pay child support, the least he can do is foot the bill for his own phone calls," Gramma said in a voice loud enough for Uncle Dad to hear in Las Vegas without the phone connection.

"I'm not doing it for him," I said. "I'm doing it for Chloe."

Chloe took the phone into the living room, giving Gramma a dark look from the corner of her eye as she went.

So much for a nice dinner.

"He's got his nerve calling at all when he doesn't have anything to do with them," Gramma started in. "It makes me so mad. They'd be better off if they didn't talk to him at all, ever. What good does it do?

He goes and tries to make them feel sorry for him so they don't see that he's so selfish he puts himself first and never even thinks about them. People treat dogs better."

"You're right," Danny said in a quiet, soothing tone that no one but us could hear. He got up with his empty dessert plate and squeezed my grandmother's shoulder as he passed her, pausing to bend near her ear. "You and I know he's a prick, Rose Nell, and he doesn't deserve those two kids. But he's still their father, and Jimi's doing the right thing."

"He's no kind of father at all," Gramma said, too riled to see the reason in his words.

"It's okay, Gram. He's not worth getting mad about," I said.

"Shannon's the wise one." She went on anyway. "She won't have anything to do with him."

"But she'll probably pay for it down the road with guilt or God knows what else," I said. "Besides, think of it this way: The girls will learn for themselves the kind of person he is. But if we say it, they just get mad at us and defend him. Even Shannon."

"I don't care. It's wrong. You're struggling to support these girls without any help from him, and now he gets away with more on top of it."

She pushed herself from the table too, but not for another slice of pie. She left the kitchen and went to her bedroom, muttering another comment as she passed Chloe, who was still on the phone.

Looked as if the honeymoon was over.

From the living room Chloe's voice carried to us. She was assuring Uncle Dad that it was okay that he couldn't help with her college tuition even though he'd promised to and she'd counted on it.

We heard her say, "Is that why Mom needed to pay

for this call too? Why did you invest in the stock market if you couldn't afford to lose the money?"

My eyes met Danny's as he sat down, and I shook my head.

"He's a jerk," Danny said softly.

"One hundred percent. But there's nothing we can do about it."

"We could set Nellie loose on him next time he comes to town."

"She'd tear him limb from limb."

"Serve him right."

"Don't I know it." But there was nothing more to say about it, and now that we were alone I knew I'd better get into the other things I needed to talk to Danny about before I chickened out. "Speaking of murder, how's the investigation of Bruce's going?"

Danny took a bite of his pie and shrugged, making me wait for him to swallow before he answered me. "Takes time. We're still looking at a lot of things. A lot of people."

"Is Clifford Silver one of the people you're looking at?" In living color in a photograph maybe . . .

"You've been talking to Beverly Runyan?"

"I'm surprised she told you," I said, walking the fine line of letting him think his assumption was right.

"There's no proof Bruce Mann and Clifford Silver were having sex, could be she's just stirring up trouble. She strikes me as somebody who'd enjoy that. She claims there's a picture of the two of them together, but we haven't found it, so I'm reserving judgment."

"Does that mean Clifford isn't a serious suspect?"

"I didn't say that. Could be there was a picture, he killed Mann, went in after the fact, and found it himself."

"I don't think so," I said, treading even more carefully.

"You don't think that he killed Mann or that he has the picture."

"I can't imagine him as a killer, and I know he doesn't have the picture."

"Killers come in every size and shape, Jimi. Did you know that one of the classes Silver's taught in the past at that technical school was home wiring? And that he does work as a handyman sometimes because he's a jack-of-all-trades around the house? And that Bruce had hired him not long ago?"

Some of that was news to me. Some wasn't. "I know that he doesn't have the picture," I repeated. "And I know he's never even seen it."

"What makes you so sure?"

"I, uh, caught him at Bruce's house on Sunday looking for it. Then Monday night he told me he's never seen it, and I believe him."

It was no coincidence that I'd made Danny's favorite pie to sweeten him up for when I had to tell him about Sunday's fun and games. But it might not have worked because he had a forkful on its way to his mouth, and when I said that, he set it back on his plate to stare at me.

"What do you mean you caught him at Mann's house?"

I soft-pedaled my way through an explanation that was almost true about looking for Steve Kraner's tax file just in case there might be something useful to Linda in it. I left out the fact that my grandmother had been in on the whole thing. No sense getting him ticked off at her too.

But he didn't actually get ticked off. He just gave

me a hard cop frown. "Do you know how dangerous that was? Not to mention illegal?"

"And almost fruitless. I didn't find the file." And I didn't tell him I'd seen Gail give one to Linda the next night. How did I know it had anything to do with Steve and Linda's finances? It could have contained cookie recipes or a diet article.

Besides, I had something better for Danny. "Just as I was leaving Bruce's den, I found this." I took the Godiva gift card out of my pocket and handed it to him.

That seemed to do the trick and distract him from my unlawful entry and the file. He read it, took that bite of pie after all, and then looked at me again. "Where exactly did you find this?"

I explained that too.

Danny read the inscription again and shook his head. "Was there anybody that guy wasn't screwing?"

"Me."

I got the frown again. Still, it didn't stop me from fishing. "Why, was he screwing Linda and Gail and Janine and Ron and Steve too?"

Danny rolled his eyes at me, but he didn't say anything.

"So did you know Bruce and Nan Arnot were doing the Goldilocks thing?" I asked.

"Who says this card is from Nan Arnot? It's only signed Nan."

"Seems logical. Did you know?"

He didn't answer me right away. He finished his pie first. Then he said, "No. I didn't know."

Score one for me.

"What do you know about Nan Arnot?" he asked then.

"Not a lot. She's young, pretty, but in a crass kind of way. She's cousins with Gail Frankin—"

That raised his eyebrows. Score two for me.

I went on. "Gail says Nan dumped Ron because he couldn't support her as a lady of leisure. I'm wondering how Steve's reduced financial position figures into that now. Maybe that's why she went for Bruce—"

"I asked you what you knew, Jimi, not what you could speculate."

"That's about it. Except I also know she now owns a watch just like one Steve gave Linda for their anniversary. He took it a couple of months ago to have it fixed and claims it was stolen in a robbery of the jewelry store."

"Oh, brother."

"Yeah, I thought it was pretty hard to swallow too."

"Do you think Steve knew Nan was playing Goldilocks with Bruce?" I asked.

"Who knows?"

"Maybe Beverly?" I was only being flip.

"I don't think even she knew about the Nan thing. She told us a lot but didn't mention that. I doubt she'd have left it out. She was trying hard to convince us to look at anyone but her."

"Nice. Is that common?"

"She has an arrest under her belt that I think she was hoping to keep us from noticing. She wasn't figuring that we already knew about it before we even talked to her a second time."

"An arrest for what?"

"She tried to shoot the balls off her first husband."

"Ouch."

Danny's pager went off just then. He stopped the beep, got up, and went to my grandmother's pink wall phone.

Then I remembered Chloe and Uncle Dad's long-distance chat. But when I looked into the living room, she was gone. I hope after ending the call.

Back in the kitchen I started to clear the table. Danny's conversation sounded work-related. He was asking quick, terse questions—when, where, who—and writing the answers on a pad he'd taken from behind the phone.

Then he said, "I'll be right there," and hung up.

"I know. I'm on my own with these dishes, right?"

He didn't answer that. Instead, he went on with our conversation as if the call hadn't interrupted it. "Any indication that Ron Arnot knew Nan was doing the Goldilocks thing with Mann?"

"None I've seen. And I'd think if Ron knew, he'd have gone ballistic. I doubt if he could have stayed civil to Bruce during the Hunter seminars."

"What do you mean by ballistic? Do you think he'd scream and holler and storm off, or do you think he would have been violent?"

Suddenly I had the suspicion that we weren't just continuing our conversation. "What's up, Danny?"

"Violent or just volatile?" he repeated, ignoring my question.

"I don't know. Ron's big on hunting and fishing and camping and being able to survive in the wilderness, if that means anything. Why?"

He paused, did more of the hard stare, and then gave in and answered me. "Nan Arnot was found dead about an hour ago."

Chapter Fifteen

DANNY WAS OUT the door before I knew it. And before I had a chance to ask him anything. All I could be fairly sure of was that Nan had not died of natural or accidental causes. Homicide detectives don't get called to the scenes of those.

As I sat there alone in the kitchen, it took me a minute to digest the news. I hadn't actually known Nan Arnot, had not particularly liked her when I'd met her, had definitely not liked the part she'd played in the breakup of Linda's marriage. Still, she was barely more than a kid—only three years older than Chloe—and it gave me a sick feeling to think not only that she was dead but that the odds were that someone had killed her. Just as someone had prematurely ended Bruce's life.

I didn't want to think there was a connection between their deaths, but how could I not? There was a connection between their lives. Between a lot of the people they knew or were related to. A lot of the same people I knew.

But that thought was an after-dinner drink I just couldn't swallow in one gulp. Instead, I went upstairs, intending to get the girls to come back down, help me clean the dinner mess, and distract me.

I was grateful that the sounds coming from Shannon's open bedroom door were not the sounds of more fighting. But I didn't expect to find Chloe, Shannon, and my grandmother all sitting on the floor playing cards again as if the Uncle Dad incident had never happened.

I was so glad to see the waters smoothed, though, that I didn't interrupt them. Better to turn on the TV to get my mind off murder while I cleaned up.

But I must not have been as silent a witness as I thought, because not five minutes after I returned to the kitchen my grandmother joined me.

"You mad at me?" she asked as she pitched in.

"Why would I be mad at you?"

"Ooh, for being a bigmouth about that call."

"No, I'm not mad at you. Do you think I feel any different? It just doesn't do any good to say anything about it."

"I know, I know. But when he lies to one of those girls or breaks another promise to them or cheats you some more, I just can't stand it. I can't be quiet."

"It took a long time for me to be able to myself. I try to think that every time he pulls one of his tricks he's toughening them up, teaching them what he's really like so they can build some defenses of their own. They aren't stupid, Gram. They see what he's doing."

"I still want to wring his neck."

"He isn't worth the jail time."

"I'm old. It might be worth it to me."

I laughed but was feeling pretty frustrated myself because I knew I wasn't getting through to her. I thought I'd try a different tack.

"You said when we talked about doing this move that you wouldn't let Uncle Dad get to you. I can't have our being here give you high blood pressure, you know."

"Aay, a little fire in my blood is good for me. Better than getting all worn out."

"Just let Jack La Lanne put the fire in your blood and try to ignore this other stuff, huh?" *For all our sakes,* I wanted to add but was afraid it would hurt her feelings.

"I'll pray lightning strikes that big jackass."

"Jack La Lanne?"

"You know who I mean."

I knew all right. "Lightning doesn't strike a moving target, so that probably isn't going to do any good either," I joked.

But I liked the idea.

Nan Arnot's death was an insomnia inducer if ever there was one. If I couldn't sleep, I decided I might as well be productive, so after everyone had gone to bed, I went into the main kitchen to bake Chloe's favorite pain-in-the-neck orange cookies. I also braced open the old cherry wood door with a chair as a sign to Danny that I wanted to talk to him when he came home. Plus I kept an eye on the rear entrance. He wasn't going to slip past me even if he tried.

It's a good thing the orange cookie recipe makes about seven dozen, each small cakey confection needing to be separately frosted, because Danny didn't show up until after 2:00 A.M.

His dark hair looked as if he'd dragged his hands through it more than once, his dotted tie hung in two strips inside his sport coat, his shirt was open down to the third button, and I caught him scratching his chest and yawning as he came in, before he realized the upper door was open and I was watching for him.

I pretended not to notice how tired he seemed and called for him to come up the four steps to the kitchen anyway.

"Big surprise that you're still awake," he said.

"Want a cookie?"

He took one from the wax paper that lined the table and plopped into a chair to eat it.

I decided to cut to the chase. It was too late for anything else. "Is Nan Arnot really dead?"

"Really and truly, one hundred percent dead."

"How?"

"Electrocution."

I started to stack cookies into a tin. "Another rigged heating vent?" I asked, almost afraid to hear the answer.

"Nothing that creative. No, this time somebody plugged a brand-new extension cord into the dryer's two-hundred-forty-volt outlet, plugged the toaster oven into that, and dropped it into her bath."

"Definitely not an accident."

"Definitely not."

"Probably not just a prowler who killed her in the act of a burglary either?" But I could hope.

"Probably not. Especially since there was cash sitting on top of the dresser drawers."

"So what does that mean?"

"We're probably not looking for strangers."

"So who will you look at? Or have you already made an arrest?"

"No, we haven't made an arrest."

I waited for him to answer the first question I'd asked, but when he didn't, I thought I'd try a different tack with him the way I had with my grandmother earlier. "Who found the body?"

"Steve Kraner. Came home, the apartment door was wide open, walked in thinking she'd gone to get the mail and hadn't closed the door after herself."

"Was there forced entry?"

"No. But he claims she was always leaving the door unlocked, that anyone could have walked in. There are some extra keys floating around too." But Danny didn't sound as if he put much store in either of those possibilities.

"Are you thinking that Steve did it?"

"He's on the list."

"Who else is?"

Danny took another cookie. I wondered if that was a signal that he wasn't going to answer me. Again. Apparently he really didn't want to get into it. Now? Or just with me?

But I'm nothing if not persistent. "Do you think whoever killed Bruce killed Nan?"

"Maybe. Maybe not. Both were electrocutions; that's a link. They were involved with each other and with several of the same people; that's another link."

"But?"

"Method wasn't the same. Lack of subtlety, lack of distance. This time the killer was right there at the time of death, face-to-face, to watch it happen. Not nearly as neat or clean or patient as the last one."

I didn't like the image that brought to mind. "So maybe it wasn't the same murderer."

"Or maybe the killer didn't have time to spare this go-round. Maybe he or she needed—or wanted—it done in a hurry for some reason. Or maybe the killer just hated Nan more than he or she hated Mann and wanted to see this one up close and personal."

I didn't like that either. "Then you do think it was the same killer?"

He took another cookie.

"Any telling evidence? A business card on the floor next to the bathtub? An ID bracelet clutched in her hand?"

"Could I tell you if there was?"

"You might tell me if there wasn't."

"There wasn't."

"Did Steve have an alibi?"

"He was running errands. Saw a few salespeople who might remember him. Or might not."

"So he might have an alibi or he might not. Or even if somebody remembers him, it doesn't mean that between errands he didn't make a quick stop at home to do the deed."

"You don't like him."

No, I didn't. I didn't like cheating husbands. It hit too close to home. But that didn't make my former neighbor a murderer, and I realized I shouldn't be casting extra suspicion on to him just because he was such a creep.

I decided to back off a little. "Was Steve upset?" I asked.

"Very. So was Ron Arnot when we dropped in on him with the news."

My stomach clenched at the mention of Ron. I thought of his tough-guy routine hiding a hurt bigger than he could deal with and wondered how he'd responded to a cop at his door, asking him the kinds of questions that insinuated they thought he might have killed his ex-wife. I hoped he hadn't done the tough-guy routine then.

"Does he have an alibi?" I asked.

"No." Danny picked up one of the cookies with his fingertips and twirled it as if it were a gambling chip. "He also looked like he needed some of that emotional support your divorce group is supposed to be good for. Guy passed out cold on me. Then came to and broke down bad."

Better that than the tough-guy routine. "Poor Ron."

"Will you feel that way if he killed her? Or her and Mann both?"

This time I didn't answer him. At least not until something else occurred to me. "If Ron were the killer, wouldn't he have been more likely to go after Steve than Bruce? He probably didn't even know about what was going on between Nan and Bruce."

"He said he didn't when we asked him. But who knows? And maybe Steve's turn is coming up. Or maybe Beverly knew about Nan and Bruce, could handle sharing him with a man but not with another woman, and that nasty streak of hers made her fix both their wagons. Or maybe she didn't like sharing Mann with anybody, and old Clifford should watch out." Danny shrugged. "Or maybe the murders didn't have a single thing to do with each other, and we're barking up the wrong tree altogether."

I couldn't tell if he believed that. I didn't think he did.

Then he said, "You, uh, see your friend Linda at all today?"

That woke me up. Not that I'd been sleeping. "I saw her this morning and talked to her on the phone this afternoon."

"What time?"

"For which?"

"Both."

"I saw her at about seven forty-five after I dropped Shannon off at school, and I talked to her a few minutes before you came home for dinner."

"Time of death appears to be one thirty-six P.M."

"Stopped clocks again?" I guessed.

"Very handy."

"You aren't thinking Linda did it?" I asked flat out because I didn't like this beating around the bush.

He just ate another cookie, breaking off eye contact with me.

"Linda probably didn't even get out of bed all day. She's sunk into a terrible depression. She isn't taking her kids to school or going to the grocery store. Ask Audrey. She and I have been doing a sort of suicide watch on Linda all week."

He raised an eyebrow at me. "She must have seen Nan as the cause of her marriage breaking up. Couldn't have been her favorite person. And you've said she's pretty desperate to get her husband back. Maybe she thought this would do it."

"I'm telling you it isn't Linda, Danny. She doesn't have the energy to wash her hair right now. Besides, she isn't a murderer. I've seen her get sick at the sight of a dead animal on the side of the road. She couldn't kill anyone—not even Nan Arnot."

Danny didn't say any more about it. He stacked three cookies in his palm and stood up. "I'd better get some sleep before I drop." Then, as if he'd just remembered our after-dinner excitement, he asked, "How are things around here? Everybody still alive?"

"And well. Gramma and the girls made up by the time you left."

"Glad to hear it. Thanks for the cookies." He held them up, then said, "Night."

But his list of suspects in both murders was still weighing on me, and I wasn't ready to let him go yet.

"Danny?" I said as he took the chair away from the cherry wood door.

"Yeah?"

"Just between you and me, do you think the same person who killed Bruce also killed Nan?"

"Without as much patience, but yeah, I think the same person did it. And I'm going to be looking real hard at anybody who knew both victims."

Chapter Sixteen

VERY LITTLE SLEEP and a lot on my mind didn't make me a great driver or a great listener as I took Shannon to school the next morning. Usually she just plays the radio and talks back to the purposely obnoxious DJs of her favorite stations, but today she had it on only as background while she explained her quandary to me and I tried to concentrate.

"I told you, it's a reverse dance," she said, impatient with my third request for clarification. "And *my* friends are going with *his* friends."

I wasn't sure which boy we were talking about but decided against asking. I knew she'd told me that too, and I'd be in for it if I let on that I hadn't retained it. With luck a name would come up again and clue me in.

"If I ask him, I can hang out with everybody," she went on. "But I'll have to ride alone with him in his car on the way, and I don't know what we'd talk about."

"What's he interested in?"

"How should I know?"

"You could ask. That'd give you something to talk about."

"You want me to get in the car and say, 'What are you interested in?' What do you think I am? A dork?"

"You could ask some of your friends beforehand, find out if he likes football or soccer or *Star Trek* or—"

"Bor-ring."

I knew when I couldn't win. "How about this: Hemorrhoids are not a laughing matter?"

"Oh, good one. No wonder you have so many dates."

She clammed up after that. Hey, I was only trying to help.

"So," I said, "how did we go from everybody being mad at each other last night to you and Chloe and Gramma playing cards again after Uncle Dad's call?"

"I don't know. When Chloe hung up with him, she came in my room and was saying how nobody understands him and then Gramma came in and said she was sorry and we started to play Bullshit again."

She just had to throw that in.

"Chloe is so stupid," Shannon added.

"She's not stupid."

"Yes, she is. She believes everything Uncle Dad says. She never thinks why does he have money to go to the movies all the time and drive expensive cars and go on trips and everything but he just doesn't have money for us. He talks about that other stuff, then does that whiny voice to say how hard his life is, and she buys it. She feels sorry for him. She's so stupid."

"It probably makes her feel better to try to believe him."

"It's just stupid."

I thought it might be easier for Shannon if she could buy into a little of it. "You have to realize that because Chloe's older than you, she spent more time with Uncle Dad when she was growing up than you did, Shannon. She was closer to him. Maybe it makes her see him in a different light. Or want to at least."

"Oh, please. He brags about his fancy life, his fancy girlfriend, who has to be taken to *special* places, then all of a sudden says he's hungry but doesn't have the money for a sandwich. Hello! If he can't afford to eat, he shouldn't have taken his girlfriend to San Francisco for her birthday. And how come he had the money and the time to go there but he can't ever come here?"

And how come my "I couldn't care less" daughter sounded hurt?

As if I didn't know.

I made a U-turn around an island median and pulled up in front of her school. "Fewer expectations make for fewer disappointments. Especially where Uncle Dad is concerned," I explained.

"I don't expect anything from him. And that's what I get."

I was batting a thousand this morning. "Maybe you ought to try it Chloe's way: accept everything he says at face value and not think much more about it."

"Yeah, right. Like anybody but Chloe could do that." Shannon grabbed her backpack and got out.

Great way to start the day. "I'll be back at three-fifteen," I said before she got away.

"I know. Bye."

I watched her walk across the student parking lot, thinking that she'd probably be better off with a little of Chloe's blind faith in their father. If she'd been able to hold on to any illusions of him before we moved into

Gramma's house, she certainly couldn't with Gramma pointing out what a jerk he was.

Shannon disappeared into the school, and I marinated in a fresh batch of guilt for a few minutes before merging back into the flow of traffic.

I'm not a morning person, and in all my years of taking the kids to school I've never done anything but drop them off and go home. No getting out of the car to chat with the other mothers. No stopping at the grocery store to beat the crowds. No nothing but wishing my car windows were tinted so I could go straight from bed, jump into my bathrobe, get behind the steering wheel, and never be seen by anybody at all.

But this week I'd broken my routine. I'd been stopping at Linda's house to check on her. Today that wasn't my only reason for going there. If she hadn't heard about Nan Arnot's death, she needed to. Before Danny or any other cops showed up on her doorstep with the news and a lot of questions.

I parked in front of Linda's house and got out. But as I closed the door, my gaze caught on my old house across the street. The new owners had hired painters, who were brushing a pinkish color on the trim.

Pink trim with red brick? Personally I preferred the scarred and peeling white to that. Which was what it would still be if we lived there, because I couldn't afford a new paint job.

I headed up Linda's walk and knocked on the door, opening it before I was invited to, calling inside as I did, same as always.

"I'm upstairs," Linda informed me as listlessly as if she were terminally ill.

I went inside and closed the front door, glancing around from the entryway to see if there were any kids I should urge out of the house or any who needed reassuring or comforting that Mom was going to be okay—things I'd been dealing with as part of trying to make sure they were faring all right through this.

To the right of the stairs directly in front of me was a formal living room decorated with pastel colors and modern furniture. To the left of the stairs was a family room with two leather couches, two matching recliners, and a big-screen television. A breakfast bar separated that room from the kitchen, which was at the rear of the house.

I didn't spot any kids, so I climbed the ten steps to the second floor.

I found Linda the way I had the day before: in bed, with the window shades pulled down between the tie-back ruffled curtains.

Only unlike the day before, Linda pushed herself to sit up against the headboard of her canopy bed when she saw me. I considered that progress.

Feeling like Scarlett O'Hara's Mammy, I raised the shades and let October sunshine flood in on the ornate early American chiffonier, the matching armoire, which hid a television if the doors were closed, the bureau, and the night tables that bracketed her bed. Come to think of it, her house was like moving from one showroom to the next in a furniture store, with no two rooms decorated in the same style.

"The kids get off to school okay?" I asked.

"Guess so," she said after listening for the telltale sounds of them.

I knew that since this depression had set in, the older of her five children were getting the younger ones dressed and ready for school and that the younger three were walking to school while the older two begged rides from friends despite the fact that I'd offered to drive them. I was keeping up on the laundry and bringing in our leftovers and a casserole here and there so the kids had plenty to eat. Life was going on without Linda.

If nobody was picking up the slack, would Linda be so apt to give in to her present state of mind? I wondered.

"How about I fix you some breakfast?" I asked.

Every other morning she'd turned me down flat. Today she seemed to consider it. But for only a minute before she blew it off. "I'll just have some cereal when I get downstairs."

That might be never.

But then she wrinkled her nose at the flannel nightgown she'd had on all week as if she'd just realized she was wearing it. "First I need a shower and to change these sheets," she said as if she really did mean to get up today.

Maybe there was hope.

"I'll work on the sheets while you take the shower," I said to encourage her.

"You don't have to."

"I know I don't *have* to. I want to. Then we can talk over coffee. I have something I need to tell you."

"Okay," she replied as if she really didn't care one way or another.

But she did get up, and I wanted to shout hallelujah when the bathroom door closed behind her, but I refrained. Instead, I decided to get that bed made before she could slip back into it.

Linda had had her gallbladder removed about three years earlier, and I'd helped around the house when she'd come home from the hospital, so I knew my way around the place pretty well. I took some nice white sheets with pink rosebuds all over them and three fresh pillowcases to match out of the linen closet and headed for the bed.

But before I got started on it, I noticed that Linda had her share of debris littering the night table, and I decided to clean that up first.

I tossed wadded Kleenex and used Styrofoam cups in the trash, then gathered the television's remote control and the week's *TV Guide* to put in the top drawer of the stand, where I knew she kept them.

I had some trouble getting the drawer open. I could get it to come out about an inch, but then something jammed it. I reached inside to work whatever it was down from the top rail and finally managed it. But when I slid the drawer completely open and saw what it was that had been holding it shut, I stopped short.

Inside, along with lotions, Chap Stick, and moisturizers, was a hot-pink file folder with Steve Kraner's name neatly typed on the tab in the same way I'd seen on every other folder in Bruce Mann's den.

Feeling suddenly like a thief in the night, I listened for sounds in the bathroom, heard the shower still on full blast, and slipped the folder out of the drawer.

Okay, so looking for it at Bruce's house in order to help Linda and taking it out of her private drawer just to have a look myself were two different things. But there was still no way I wasn't going to have that look.

I sat on the bare mattress, set the file on my lap, and opened it.

Bruce had been a wonderfully well-organized, succinct record keeper. What I found laid out clearly was the slow progression of Steve Kraner's depletion of nearly every penny he and Linda had, beginning when he'd started his own furniture store.

The money had been paid to three companies: the Tonra Corporation, a furniture broker; Van Wise Enterprises, a furniture distributor; and the Wheatley Company, a furniture manufacturer. Three different letterheads. Three different addresses around town. Complete with invoices and receipts for funds due and collected.

It all looked very much on the up-and-up. If I were a judge, I would have believed they were legitimate organizations that had provided legitimate goods and services to Steve Kraner and had been paid accordingly.

But then, if I were a judge, presumably I wouldn't be seeing the three separate ledgers I found in the file for each company. Ledgers that kept track of the moneys paid into their three separate bank accounts.

Oh, yeah, Bruce had laid out everything very clearly.

At the top of each ledger were the name and address for the bank that held the account, the account number, the name of the business, and the name of the sole proprietor. Nan Arnot owned the Tonra Corporation—a neat anagram of her last name, I suddenly realized. Nannette Alicia Arnot owned the Wheatley Company. And N. Alicia Arnot owned Van Wise Enterprises.

Well, wasn't that convenient? Almost every penny poor Steve had supposedly spent to make his store a success and keep it afloat had been paid to his girlfriend. The twenty-two-year-old manicurist. Guess the furniture business was just her hobby.

But that wasn't all that was in the file. I flipped past the ledgers to see what else was there and found a copy of a will, Nan Arnot's will.

Of course. Didn't every young manicurist-slash-entrepreneur have one?

It was dated only shortly after the transactions with her busy-beaver companies began.

I wondered why Bruce had been keeping Nan's will, then remembered that I hadn't found the file at Bruce's house. Gail Frankin had given it to Linda. Who knew where she'd gotten it?

I heard the water in the shower go off and frantically scanned the document. Luckily I found what I was most interested in right away: In the event of Nan Arnot's death, all her worldly possessions and assets went to Steve Kraner. So if something happened to her, he got his money back.

On the other hand, there were no provisions if she decided not to return it to him once his divorce from Linda was final. Like if Goldilocks were to run off with the big bad bear.

The squeak of the shower door opening told me what was going on inside the bathroom, so I closed the file in a hurry and put it back in the drawer. Then I got busy making the bed.

But Linda didn't come out of the bathroom, and my mind started to wander.

What would Danny think if he saw what was in that file?

Nan Arnot was dead. Murdered. And my friend was on Danny's list of suspects. Everybody knew Linda hated Nan. She couldn't say her name in a normal tone of voice, for crying out loud. But with Nan dead, not only was she out of the way of a possible reconciliation between Linda and Steve, but all the money reverted to Steve and put Linda back in line for her half of it even if she didn't get him to come home to her and the kids.

Or at least, I thought, that was how the cops would see it. And they'd be even unlikely to believe that Linda hadn't budged from her house, much less her bed, in the last twenty-four hours.

But what if I did something with the file that didn't

link it so closely to Linda? What if I took it, handed it over to Danny, and refused to tell him where I got it?

Finding it here, in Linda's bedroom, might tip the scales against her. But by itself the file gave Steve a stronger motive than it gave Linda. And for more than just Nan's murder. For Bruce's too. If Steve had found out that something was going on between Bruce and Nan, that they'd planned to keep his money once the divorce was final, that could have set him off. He could have killed Bruce, then done in Nan too and, in the process, ensured that he'd get his money back.

Taking the file, giving it to Danny without letting him know where it had come from, might spread the incrimination around a little, the way I thought it should be.

So take the damn file, I told myself.

I shot a look at the bathroom door and reached for the drawer knob.

But before I had actually pulled it, the doorbell rang and Linda came out of the bathroom almost at the same time.

She went to the window and looked outside. "The police are here," she said as if it confused her. "A lot of them."

That meant they hadn't come just to talk. And it was too late for me to snatch the file and spare my friend the bumpy ride she was in for when the boys in blue discovered what they would certainly consider a motive for murder.

Chapter Seventeen

"NAN IS DEAD?" Linda said, sounding dazed.

But then, who wouldn't be? We were sitting on her front porch the way we had on many a summer night. Only this time we'd been banished there and were under the watchful eye of a homely cop with a nose the size of Canada. He was standing a few feet away while, inside, her house was being searched by Danny and more cops.

Searched and destroyed if the crash we'd just heard meant anything.

I was trying hard to trust that the Danny I knew and Danny the cop were enough alike that he wouldn't let any real damage be done to Linda's belongings and that he had a good reason for having obtained a search warrant. But it wasn't easy.

"When did she die?" Linda asked.

"Yesterday. She was killed."

"Killed? Like Bruce?"

"They both were murdered, yes. But not in exactly the same way," I said, hedging. I didn't want inadvertently to give her a detail she might repeat when she was interviewed. If she told Danny something she wasn't likely to know, he'd take it as evidence that the reason she had inside information was that she'd done the deed.

"Linda, I think you ought to call your lawyer."

"Why?"

"I don't know what they're looking for in there." But I knew what they'd find: that file. "But they don't come with search warrants and go through your house without a reason. And when they're through, they'll be talking to you. Asking questions. You should have a lawyer with you for that. Just in case."

The sweat suit she had on was not her best. It was a faded navy blue job with quilting in saddlebags over her shoulders. The quilting was in varying degrees of unquilting. Her hair was still damp from her shower; her face was scrubbed clean and so pale her eyes seemed to pop out of it.

"Do they think *I* killed *Nan*?" she asked.

"They're wondering about it. Why else would they be here like this?" I took it as a sign of just how lost Linda was that this hadn't occurred to her.

"Oh, my God," she whispered.

It seemed particularly cruel to be putting her in this position when she was already so beaten down and out of it. Almost like accusing a child of something she doesn't even have a concept of, let alone the capability to have done. Danny had better have a damn good reason for this.

"Were you alone here all day yesterday?" I asked her.

"You mean, after you left in the morning?"

"Yes."

"The kids got home from school around three."

"But between when I left and when they came home, did anyone see you?"

"See me?"

"Come over. Visit." She really was in a daze.

"I was alone," she said as if she weren't really sure.

"Did you talk to anyone on the phone?"

"Just you."

"But that was after six. How about Audrey? Didn't she call? She must have if you knew she was stopping by last night."

"She called just a few minutes before you did."

"But not earlier?"

"She said she'd called in the morning, but I must have slept through it. I don't even remember hearing the phone ring."

"How about TV programs? Did you watch TV?"

"Sure. It was on all day. Maybe that's why I didn't hear the phone; maybe the TV was on too loud."

"Think about the shows, what was on, everything you watched, and tell Danny when you talk to him."

"Tell him what I watched on TV?"

"Every detail you can think of."

She looked at me as if I were nuts. But before I could explain that being knowledgeable about the previous day's television programs was going to be her only alibi, Danny came out and asked her back in the house.

I stood up to go with her, but as soon as Linda went through the door, Danny stepped in front of it and frowned down at me. "I can't have you in on this, Jimi."

"She didn't do it," I told him in no uncertain terms.

"Why don't you go on home?"

"Why don't I just wait out here until you're finished?"

He gave me a solemn shake of the head. "Go on home."

The homely cop stepped forward to reinforce his order, but Danny stopped him with one raised hand, palm out like an Indian chief.

"Go on, Jimi. It'll be okay."

Okay for whom? Not for Linda, I didn't think.

I stared at him, searching for reassurance that I could trust him to be fair, to be objective, to go easy on her, to see that she couldn't possibly have committed murder yesterday. Or any other day, for that matter.

But as hard as I tried, I didn't find any reassurance in those old familiar features. In fact, what I saw was a cold aloofness behind his eyes that I'd never seen there before, something I'd only imagined as his cop face. I really didn't want to leave Linda to it.

But I didn't have any choice. There he was, blocking the door, and he wasn't going to let me inside. "Home, Jimi."

That one had an edge to it. Maybe he'd let the homely cop drag me off after all.

"When can I come back and see her?" I asked.

"I can't tell you that because I'm not sure. We might not even stay here. We might need to move this to the station."

"What does that mean? That you're going to arrest her?"

"We just need to talk to her. For now."

"So you aren't going to arrest her."

"I didn't say that. I'm not sure how it will play out."

Play being the operative word. He'd play Linda, see

what he could get her to say, and if it wasn't the right thing, she was in for it.

"Keep an open mind, Danny, no matter what you found or what she says. She didn't do it. She couldn't even get out of bed yesterday, and I'm not sure she's mentally capable of understanding what's going on today."

"I'll keep it in mind." He didn't sound as if he really would.

"Let her call her lawyer. She needs some support."

"She'll have that option. It's her right."

"Make sure she understands that. And encourage her to do it."

He didn't say anything to that, one way or another. But surely Danny, *my* Danny, wouldn't take advantage of someone in the state Linda was in. Someone who was my friend.

"Go home now, Jimi," he repeated yet again.

I still didn't want to. But there was nothing else I could do. So I gave him one of his own hard stares, turned, and left without so much as a good-bye.

That'd teach him. Or so I told myself, so I wouldn't feel as impotent as a ninety-year-old man.

I didn't know whether to be mad or worried or what by the time I got home. Gramma was working out with Jack La Lanne, hanging on to the back of a kitchen chair and doing side leg lifts. Not an easy thing in a slip and housedress.

I didn't disturb her even though I was inclined to. I wanted badly to do some ranting about Danny and cops in general not knowing their heads from holes in the ground if they honestly thought Linda was a murderer. But I know how Gramma loves her time with Jack and refrained. Instead, I went up to the attic.

My answering machine is on the kitchen counter that runs right up to the door, and as I walked in, I noticed the message light blinking.

Probably Shannon calling from school because she'd forgotten something.

Good. Anything would be welcome to take my mind off Linda and Danny and Bruce and Nan and murder.

I hit the button and heard Ron Arnot's voice, although if he hadn't identified himself, I'd have never guessed who he was. He sounded like a little boy. A scared little boy.

So much for taking my mind off the mess that was swirling around me.

"I told the police somethin' maybe I shouldn't of," Ron's message began. "Somethin' 'bout Linda. I know you're friends with that cop guy. Maybe you can fix it . . . ." Pause. "I'll be home all day; I couldn't go to work. Could you call me or somethin'?"

I rewound it and listened again, hoping I'd heard it wrong the first time. What could he have told Danny? Something bad enough for Danny to get a search warrant and go after Linda?

The message played again. I'd heard it right the first time.

"Shit," I muttered to the machine. The last thing Linda needed was someone to say something to the police that made her look bad.

But I was worried about how Ron sounded too. Worse than how Danny had described him the night before. His words had slurred slightly and come so slowly it was as if he'd barely had the energy to get them out. His voice sounded flat enough to belong to a corpse. If corpses could talk.

I'd intended to check in with him today anyway to see how he was doing since Danny had left him. Feeling as edgy as I was, I knew I wasn't going to get any work done, so rather than pick up the phone and call him back I decided to look up his address in the Hunter group roster and pay him a visit instead.

Still, as I threw my own bed together and headed for the tub for a quick bath, I couldn't shake the sense that things had started to snowball in the wrong direction.

And that I couldn't stop them.

Chapter Eighteen

RON ARNOT HAD moved back home with his parents. Sort of. His folks lived in a brick house built to look trendy in the fifties. The roof sloped dramatically, peaking in the center of the many-paned floor-to-ceiling living room window and then trailing off the other side at a more leisurely angle all the way over the carport.

Someone—I assumed the Arnots—had added a second slab of concrete to the original single-car driveway to accommodate a mobile home, and it was in that mobile home that Ron had taken up residence since his divorce from Nan.

I parked at the curb in front, wondering as I walked up the drive if decorum dictated that I check in at the main house before visiting the trailer. But there was loud Pearl Jam music coming from the mobile home to tell me that was where Ron was, so I decided to ignore decorum and just went to the aluminum door at the rear of the house-on-a-truck and knocked.

It didn't have much effect against Pearl Jam's drummer at 130 decibels.

I pounded hard the second time.

"Yeah, I know, turn it down," Ron yelled from inside.

The music went to a roar, but he didn't open the door.

I knocked again. Or at least halfway between knocked and pounded.

"I turned the goddamn sound down! What do ya want from me anyway?" he demanded as he finally yanked the door open.

For a minute he glared down at me through bloodshot blue eyes. Then he realized I wasn't whoever he'd thought I was, and he looked like a kid caught mouthing off.

"Jimi."

I said hi and did a quick once-over of him. He had on a crew-neck undershirt tucked into faded jeans with the waistband button left unfastened. His sandy hair was sticking up in odd places as if he hadn't slept on a pillow and had moved around so much his whole head had had an equal opportunity to be mussed up. There were bruised-looking crescents under his eyes, his skin was the color of chardonnay, and his lips were dry and cracked. Handsome kid though he was, he looked like hell.

"You didn't have to come over. You could've called. My mom woulda come out and got me to talk."

"I wanted to stop by."

"C'mon in."

He moved back into the trailer so I could. I climbed the three steps that took me past the truck's bumper and into the mobile-home part of the vehicle. It smelled of beer. Fresh beer. Breakfast of champions.

I'm claustrophobic, and all it took was a few steps into that trailer to kick off the anxious, penned-in panic I get. I fought it, but rather than close the door behind me I said, "Do you mind if I leave this open?"

"Jeez, I'm sorry. Does it stink in here?"

"No, I'm just not good with small spaces."

And this was definitely a small space. Close, cluttered quarters. A narrow walkway bisected it, a straight shot back to a bed that was just a bunk over the truck cab. It spilled sheets and blankets as if Ron had slid out of it and taken them part of the way with him in the process.

His kitchen was to the left. A few cupboards above a minute refrigerator and a stainless steel minisink littered with dirty dishes. The bathroom was just beyond that, a toilet in a closet; the door was open to show it off or air it out, I wasn't sure which.

The right half of the place was taken up by a U-shaped bench seat cushioned in brown vinyl and a Formica table that held a five-inch black-and-white television and twenty-seven beer cans. I counted. One for every year he'd been alive. Presumably not all consumed this morning. But maybe.

I perched on the end of the bench seat nearest the door, my knees out in the walkway. I hoped being that close to the exit and some fresh air would help the claustrophobia.

"Could I getcha somethin'? Coffee or tea or a pop or somethin'? My mom has stuff like that. I could—"

"No, thanks. I'm fine. I came to see how you are."

He shrugged and sat the same way I was on the opposite side of the U, legs apart, elbows to knees, staring at the floor. "Nan's dead, you know?"

"I know."

He shook his head a couple of times and then rolled his gaze down the walkway and out the door like a bowling ball. "Man, how'd things get so fucked up?"

Good question.

"Sorry," he added. "My mom'd kick my butt for sayin' that to you."

"It's okay." Hey, he wasn't my kid.

He aimed a nod out the door. "That's how I always thought things were s'posed to be, you know, like it is with my folks? I was never good with books or school or stuff. I was okay with tools an' fixin' things, but payin' attention to some boring teacher in a classroom? Man, I couldn't do it. So I knew I wasn't goin' to college. But then, my dad didn't, an' he did okay for himself. For all of us—my mom an' me an' my two brothers—workin' construction. An' I could do that. So that's how I figured it'd be: I'd get outta school, go work with him, marry Nan, an' we'd be like Mom and Dad. Get ourselves a little house. Have some kids. Take care of each other . . ." His voice trailed off as if he'd been talking to himself and just realized he'd had an audience the whole time.

"That was pretty much what I figured life would be like too. Get married, live happily ever after," I said, hoping it would encourage him not to clam up the way he usually did to hide his feelings.

"My folks never got no damn divorce." He looked down at his feet, and I could see him blinking fast, fighting tears.

"Mine didn't either. It was hard for me to accept that I wasn't going to have the same kind of life they had. It was what I wanted too."

"Nan wanted a lot more. An' she got it."

She got a hot-wired toaster oven in her bathwater. But I didn't think that's what he meant.

"She was doin' real good." He went on. "Lotsa clothes, like she liked. Havin' her hair done up by better girls than she used to work with. Not workin' at all herself. Talkin' 'bout travelin'. Buyin' a sports car. Stuff I couldn't give her. Maybe ever. But then, I wasn't an old fart either; that shoulda counted for somethin'."

Steve Kraner is only five or six years older than I am, but I tried not to take offense at being categorized as an old fart by association. Besides, I had kids; I was used to being considered ancient.

Ron looked up at me over a work-honed biceps. "She was leavin' him, you know. Soon, she said. I got all excited, thought cuz she'd told me, she'd be comin' back to me. But she had some other guy already. Wouldn't say who he was. But I knew. I found out."

Only he'd tried not to let Danny know that.

Ron's hands weren't just hanging loosely between his knees anymore. They were in white-knuckled fists, and his jawline was suddenly clenched. "You won't believe this; it was Bruce she was doin'. From our group, for chrissake. She hooked up with him through Kraner, and she was gonna dump Kraner for him. Man, I hated that prick."

"Steve Kraner or Bruce?"

"Both of 'em. But especially Bruce. At least Kraner treated her good."

"But Bruce didn't?"

He shook his head ominously but didn't answer my question beyond that.

I tried another one. "How did you find out Nan was ready to jump ship again with Bruce?"

"The week before he died the prick comes up to me before the meeting an' says he didn't know what I was so broke up about, that he'd had Nan an' she wasn't nothin' great. That I should give him a chance to turn me on to a whole lot better than that. Bastard. I was so pissed I coulda beat the hell out of 'im. Clifford an' Janine held me off. I figured they were just savin' his ass but turned out they hated him as much as I did an' didn't want to see me get in any trouble because of him."

"Janine hated Bruce?"

"Bad."

"Are you sure about that?" Were we talking about the same Janine who'd been nearly hanging on Bruce from day one of the group?

"I'm sure all right. I don't know why she hated him so much, but she said he was too much of a shit for me to get upset over, an' she really meant it. It was like she wanted to spit on him or something. More even than me."

I filed that bit of information away with my amazement, figuring I'd take a look at it later on, so I could keep up as Ron started to talk again.

"I told Nan what Bruce said about her. But she laughed in my face. Said it was another one of my bullshit tricks to try gettin' her back. Said she knew Bruce wanted her. He wanted her bad, an' he was gonna get her."

Along with all the Kraners' money probably.

"When I saw her a couple of days after that, she said her an' him'd had a good laugh at what a sucker I was."

He said that through gritted teeth, and I watched the rage it sent through him ripple like a big stone in a still pond.

"I'm sorry, Ron."

A laugh that wasn't a laugh jumped out of his

throat. "Yeah, me too." He stared at the floor again. Shook his head. Said in a quiet voice, "So you want to tell me how I could hate it so much that she's dead?" Then he buried his face in his hands, and I knew the tears had won the battle.

I thought about going to him, putting my arms around him, or at least patting him on the back to comfort him. I wanted to. But I knew from the Hunter group that it was more likely to set him off than do any good.

The tears' victory was short-lived. After only a few minutes he sniffed and scrubbed his face with his hands, then rubbed his palms hard against his thighs, leaving a damp trail.

Even though I hadn't breached his tough-guy etiquette by comforting him, he still seemed to want me out of there. He sat up as straight and stiff as any high-powered executive signaling to an underling that the meeting was over and stared out the window over the minisink, which was directly in front of him.

"It don't matter," he said with finality, then did a quick change of subject that got down to business. "Look, the reason I called you was cuz I had to talk to that cop friend of yours last night an' I mighta said somethin' I shouldn't of."

"What was that?"

"Well, yesterday around noon I was on my lunch hour an' not workin' far from Linda's house, so I went over there. I know she's been in a bad way for some reason, an' I thought I'd see how she was doin'. But she wasn't there. An' I told the cop that, an' then I was sorry I did. I got to thinkin' that it was a bad thing to've done. I shoulda just kept my mouth shut. But he asked me where I was about then, an' I went an' told him. Didn't seem like any big deal except when he started askin' a lot of other stuff about Linda confidin' in me an' not likin' Nan, an' then I got to thinking that it wasn't only me bein' checked out but Linda too. So I thought maybe you could fix it with him."

"It's okay," I said, even though it wasn't. "Linda was there; she just hasn't been getting out of bed for much of anything. I'm sure she figured you were a delivery person or a salesman, and she didn't bother going downstairs to answer. Or she might have had the TV on too loud and not heard the doorbell."

"See, that's where it gets worse. The upstairs window was open, an' I knew she'd been stayin' in bed most of the time, so I hollered up for her. She still didn't answer. An' I didn't hear no television sounds either."

Great. "She might have been in the bathroom."

"I was there about twenty minutes, tryin' to get her to let me in cuz I was worried 'bout her."

"Did you tell Danny all that?"

"I shouldn't of, huh?"

"You had to be straight with him." I reassured him, all the while wishing he hadn't been.

"Can you fix it?"

"I don't know. I'll try. I'm sure it'll be okay."

He didn't look convinced. Probably because I wasn't.

I really knew I'd outstayed my welcome when silence fell between us and he didn't do anything to fill it. I stood up. "I'd better take off."

He nodded.

"Are you spending time with your folks? Your buddies?" I asked, still worried about him.

"Yeah. I guess. My mom keeps comin' over here an' tryin' to get me to eat. An' my brothers been hangin' round the house too, after work and stuff."

I was glad to hear that. "If you need anything, Ron, or just want to talk to somebody who isn't family, call me."

He just fidgeted.

I thought maybe it would be better if I put it on a different level. "Or you could come by, have dinner with us. My grandmother cooks like nobody in the world. You could meet my girls—"

"Yeah. Maybe sometime," he said just to shut me up.

"You'll be at the meeting at Audrey's on Monday night, won't you?"

"I don't know. I don't see the point now."

"I wish you'd come anyway. I think it would still do you good."

"I don't know."

I recognized a stone wall when I saw one. So, with nothing else to say, I said, "Okay. Well."

I climbed out of the mobile home and felt better being in the open air again even if I didn't feel better about Ron.

"I'll check back with you," I said.

He nodded again, and I could envision him having his mother tell me he wasn't home when I did call rather than let my good intentions stir up feelings he wanted to pretend he could bury. But that was just another thing I couldn't do or say anything about. Instead, this time I said, "Take care of yourself."

"You too."

Then he closed the trailer door on me.

I stood there like a dummy for a minute, feeling frustrated and bad for the kid inside that tuna can on wheels. This was turning out to be a day that would not go down as one of my better ones.

But standing there wasn't accomplishing anything

either, so I finally headed down the driveway toward my car. The orderliness of my computer and the Kiwanis newsletter were suddenly very appealing.

But just as I was about to step off the curb to go around to the driver's side, another car pulled up behind me. A neat little compact blue Nissan. Driven by Gail Frankin.

And curiosity reared its ugly head to keep me right where I was. Looked as if the Kiwanis were going to have to wait a little longer for me to get to their new members' list. Because there were some things I wanted to know from Gail Frankin.

Beginning with how she'd gotten hold of Bruce's file on Steve Kraner to give to Linda.

Chapter Nineteen

GAIL WAVED and smiled as she turned off her engine. The smile was tight-lipped. She'd made it clear at Bruce's funeral that she wasn't fond of her cousin, but I doubted she'd disliked Nan enough to want her dead.

As always, Gail looked good otherwise. She had on perfectly pressed navy blue slacks and a crisp white blouse with a lacy Peter Pan collar. Her hair gleamed with red highlights in the morning sunshine without so much as a single split end, and her makeup was masterfully understated.

I always envy women who can put themselves together that way. My makeup usually melts off by noon even if I don't put it on until ten, my standard blue jeans and turtleneck attire never garners compliments, and split ends and I are old acquaintances. But hey, I try.

Gail got out of her car and joined me on the sidewalk. "Paying a house call on Ron?" she said by way of a greeting.

"I just left him," I answered, and went on to relay my condolences.

"I can't believe it's happened," she said. Then she nodded toward the mobile home. "How is Ron taking it?"

"Not too well."

"Poor kid." She stared at the back of the truck as if there might be a sign posted to it. Then she shook her head and looked at me again. "I was visiting my husband . . . maybe I should say my *ex*-husband since that's what he'll be pretty soon. Anyway, he's in a nursing home a few blocks from here, and I thought I'd stop in and see Ron while I was nearby."

"I didn't realize your husband was in a nursing home." Probably because she hadn't said it. When she'd talked about divorcing him during the Hunter meetings, she'd admitted he had a progressive disease but hadn't said how far it had progressed. She'd given the impression that she just hadn't been able to face what the future held. Now it seemed as if that future was the present.

"He had to be put in Mount Claire's about six months ago. He's lost control of everything, and he needs twenty-four-hour care. There wasn't a choice."

"Still, that must have been a hard decision to make."

She nodded almost imperceptibly. "He didn't want to go. I don't suppose anybody does. But I try to visit every day and make sure he gets anything he wants. That he's being well taken care of."

Seemed kind of odd for someone who was divorcing him. "Are you the only one there is to look in on him?"

"He comes from a big family actually. Two brothers and two sisters. There're his parents too. We're all really close. I hope that won't change."

"Sometimes that kind of relationship is difficult to maintain." At least it had been for me. Not that my former in-laws and I hadn't tried.

"I think we might be able to, though. The divorce wasn't my idea. Jeremy's family had me over for a barbecue at the start of the summer and said they'd talked about it and thought that that's what I should do. They said I was young and deserved a full life, and since Jeremy wouldn't ever recover . . . I should be free to start over."

"And Jeremy agreed?"

"The disease and the drugs he's given to help control it affect his mental capacity at this stage. We had to have him declared incompetent, and one of his brothers was given his power of attorney. I'm not even sure he understands what I'm doing. Especially since I show up every day. He still just cries and begs me to get him out of there . . . on the days he can talk at all."

God.

"Still, though, I feel like I'm abandoning him. 'In sickness and in health,' you know. But he could live this way for a long, long time and . . ." She just shook her head. "I don't know why I'm talking about this now. I didn't want to be the pity case in the group, so I've avoided it, and this is a terrible time to bring it up. I guess I'm just feeling maudlin."

Death and disease will do that to the best of us. Frost it with divorce, and I was amazed she was still standing, let alone checking in with her ex-cousin-in-law to make sure he was okay.

"Is it helping at all to go through the Hunter

group?" I asked because for the first time I'd heard a divorce story that didn't get covered in the seminar.

She laughed a little, genuinely. "It makes me see that people get divorced for more minor reasons than I have."

Ain't that the truth?

"It's been good, though," she went on, "to go see that some of what I'm feeling isn't any different from what everybody goes through. The support is nice too. Every time you call me just to see how I'm doing or because you've remembered a lawyer's appointment I have to keep, I don't feel so bad. And I'm seeing Audrey privately for counseling too, so that helps."

Now there were two members I regretted not having called more often, but I was glad she was talking to Audrey at least.

She glanced at the trailer again. "I should go see Ron," she said by way of an exit line.

"Before you do, I have to ask you a question," I said in a hurry, afraid she was going to get away before I'd done my nosy best.

"Sure."

I couldn't think of a subtle way to glean the information from her, so I decided to go with point-blank. "I know that Bruce was helping Steve hide all of his and Linda's assets, and I know how Bruce and Steve and Nan were doing it. I also saw you give Linda the file that proved it. I just wondered how you got it."

It didn't seem possible to make her look more troubled, but I'd managed it. Some accomplishment. If she'd have smacked me for it, I'd have felt it was my just deserts.

Instead, she said, "I took it from Nan's apartment."

"Nan and Steve had it? I thought Bruce did."

"He did, but Steve had gotten it from him. Just

before Bruce was killed, I think. Steve and Bruce had some sort of falling-out. Over Linda, Nan said, but not exactly why."

"How did you know there was a file at all? I wouldn't think it would have been something they'd talk about."

"Nan bragged to me about what they were doing at a family picnic about two months ago. She said she knew a way I could fix it so I got all of Jeremy's and my assets from the marriage and then proceeded to explain the brilliant scheme that was making her rich—that's how she put it."

Gail seemed to bite back the scorn that had crept into her voice. Apparently she didn't like to speak ill of the dead. Even if they deserved it.

"It was before I started the Hunter group." She went on. "Before I actually knew Linda. Or Bruce. I didn't approve of what she and Steve were doing, but when I got to know Linda and watched Bruce being friendly to her all the while he was helping them steal from her and her kids, well, it just ate at me. I went to Nan and said if they didn't give Linda what she had coming to her, I'd tell her myself what was going on. That was when Nan said it wouldn't do any good. The only proof was the file, and she had it. Then the phone rang, and she went to answer it. And I did some snooping until I found it." She added that with a glance at the ground, apparently ashamed of what she'd done. She couldn't know we were cut from the same cloth in this regard, if not in our fashion sense.

"I don't like to cause problems," she continued, "but I had to do something. So I took it and snuck out while Nan was still talking on the phone."

"And gave it to Linda."

Her expression clouded over like the Colorado sky before a June tornado. "And now Nan is dead."

No disputing that.

"I don't want to think this, Jimi, but ever since I heard, I can't help it. What if Linda got so mad when she saw what was in the file that she killed Nan?"

"Linda isn't a murderer." But I was beginning to wonder if I was the only person who knew that.

"Who else would have wanted Nan dead?"

I could think of a couple of people, but instead of getting into it I said, "Did you know Nan was personally involved with Bruce?"

"I'd heard something about it. He told me it wasn't true."

"*He* did? When?"

She didn't answer that one too readily. She didn't seem to want to look me in the eye again either. Finally she said, "Bruce tried to . . . date me."

"Tried and failed?"

"I knew what kind of man he was from what he was doing with Nan and Steve and that money. There was no way I wanted anything to do with him. Somehow he got the idea that the reason I wouldn't go out with him was Nan, and that was when he swore he wasn't interested in her. He said that she had the hots for him—that was how he put it—and kept trying to seduce him every time Steve's back was turned, but that he didn't want any part of her."

Good ol' Bruce. He'd had way more than both ends of his candle burning at the same time.

Gail shivered visibly. "That man made my skin crawl. If he's an example of what's out there for single women to start over with, I'd rather stick with a sick husband."

I considered putting in a pitch for Danny but refrained. It didn't seem like the right time or place. Besides, maybe I was mad at him.

Then Gail went on, although it seemed reluctantly. "That man was dangerous. Did he ever . . . bother you?"

"Bruce? No, why?"

"I just wondered."

"Did he do something to you?"

She hesitated again, making me sure she was reluctant. Finally she said, "He didn't actually do anything, but I think he would have."

"What do you mean?"

"He showed up at my house the week before he died. Without calling first or anything, just out of the blue. I wasn't even going to ask him in, but he sort of pushed past me. He wanted a drink. I said I was just on my way out even though I wasn't. He said he wanted a drink anyway and started looking through my cupboards, trying to find the liquor. All the while he was saying some really offensive things to me. First I laughed them off. Then he said even worse things, about how he knew I had to be really *horny* because Nan had told him my husband couldn't *get it up* for years now, and even worse—pure filth. I told him I didn't appreciate it and asked him to leave. But he wouldn't go. Instead, he came after me."

"What do you mean, he came after you?"

"It was the closest I've ever come to being raped. In fact, I think I would have been if Ron hadn't happened to show up unexpectedly right then. Thank God." Just the memory made her shiver again. "What kind of man was Bruce anyway?"

"Not a nice one."

"I hate to say this—and I've never said it about anybody before—but I can't feel as if his dying was a loss to the world. I know I slept better not having to think he could show up at my door again. As it was, Ron spent two nights after that on my couch."

"I didn't realize you and Ron were so close."

"He's a good kid. He even visits Jeremy once a week at the home."

That seemed to remind her why she was here in the first place, because she cast a glance at Ron's temporary housing once more. "I'd better go up. I still have to pay a visit to my aunt and uncle today too. They may want me to sit at the house while they make funeral arrangements. I still can't believe Nan is dead."

I let Gail go this time, but even after I had, I felt a heavy pall had been left behind.

Chapter Twenty

BY EIGHT O'CLOCK that night I still couldn't reach Linda, and Danny hadn't come home yet. So when the phone rang in my attic room, I was hoping it was one of them. I picked up even before the machine could do its ditty; that was how eager I was for the caller to be either of my friends.

It wasn't.

It was Bruce Mann's young widow, Melanie. Surprise took the place of disappointment as soon as it sank in who my caller was.

"How are you doing?" I asked.

"Okay and not okay," she said. "The not-okay part is why I called you. It's about someone in that divorce group Bruce was going to."

Melanie didn't sound too okay at all. At least I didn't think she did, but it was a little hard to hear her over the kids' commotion in the background at her end and the printer's hum as it rolled off the Kiwanis roster I'd just finished at mine.

"What's up?" I asked.

"Well. I knew a woman in your group was bothering Bruce. He'd complained to me about it—not in any kind of detail; I didn't really know what he meant, and to tell you the truth, I didn't ask. I had enough of my own problems with him to care. But I do know he said she'd never even been married and he couldn't figure out why she had joined except to bug him—"

I broke in there. "Are you sure about that, that he said someone in the group had never been married?"

"Pretty sure. He said that he'd expose her as the liar she was but that she could get him in a lot of trouble. I didn't know why *he'd* be in trouble because she'd lied about getting divorced, but that's what he said."

Something crashed. At her end, not mine.

"Elizabeth Marie, you quit chasing your brother!" Melanie shouted, her mouth apparently away from the phone because she didn't shatter my eardrum. Then back to me she said, "Anyway, now this woman is calling me."

"Why?"

"She's demanding money."

"What for?"

"She claims Bruce owed it to her. He didn't tell me that when he was griping about her, but she keeps saying he agreed to pay her just before he died. When I said I didn't know what she was talking about, she got really insistent that I make good on his debt anyway."

"Does she have proof of the debt? An IOU? Something written down?"

"No. She says that it was only a verbal agreement but that they're binding and I have to pay her. Nathan Thomas Mann, don't you hit your sister! I'm sorry.

These kids were sitting watching television before I called and now—"

"I know. The minute you get on the phone they go wild. My kids always did. Sometimes they still do. It's okay." Besides, I didn't care what kind of roughhouse her kids were playing; I was too caught up in what she was telling me. "How much money are we talking about?"

"She says she isn't sure exactly how much she has coming, but she'll take fifty thousand dollars because she knows it wasn't less than that—like I'm getting a bargain."

"Wow."

"I'll be honest with you: I inherited quite a bit of money from my parents when they died not long ago, so I could handle losing this if I had to, but I don't know, I can't—I don't *want* to hand over that much money to some strange woman I don't know from Adam, just because she says she has it coming. She won't even tell me why."

"I don't think anybody should hand over any amount of money, let alone so much, without more to go on, Melanie."

"I wondered if you knew something about her. She's not very nice when she calls, and she gets really angry when I don't just accept what she's saying. She scares me a little."

"You haven't told me who she is yet," I said.

Melanie laughed weakly. "No, I guess I haven't, have I? I'm sorry. These days I think I'm losing it."

A louder crash sounded in the background, followed by a prolonged scream of genuine pain and another of a fright-filled "Momma! Momma!"

"Oh, my God, I have to go, Jimi. I'll call you right back."

Boom, she hung up.

The Kiwanis roster was through printing out, but I didn't go to sort the pages. I stayed leaning against the countertop near the phone, waiting for that call-back that couldn't come too soon to satisfy my curiosity.

The trouble was, it didn't come at all.

When I hadn't heard from Melanie by eight-thirty, I dug up her phone number and called her, figuring I could ask if everything was okay as a segue into the conversation again.

But there was no answer. I checked the number and redialed. Still no answer. Damn.

As I put the phone down after my third try, a knock on the outside door to my attic apartment made me jump a foot. I didn't know who would use the entrance at the top of the stairs that ran up from the backyard, and the fact that two people I knew had been murdered in less than two weeks sprang to the front of my mind. I was glad my door-locking habits didn't leave a doubt in my mind that the dead bolt and the chain were securely in place.

But when the knock came again—louder this time—I also knew I had to see who was out there.

With my heart in my throat and wishing whoever it was would just go away so I could keep trying to reconnect with Melanie, I went to the window on the same wall and peeked through a tiny slit I made by barely pulling the shade away from the sill.

Danny was standing out on the landing.

That was as good as reconnecting with Melanie, and I rescinded my wish that he'd go away.

I unlocked the locks and opened up. "What are you doing using this door? Why didn't you come through the house?"

"It's all dark except up here. I thought maybe the girls and Nellie had gone to bed."

He hadn't had enough experience to know teenagers keep vampire hours even on school nights. "They went for ice cream."

"Why didn't you go too?" he asked as he came in, shrugging out of his tie and his top collar button on the way.

He plopped down on the plaid love seat of the love seat–easy chair combination that made up my living room in the attic. He looked tired and as if he didn't want to be doing this at all. As if he were paying a duty call and would have liked it better if he'd found I was out having ice cream too.

I didn't care so long as somebody finally gave me some solid information. I was sick of being left dangling.

"What happened with Linda?" I asked without ceremony.

"I just let her lawyer take her home."

"From this morning? From jail?"

"From the station."

"From this morning?" I repeated.

"We got there at about one this afternoon."

"And you've been interviewing her all this time?"

"Off and on."

"I suppose you found the file at Linda's."

"The *tax* file you were looking for at Mann's house on Sunday? Yeah, we found it. How'd you know it was there?"

"By accident. I was cleaning up just before you got there, opened the drawer to put something in it, and came across it."

"And looked inside," he said, no question in his tone at all, so I didn't answer it.

"Looks bad for your friend, Jimi. Looks like maybe she hatched a pretty neat plan: get rid of Mann out of spite for what he did to help her husband and his girlfriend cheat her, and so Goldilocks and the big bad bear couldn't make off with the dough. Then kill the girlfriend, so the money reverts to her husband. Now, if she can just get rid of the husband, she ends up with all the marbles."

"That doesn't wash. Linda didn't know anything underhanded was going on with the money until Monday night."

"When Gail Frankin gave her that file. Or so you think. But what if Mann told her about the money earlier?"

"Why would he have done that?"

"Guilt. Maybe they got close. He started feeling rotten about cheating her and confessed."

"Somehow from what I've learned about him since his death I can't picture Bruce Mann as repentant. Besides, Linda wasn't that close to him."

"They were pretty close."

He knew something I didn't. "God, don't tell me he slept with her too?"

"Okay, I won't tell you. I also won't tell you we have phone records that prove they were very chatty with each other. Or that I have someone who was at her house yesterday at the time of the murder who's pretty sure she was out."

"So Linda and Bruce were closer than I thought. She was vulnerable and needed the attention. That's not a motive for murder. Plus Linda can barely change a lightbulb, let alone rig a heating vent to kill somebody. And just because Ron couldn't get her to show her face doesn't mean she wasn't in the bathroom.

Also, even if she was out, she could have been anywhere. It doesn't mean she was killing Nan Arnot."

Danny just stared at me, his chin nearly on his chest, his eyebrows meeting over the bridge of his nose, looking up from under his forehead. "I had enough to hold her, Jimi."

"But you didn't."

"Because she's your friend."

"Don't give me that. You'd put *me* in jail if I looked reasonably guilty."

That had come out a little caustically. I regretted it.

"Linda Kraner is a long-standing member of the community with five kids she isn't going to abandon," he said, "And I want to take a closer look at Steve Kraner. That's what I'll say if I get called on the carpet for letting her go home. But I let her go home because she's your friend."

I swallowed some pride and said, "Thank you."

"But unless Steve Kraner or somebody else starts to look as good, I'll haul her back in."

"I know."

He stood up and met me eye to eye. "This is all between you and me."

That was the second time in the last few days that he'd said that to me, and I was beginning to take it as an insult. But since I had one coming, I swallowed that too. "I always figure anything you say to me is just between the two of us."

"Good." He went back to the outside door, opened it, and said goodnight.

I followed behind to lock up after him. As I did, I remembered Melanie Mann's aborted phone call and thought about trying to get hold of her again. But the truth was, I'd just plain had enough for one day.

Chapter Twenty-one

By late Monday afternoon, as I was getting ready for dinner and the Hunter meeting at Audrey's apartment, I was seriously wondering if Melanie Mann had disappeared into thin air.

Since the conversation she'd cut short on Thursday night I'd called her at least two dozen times, left as many messages on her answering machine, and gone by her apartment twice, all without ever connecting with her or with the friend whose home she was sharing.

At least I was reasonably sure she was still sharing it since I'd also tried the phone number at the Mann house and then taken a drive up there too, only to find the crime scene tape in place and no signs that she'd moved back in.

I was beginning to wonder if I should tell Danny about her call and the fact that she seemed to have disappeared. And I might have, except so had he.

Not quite as mysteriously; he was only working day and night. I hoped it was on finding the real killer or killers of Bruce Mann and Nan Arnot in order to get Linda off the hook.

Still, if I didn't reach Melanie really soon, I was either going to camp out on her doorstep until somebody told me where she was or going to get Danny in on it.

I tried Melanie's number one more time at five-thirty. The machine answered again, and I left yet another message, telling her I'd be home around ten and wouldn't go to bed until midnight if she wanted to call back late. Then I went out and started my car.

Since Chloe had taken Shannon to school for me that morning and I'd worked at the computer all day, my car hadn't been run and it needs a good five minutes for the engine to warm up or it chugs along miserably.

As far as I knew, I was going to be Audrey's only guest for dinner. She'd invited me for a premeeting supper as compensation for volunteering for this particular group. I didn't have any time to spare, so as I went back in the house, I was thinking about whether I needed gas or could wait until I went to pick Shannon up from school the next afternoon.

I hadn't really decided, when I heard Shannon's drippingly snide voice coming from the kitchen, where Gramma and the girls were having dinner alone since Danny wasn't making it home for meals these days.

"He wants us to come spend Christmas with him. If *Mom*'ll pay for the plane tickets. We're supposed to ask for them for our presents," my younger daughter was saying.

"God, you have a big mouth!" Chloe said. "I haven't even asked Mom yet."

That was why what I was overhearing was news to me.

"I don't care." Shannon again. "I'm not wasting my whole Christmas present on a plane ticket. Especially not one to see him. Why should we? He never cared about seeing us on Christmas before or he'd have come here."

I went into the kitchen, where they were eating chicken-fried steak with brown gravy—Gramma hates white gravy—garlic mashed potatoes, homemade rosemary focaccia with peppered olive oil for dipping, and creamed corn—Shannon's favorite.

But my grandmother seemed to have stopped eating. Her back was up—literally. She was sitting ramrod straight in her chair, and I could tell she was trying so hard not to say anything to the girls about this subject that she was ready to burst.

"It'd be a *trip,* Shannon," Chloe said. "Who cares if it's to visit Dad? We'd get to see Las Vegas."

"Oh, big deal. Like we could do anything there."

"It's the desert. Maybe it'd be warm enough to swim or get a tan. Dad said there was a bunch of stuff we could do."

My grandmother couldn't hold it anymore. "You'd leave your mother alone for Christmas?"

"I wouldn't," Shannon said.

No one seemed to have noticed me standing in the doorway before, but just then Chloe gave me a guilty glance. "She wouldn't be alone. She'd have you and Danny and everybody else, Gramma."

Shannon started to explain to me what they were talking about.

"I heard," I said, not crazy over the knot that was in the pit of my stomach at the thought of the girls being gone at any time, let alone for Christmas. "It's over two months away. Why don't we talk about it later?" I added. Like when Gramma isn't sitting right there, fuming.

"Dad says we need to get plane reservations soon because Christmas is a busy travel time," Chloe said as if this were a done deal.

"Then let him get them and pay for them," Gramma said.

"He can't. He doesn't have the money," Chloe answered under her breath. We all knew what the mention of Uncle Dad's purported poverty set off in my grandmother.

"Well, I'm not going, so I don't need to be here for this," Shannon said, taking her plate to the sink and once again making a hasty exit out of the fray, this one of her origination.

"The kitchen needs to be cleaned," I called after her.

"I'll be back."

That left Gramma and Chloe head to head.

And me with my car running.

"This doesn't have to be discussed right now," I said, feeble defuser that it was.

"Yeah, right, like it'll ever get *discussed.* Why don't you just say no and forget it?"

"I'm not going to say no. If what you want for your Christmas gift is a plane ticket to Las Vegas and you're perfectly clear that that'll be your whole gift, it's up to you. That's what I'll give you."

"I never heard anything so terrible," Gramma said. "He doesn't have anything to do with you, Chloe, and you'd leave your mother to spend Christmas with him? Where was he when you were sick with the flu last month? Or when you needed winter tires two weeks ago? Where was he when you were upset over that boy last summer? Where was he—"

"It's okay, Gram." I interrupted because this could go on forever.

"It isn't okay! These girls should be grateful for all you do for them and spit in his face for what he doesn't do. But no, they want to run off and spend Christmas with him."

"Not me," Shannon said from the living room, where she'd landed in front of the TV.

"Let's just put this subject on hold for now, can we?"

"Never mind! I just won't go if it's such a big deal," Chloe said in a huff, taking her plate to the sink too.

I knew this wasn't the last I'd hear from either her or my grandmother, but all I cared about was ending it for the time being.

"Can Shannon help with the dishes tonight and I'll do it tomorrow night? I have a test to study for," Chloe said, letting it be known that she was the injured party here.

"I helped last night." This from the living room again.

"Yes, you can go study," I said, knowing it meant Chloe would lock herself in her room for the evening, and glad of it. "And, Shannon, you can help with the dishes. Chloe can do it the next two nights."

That still left my grandmother, her cheeks beet red with unvented anger.

"It's okay, Gram. It really is," I said, waiting for Chloe to leave the room before I added, "You know Uncle Dad is all talk. As soon as she says she's coming, he'll come up with a reason why she can't." I wasn't sure about that, but it seemed a good way to put off the problem until I had more time to deal with everyone. And my own feelings about it too.

"Ha! That's true all right," Gramma said, and the high color in her face started to fade.

"I have to go, Gram," I said before she could get started again. "Would you do me a favor?"

She just looked at me. I took it as a tacit agreement.

"Don't talk any more about it tonight. Don't even think any more about it. Let's just see if it really pans out, huh?"

I could tell she had plenty more to say on the subject, but she didn't. "Aay, whatever you want," she said.

"I'll see you all later, then," I said, not waiting for a good-bye before I left through the living room, reminding Shannon to go back to help clean up.

And hoping everyone stayed in her separate corner while I was gone.

I knocked on Audrey's apartment door twenty minutes later, having broken only a few speed limits so I could fill my tank and still get there on time.

She opened the door and said, "Come on in, Jimi. Take off your shoes and meet me in the kitchen, would you? I have a sauce on the stove that'll burn if I leave it."

"Go ahead," I answered as I stepped inside and closed the door behind me.

I hadn't been in Audrey's apartment in a while, and I was struck all over again by how small it was. The living room was barely big enough for a love seat, one wing chair, and the TV stand that held her nineteen-inch television, her VCR, and a boom box that pretended to be a stereo system.

Plants were her main accent. A feather fern hung in a basket from the ceiling in front of the single window, a rhododendron sat on the end table keeping a bean pot lamp company, twin violets took up the center of each of two tiny tea tables that served as the coffee table, and a four-foot-tall topiary occupied one corner.

In spite of the room's modest dimensions, the plants and the pale cream and sky blue color scheme helped open up the space and leave it with an airy feel, not at all what I'd expected when I'd first come here. As a kid I'd had to be tutored in my catechism after getting a late start in studying for my confirmation. I'd had to go to the nuns' home, an old house where half a dozen of them lived together.

My memory of the place was vivid. Liberty green walls that had cracked above the doorjambs. Dark, scarred paneling and woodworking. The smell of mentholatum seeping out of the corners. And the only decorations religious pictures and crucifixes—wooden crucifixes, plastic ones, even a few braided out of Easter palms.

I'd hated it. It was enough to chase the fantasy of becoming a nun right out of even the most devout, of which I had not been one.

But Audrey's home wasn't like that at all. She did have a small silver crucifix over her TV, but there wasn't a portrait of a thorny-headed Jesus to be had.

"I'm sorry I'm late," I called in to her.

"You're fine. My last session ran over, so I'm running behind too."

As she'd reminded me, there was one rule of the place, and that was that everyone had to take off his or her shoes at the door. I wasn't sure if it was to put people in a more relaxed and comfortable frame of mind or to spare her biege carpet from all the feet that came with her therapy clients since she used her living room as her office. But I took mine off anyway and then headed for the kitchen.

It was straight back and no bigger than most laundry rooms. I realized that she'd be hard pressed to have more than a single dinner guest at a time, because her kitchen table was only about three feet square, set in a U-shaped alcove formed by two corner walls and the end of a row of cupboards. There were only two cane-backed chairs, one in back, one in front, and maybe eighteen inches of space between the table and the cupboard side to get to the one in back.

"Would you mind if I call home real quick? I left a minicrisis, and I'd just like to check on things."

Audrey pointed to the narrow hallway off the kitchen. "The phone's down there."

On a stand the exact size of the phone-answering machine itself.

I dialed the girls' number, looking around as I waited for one of them to answer. The bathroom was directly in front of me, yet another dinky space that would require stepping out of the way to get the door open or closed from the inside.

Audrey's bedroom was a few feet to the right of that. I could see almost the whole room from my vantage point. It took only a twin bed, a low antique dresser, and a stiff-backed chair in one corner to fill it.

I remembered Audrey's saying she'd raised her niece here after her sister and brother-in-law died, and it boggled my mind to think of two people, one of them a teenage girl, living in such close quarters. Maybe Audrey wasn't a nun after all. Maybe she was a saint.

Chloe answered on the fourth ring. She must have been far, far away for the phenomenon of multiple rings to occur. I'd been hoping Shannon would pick up, because she was more likely to tell me what was going on with both Chloe and my grandmother, but instead I got my older daughter, whose cheery hello transformed into a sullen "Oh" when she heard my voice.

I asked how she was doing, and she started the one-word-answer refrain. What I gleaned from it was that Chloe was indeed keeping her distance from Gramma and no more fireworks had broken out since I'd left.

That was all I wanted to know. I encouraged her to study hard—translation: Stay in your room—and hung up.

"Trouble at home?" Audrey asked when I rejoined her.

I filled her in, not leaving anything out as we sat down to a dinner of broiled chicken and sherry sauce, peas, buttered noodles, and iced tea. I didn't want to turn our meal into a therapy session, but by the time I recounted the end of the honeymoon phase of moving into my grandmother's house, that was what it sounded like.

If it bothered Audrey, she didn't let on. She listened, commented periodically, laughed in the right spots, and left me feeling as if I were just confiding a problem to a friend. But then, that was her gift as a therapist.

"It isn't that I don't understand how my grandmother feels." I finished up. "I feel it myself every time Uncle Dad pulls something. And I know it took me a long time to get to the point where I didn't make some nasty comment when it happened. I just don't know how to get it through to Gramma that it's better to keep quiet."

"I don't mean to diminish anything you've been through, Jimi, but I can tell you from experience that in some ways it's as hard to be on the sidelines of these things the way your grandmother is as to be in the middle of it the way the divorcing couple is. Those protective instincts your grandmother is feeling are powerful."

"So how do you deal with it?"

"When it happens to me, I say a lot of acts of contrition for what I'm thinking about the person causing the hurt and try to leave everything in the hands of God. But I have to tell you, sometimes, when I see somebody really close to me being wronged, words fly out of my mouth too. It's that old deal about its being harder to see your loved ones hurt than to be hurt yourself. Some pretty uncharacteristic behavior can come out of it."

"I just wish I could get it through to Gramma that the comments do more harm than good. The trouble is, in the meantime all of us living under the same roof are not getting off to a good start."

"Would it help if I tried talking to her?"

"As a therapist? I don't know about that. She doesn't believe in airing dirty laundry; that's what she says therapy is."

"I'll bet she'd talk to me as a nun."

"Maybe. But how would you get around to the subject of her not putting in her two cents' worth about Uncle Dad in front of the girls?"

"Getting around to subjects people don't want to discuss is my job, Jimi."

I laughed. "I guess that's true."

"What if we arrange a time when you know she'll be home alone? If I drop by to see you and you aren't there, will she invite me in?"

"No doubt about it."

"Then let's set that up, and I'll take it from there.

Maybe it'll help. Maybe it won't. But we can give it a try."

I thought about it and didn't actually feel very confident that it would. But if Audrey was willing to do it, I didn't think it would do any harm either. Except maybe to my immortal soul for inciting a nun to subterfuge. But I was willing to risk it for peace on the home front.

"Okay, let's do it. And I'll pay you on the sly, so she won't know we plotted this."

Audrey laughed wryly. "I couldn't take money for it. Let's just say I'm volunteering and call it a fair trade for everything I've gotten you into with this Hunter group."

I didn't argue with that. And the reminder of all that had been going on during this round of seminars made me feel less guilty about talking about my family problems with her.

Better that than the other topic that was uppermost on my mind these days. Or as my grandfather would have put it, better the living than the dead.

Chapter Twenty-two

LINDA WAS THE first of the group members to arrive. Audrey and I were just finishing the dishes when Linda's big silver minivan pulled up outside the living room window.

I'd stopped at her house at least once a day on all three days since Nan Arnot's murder and watched my friend slowly pull herself together. Not completely—she still wasn't paying much attention to her appearance—but she was getting up every morning and staying up, wearing clothes that weren't ragbag rejects, and today she'd even driven her kids to school again. Her mood was slowly climbing out of the pits too. Also nothing dramatic, but enough not to seem like a zombie anymore.

On the basis of what I was expecting her to show up in—one of her designer sweat suits, no makeup, her hair clean but not poodle perfect—I was surprised to see her walk into Audrey's apartment dressed to the nines, her hair freshly cut and styled in a way that relaxed the perm, and her makeup looking as if a pro had applied it.

My initial thought was that she looked as if she were on her way to a wedding.

My second thought was that I was glad Danny wasn't around to see it. She was still bobbing to the top of his suspect list, and I didn't know how he might construe such a quick and vast improvement.

It didn't sit terribly well with me. Or with Audrey either if her troubled expression was any indication. But not because being all gussied up made Linda look guilty. Just because it was yet another drastic overnight change.

One look at her, and it occurred to me that maybe she was manic and I shouldn't have been lulled into thinking her mental state had been slowly improving. Maybe this was just the high before the next crash.

"Wow," I said, taking in the new navy blue crepe pantsuit and the closer-to-the-head haircut. "You don't look like a woman with a divorce seminar on her agenda."

She smiled like a young girl with a secret she couldn't keep much longer. "I have a date after the meeting."

"With who?" I didn't mean to be obtuse, but at that point I thought anything was possible.

"With Steve. Who else?"

Audrey started putting away the dishes I'd dried and didn't say anything.

I was not so reserved. "What do you mean, a date? As in he called and asked you to a late candlelight supper?"

"No," she said with a laugh that was nearly a giggle. "We're meeting for coffee."

So why was she dressed for the candlelight supper?

"How did this come about?" I asked.

"He stopped by the house last night, and not just to see the kids; he came in and talked to me too. Then he called in the middle of the night. He couldn't sleep. He was upset. He needed to talk some more."

"In general or about something specific?"

"In general. He's feeling lost. Alone. Scared."

This seemed to delight my friend. Though not as if she were glad to see him suffer, which I would have thought more healthy.

"The woman he was involved with has just died," I said. "I'm not surprised that he isn't in tiptop shape."

"But don't you see what this means? He's bottomed out, and he's turning to me. He's ready to come home."

I almost said, "Here we go again," but refrained. Instead, I said, "Did he say that?"

"No, not in so many words. He doesn't have to. In times of trouble you turn to the people you love, the people who love you, the people you trust. I'm that person for Steve. Just the way he's that person for me. He sees that now."

"Did he say *that*?"

"He doesn't have to," she said slowly, as if I could better understand that way.

"Did he say he wanted to move back in?"

"No, but he wouldn't. Steve has a lot of pride. He's waiting for me to invite him. This has all just worked out beautifully."

"Oh, Linda." Me again.

Linda waved away my concern as if she were flicking off gnats. "I didn't mean that the way it sounded.

I'm not glad *Nan* is dead. I'm just saying that it's as if fate fixed things to save my marriage. There was only one thing keeping us from being together the way we're supposed to be, and fate took it away. Things happen the way they're meant to; you say that yourself all the time, Jimi."

"I don't think a young girl's being murdered qualifies as things happening the way they're meant to. Or that it's *fate* fixing things up."

"No, I suppose if you want to be literal about it, it was somebody else who fixed things. But the important thing is that it looks like they're going to be fixed. Like Steve and I and the kids can be a family again after all."

Audrey still hadn't said a word, but she had settled in to lean against the countertop, and she watched Linda with a troubled frown that pulled her bushy eyebrows together over the bridge of her nose.

I, on the other hand, had more difficulty just observing. "Whatever you do, don't repeat any of this to anybody," I said.

"What do you mean?"

"The police are looking for the person who killed Nan, Linda."

"Well, I didn't do it."

"I know that, but you don't want to look as if you're the one profiting from her death, or that might be hard for them to believe." Harder than it already was since the file proved she benefited financially.

"Oh, I wouldn't say any of this to anyone but the two of you. Don't worry about it." She pulled back on the cuff of her new suit and checked her watch for the time. "I wish everybody would get here so we could start. If tonight runs late, I'll have to leave no matter where we are."

I stared at that watch for about half a second before I blurted out, "Where did you get that?"

She held up her wrist, the better for me to see the antique silver timepiece with the opals on either side of the face.

"Isn't it great? It should have been my first sign that everything was going to work out after all. Steve brought it with him when he came in last night. He said some of what had been stolen from the jewelry store had been recovered, and my watch was part of it, so he got it released and returned it. I was just so tick-led. It was another good omen."

I didn't know what to say to that, so I took my cue from Audrey and finally kept my mouth shut.

Grief was the subject of the evening's meeting, and it was appropriate in more ways than one. Not only be-cause discussing the stages of grief and accepting the loss divorce brought applied doubly now to Ron Arnot but because the material also dealt with mood swings for which Linda could be the poster child.

Audrey stayed in the background more than she usually did and had me lead most of the meeting. Clearly this latest switch in Linda's mood had her con-cerned too. And slightly preoccupied. But then, she was Linda's therapist, and I thought maybe she needed to do some observing and some thinking about what the best way to proceed with Linda's treatment might be. I wondered if locking her up was an option.

After the coffee break we pushed all of Audrey's furniture as much out of the way as was possible and sat in a circle on the floor. A close circle in the small confines of that living room.

The homework had been to write a letter of good-bye. During the second half of the meeting the members were to read them aloud and then drop them into an old shoe box that Audrey would burned later on.

I knew from experience that if done right, this exercise had a strong cathartic effect, but it was also one of the most difficult things the group members went through because rather than rehash what had gone wrong in their marriages the way the meetings had up to that point, this was a final admission that their marriages were over.

I asked Linda to go first just in case she might leave before we were too far into it.

"I didn't write one. I'm not saying good-bye to Steve and giving up," she answered—with too much conviction, I thought.

No one, including me, said anything to that. I just moved on and asked Ron to get us started. For the first time in the group, he broke down and wept openly as he read his letter. I hoped the good-bye it entailed and the uncontrollable display of emotion that went with it would have the same freeing effect on him that I'd seen it have on others before him.

Gail went next, her letter as heartfelt as Ron's, bidding adieu to a lot of hopes and dreams that I crossed my fingers for her to regain in the not too distant future.

Clifford's letter was more vituperative, missing the point altogether and clearly showing us all that he wasn't ready to let go of any of his anger yet.

Janine cried through her reading as well. Pretty tears to go along with a missive that, while not as venomous as Clifford's, still gave the sense that she was hanging on to the past.

As time went by and one member after another took their turn, I found myself wondering more and more who had been Melanie Mann's caller. Who was putting us all on with tales of a marriage that never existed?

Beverly was the likeliest candidate, I thought. Melanie's description seemed in line with Beverly's gruff, aggressive style. Then there was the fact that I knew she'd been involved with Bruce and even though she hadn't said anything about his owing her money, maybe some sort of debt had come out of their brief interlude.

I pictured the way she acted through each meeting: irritated by everybody else's emotions, annoyed that she was expected to contribute or participate at all. Even her letter when she read it was coldly dismissive and lacking in any expression of pain or emotion.

What I didn't understand was why she'd have joined the group in the first place if she wasn't married. Granted she'd covered her attitude problems with that story about her boss's forcing her to come, but what was the point? It wasn't as if the seminar was a barrel of laughs.

Unless she'd joined the group *because* of Bruce.

Even then it just didn't make sense to me.

I would have nabbed Beverly at the end of the session to ask her a few questions, but the minute Audrey finished her comments and reminders, Beverly was out the door. Maybe I'd studied her too openly and tipped her off.

That still left Melanie to tell me if Beverly was the one, so I didn't hang around after the meeting either. Instead, I thanked Audrey for dinner and left when Linda did. She was in more of a hurry than I was, so I said that I'd talk to her the next day but that if she needed me before then to call, and we went our separate ways.

All was quiet on the home front when I got there. Gramma was already in bed asleep, and the girls were in their own rooms. I went to Chloe's first. She was on the phone, gave me a curt "Fine" when I asked if everything was okay, and went back to her conversation.

I knew everything was not fine but decided to accept it at face value for the moment.

Shannon was on her knees next to her stereo, playing and stopping a CD every few minutes so she could write down the lyrics to a song. Some droning, moaning dirge is what it sounded like to me, but what do I know? At any rate she wasn't any more interested in rehashing her evening than Chloe had been so I said goodnight and climbed the last flight of stairs to my attic.

No messages on the answering machine.

I didn't care if it was ten twenty-three. I dialed Melanie Mann's number anyway. She picked up on the third ring, one short of her machine.

"Melanie! I'd about given up on you. This is Jimi Plain."

"Oh, Jimi, hi. I was just noticing how many messages my roommate has written down from you."

Taken from the machine, because I'd never talked to a roommate or I'd have known what was going on. "Is everything okay?" I asked.

She sighed, sounding exhausted. "It is now. I've been at Children's Hospital since I talked to you before. I've barely been coming home to change clothes, and I didn't even check my mail or the answering machine or anything."

"What happened?"

"You know how the kids were horsing around when we were on the phone? Well, my son had fallen off the top bunk bed in their room, and he broke his arm. I guess he landed just right because it was on carpeting, but he broke the bone so badly he ended up having to have surgery, and then he got sick from the anesthesia, and I've been at that hospital day and night since I hung up with you."

"Is he all right?"

"He'll be in a cast for two months or more, but he should have full use of his arm and hand after that. For a while we weren't sure if he would, but today he wiggled his fingers, so it looks good. They're letting him come home tomorrow, and I just came to pack him something to wear before I go back for one more night of sleeping in a chair."

After all that, a fake divorcée trying to get money out of her and my curiosity about who it was took a backseat.

"Is there anything I can do?"

"No, but thanks for asking. I think we're finally on top of things. At least I hope we are. When it rains, it pours, you know."

If I weren't so damned nosy, I'd have left it at that and let her go. As it was, I said, "I won't keep you, we can talk about the woman from the Hunter group who's bothering you later if you want, but I'm going nuts wondering who she is. Would you mind telling me that before you go?"

Melanie laughed, sounding loopy. "I feel terrible for leaving you hanging all this time. Her name is Janine Cummings, and I do want to talk about what's going on with her as soon as I have a minute to myself. But that isn't now."

"Anytime." I repeated my offer to help and then hung up.

Janine Cummings. Not Beverly Runyan. So much for my powers of deduction.

Chapter Twenty-three

I HADN'T BEEN in the house five minutes from getting Shannon to school the next morning when Linda's eldest daughter called from the counselor's office to tell me she thought her mother might be sick and to ask if I'd go over there later to check on her. I didn't like the sound of that.

By the end of the week before, when Linda had seemed to be coming back to herself, I'd stopped hovering over her. I'd called only once on Friday, Saturday, and Sunday afternoon. Monday I'd left her completely alone, figuring I'd see her at the meeting. Today I'd figured I'd call around nine to see how the date with Steve had gone.

But after talking to her daughter, I decided to throw on my jeans and turtleneck, and I headed for the old neighborhood.

When I got to Linda's, I knocked on the front door

and tried to open it simultaneously the way I always did. But it was locked.

Linda locked it only when she left.

But her daughter had said she was sick.

I rang the bell this time, knocked again, and shouted, "Linda? It's me."

Still nothing.

I dug her emergency key out of my purse and decided to use it. I was too worried something had happened to her not to.

Once I had the door open I called inside. No answer again. I went in anyway.

The drapes downstairs were all open. I took a quick look around but didn't find anything except a lot of kid messes.

"Are you upstairs, Linda?" I called as I climbed the steps to the second floor.

Still no answer. And a lot less light as I reached that level because all the shades were pulled.

Her bedroom door was open, but I tapped my knuckles on it anyhow. Then I spotted her. She wasn't in bed as I'd expected. She was sitting in a chair in the corner of her dark room, still wearing the new pantsuit she'd had on at the Hunter seminar the night before. Not a hair on her head was out of place. Her elaborate makeup had barely faded. She hadn't even taken off her shoes.

It was kind of eerie, actually, and I thought that it was no wonder her daughter had called me to check on her. She looked like a wax figure occupying that chair until her spot in the museum was ready. Very creepy.

"Linda?"

Her only acknowledgment of me was to look up, her movement as slow and robotic as the president in

Disneyland's Great Moments with Mr. Lincoln. She didn't say anything.

I turned on the light. "Are you okay?"

She shook her head but just barely, as if she didn't have the strength or the inclination to respond.

I went into the room and sat on the edge of the bed not too far from her. "What happened?"

Her shoulders rose with three jerks and then fell back in place. "He doesn't want me, Jimi."

"Steve said that last night?"

"He said he didn't think he had ever loved me. That he didn't know what real love was until he met *Nan*. He said he cares for me, but like he cares for his mother, not like he loved *her*."

"I'm sorry."

"That's what he said too. He was sorry if he gave me the impression that he had any other feelings for me. He'd just wanted to talk to me Sunday because he was so upset about *her*. It didn't have anything to do with me really. It's like he loves *her* more dead than me alive. Like he'd be happier with *her* in the grave than with me and the kids here."

"He's grieving," I said because I didn't know what else to say, although I was a little afraid she might take it as encouragement that Steve hadn't meant what he'd told her, that his feelings would change when he was over Nan's death.

But Linda shook her head again. "He doesn't love me. He couldn't love me and hurt me this way. It's like he doesn't even know what he's doing to me. What I'm going through. Like he can't see beyond himself. Like I'm nothing."

"I know, Linda."

Discovering that for herself had done something to her. I hadn't thought it was possible, but she was deeper into the pits than she had been so far. Her despair was so strong, it was almost an odor in the room.

"I don't know what to do," she said.

"You need to think about yourself, about the kids. Take care of yourself. It's all you *can* do."

"And just give up?"

"On the marriage. On Steve. But not on yourself. You can do only so much to hang on, Linda, and then you just have to accept things the way they are and go on."

"I'm no good at accepting things the way they are when they aren't the way I want them to be."

"Nobody is. But when you can't change it, what else can you do?"

"Something. There has to be something," she muttered, staring straight ahead at nothing in particular.

I couldn't tell what was going on in her head. Her expression was dead blank. She looked like a wax figure again. So much so that I had the urge to touch her cheek for signs of warmth. I resisted, but I didn't like the way she was behaving.

"Maybe you ought to get a little sleep," I said, not knowing if putting her to bed was a good idea. She might not get out of it again. Still, I hoped that exhaustion accounted for her strange behavior.

But she shot that down with a firm "I'm not tired."

"How about a shower, then? I'll make some coffee, fix you something to eat, and have it all ready when you get out?"

"I'm not hungry either. I think I want to be by myself, Jimi."

"I'm worried about you. I don't want to leave you by yourself."

"I'm all right. I just need for everything to sink in. I need to figure out what I'm going to do next."

That was the most reasonable thing she'd said in weeks. It even sounded as if she'd partially come to her senses and meant it. But I still wasn't sure I should go.

"Why don't I just sit downstairs, let you be alone with your thoughts until you're ready, and then we can talk or go somewhere or something?"

She shook her head again. "I don't need a babysitter."

"I'll leave, then, and come back to get you for lunch. We can go out somewhere nice. You'll be hungry by noon."

"Just go home, Jimi, and don't worry about it. I only want to be by myself."

I sat there and stared at her, wondering what to do, wondering what she might do if I left.

"Go, Jimi."

It occurred to me that even if I didn't know what to do, I knew who would. "Okay," I said. "If you're sure."

"I'm sure."

"I'll check back with you."

She nodded without looking at me, and I had the sense she'd tuned me out as completely as if I were already gone.

I made a beeline down the stairs and out the front door, leaving it unlocked and went to my car. Blessing Danny yet again for insisting on that cellular phone, I found Audrey's number in the mini address book in my purse, dialed it, and put in a call for help.

Chapter Twenty-four

IT TOOK AUDREY half an hour to get to Linda's house. I'd sneaked back in after I'd called, gone up a few steps, and sat where I hoped I could hear if Linda made so much as a moan. She hadn't.

When I heard Audrey's car pull up, I slipped back out the front door to meet her.

I'd filled her in on the phone, so after telling me she'd go visit my grandmother when she got things under control with Linda—rather than at one o'clock, as we'd agreed upon earlier—she headed up the walk, and I went to my car.

I knew Linda was in good hands, and there was nothing I could accomplish by sitting on her doorstep. I couldn't go home and risk being there when Audrey moved on to our plan, so with time to kill, I started my engine and aimed the car in the direction my thoughts had been traveling since talking to Melanie Mann the night before: Broomfield and Janine Cummings.

I took a leisurely drive around Broomfield when I got there because I didn't want to drop in on Janine until just before noon. Broomfield is a small suburban town that I don't have cause to frequent, so I hadn't realized so many new homes had been built or that Colorado's growth spurt had hit there too.

Its main claim to fame is traffic court, a family-owned car dealership, and the Broomfield Manor motel, complete with coffee shop, just off the highway. When I ran out of sights to see, I spent an hour in the coffee shop watching the clock. At eleven forty-five I paid for my cup of tea and went the three blocks farther east to the old two-story blond brick building with the Broomfield Animal Clinic sign out front and Janine's ruffled curtains on the windows of the upper level.

There were no patients or owners in the waiting room, but as I went in, I heard a low, mournful howl from somewhere behind the closed door to the right.

At first glance the reception counter looked deserted too. Not until I stepped up to it did I discover Janine kneeling on the floor beside a wire cage butted up against the bookshelves. She was murmuring in a soft voice to a Persian cat in the cage. The cat looked up at her with soulful eyes and did a pitiful part purr, part moan as if to confirm that it was miserable but appreciated the sympathy.

There'd been a bell on the door to announce me when I'd come in, so I knew Janine had to be aware of the fact that she had someone waiting for her, but she stayed with the cat anyway.

I didn't mind. The cat seemed to need her more than I did at that moment.

I stood there for a full five minutes before she got up and turned around to me. She had on pink chinos with a pink-striped white blouse tucked into them. I couldn't help noticing that the blouse was slightly frayed around the collar.

Surprise registered in her petite features when she realized I wasn't the owner of the next patient. "Jimi! Hello."

I got the greetings out of the way, then answered the curious look on her face. "I had to meet my daughter at court for a speeding ticket," I explained, stretching the truth by a year, "and since I was in your neighborhood, I thought I'd stop in and see if I could buy you lunch."

"How nice," she said, smiling as if I'd made her day and making me feel guilty. "I don't usually go until twelve-thirty, but the doctor probably won't mind if I leave a little early today. Just let me check."

The cat watched her go and then turned accusing blue eyes up to me. I knew it was peeved only because I'd taken Janine away from it, but I felt as if the white puffball knew I was operating with ulterior motives. Shame on me.

Janine returned a few minutes later. "It's okay. I don't even have to hurry back. Where shall we go?" She sounded as excited as a kid set free for an adventure.

"You pick. I don't know my way around Broomfield. Somewhere nice," I added even though somewhere nice might mean somewhere expensive, and that wasn't in my budget. Still, if I had to charge it and take a month to pay it off with interest, it was nothing more than I deserved for the false pretense of a friendly lunch when I had something else up my sleeve.

"I know just the place," she told me as she took her purse out of a drawer beside the computer.

I drove the half mile Janine directed to an old house, a Victorian painted Salem blue and trimmed in white gingerbread lattices. The sign hanging from chains from the porch roof said it was Katerina's Kafe, and I expected waitresses with their hair in braids and lots of elderly ladies inside.

I was right about the elderly ladies, but the waitresses wore their hair any way they wanted, along with plain dresses the same color as the house paint, covered with white ruffled aprons.

The place was decorated with replica antiques and had a cozy, old-fashioned parlor feel to it. I relaxed about the cost, figuring it wasn't going to set me back astronomically and enjoyed the smells of yeasty bread and what I thought was chicken pot pie with a hint of tarragon.

Janine knew the hostess, so we were seated right away at a small table in a beveled glass alcove. She also knew most of the waitresses and several of the women dining there. She exchanged greetings with most of them as we wove through the place. Clearly I was on Janine's home ground. I hoped my nosiness didn't cause a scene and turn the whole place into a lynch mob.

There were no menus. Our waitress explained the day's offerings, recommending everything. I was right about the chicken pot pie with tarragon and ordered it. Janine opted for a ham and cheese brioche that sounded good too, and I wished I were there with someone I knew well enough for me to snatch a bite.

We made small talk over our salads, and then I said, "There was something I wanted to talk to you about."

Her eyebrows rose with bright expectation, as if she

were having a good time and couldn't wait for what came next. I had second thoughts but went on anyway.

"Bruce Mann's wife—widow—is a friend of my family."

Janine's light-colored eyebrows went back into place, and the expression of expectation on her face turned into one of wariness.

"Melanie called me, concerned over your claims that Bruce owed you money."

Janine seemed to freeze in place.

"That's what I wanted to talk to you about."

I could tell she was considering denying the whole thing. In the end she let out a breath that deflated her, and her pleasure in our lunch seemed gone for good. She looked at me as if I'd betrayed her. I was sorry I hadn't at least let her enjoy her brioche before I brought this up.

"Small world," she said in a resigned tone of voice.

"Melanie doesn't know anything about Bruce's leaving a debt to you."

"So she said."

"I was surprised to hear that he did. Was this money you loaned him after you got to know him at the Hunter group?"

Lunch arrived, and even after the waitress had left us, Janine didn't answer me. I had the impression she was debating with herself again.

I poked a hole into the center of the top crust of my pot pie to let the steam out.

She didn't lift her fork.

Finally she said, "Bruce didn't borrow the money. He stole it."

"From you?"

"Basically."

I glanced at her frayed collar. I didn't mean to, but I did. And she caught it.

"Not now. I don't have anything worth stealing now. This was from seven years ago."

"So you didn't just meet up in the group?"

"Yes, we did. Seven years ago we never had reason to cross paths. I just knew *of* him."

"Then how did he steal money from you?"

She finally picked up her fork and cut into her brioche. "It's a long story," she said.

"I have time."

She ate some of the brioche but didn't seem to taste it and gave no hint if it was good or bad. She also didn't look at me or say anything. Not until she was about a quarter of the way through the flaky bun.

"Bruce deserved to die," she said. "He was a bastard."

General consensus. "What did he do?"

"Eight years ago I was involved with a married man. Bob Humberger. A wonderful man. Wonderful. His marriage was terrible for him. His wife was a cold stick of a woman. She wanted him only for the money he brought in, so she wouldn't have to work, which she'd never done a day in her life. She just cooked and cleaned and expected him to take care of her without reciprocating or meeting his *needs*—if you know what I mean. They'd been together for seventeen years by the time I met him, and he was so down in the dumps about it that my heart just went out to him."

She told that story as if it were original. And as if she'd believed it.

I played along. "How did you meet him?"

"I was managing the doughnut shop where he stopped for breakfast every morning. He was the head of the tax department at Colorado State Bank downtown. We just hit it off. On the outside it might not have seemed like it, but we had a lot in common. And he was so unhappy at home. He liked to talk to me about it. He said it made him feel better to get it off his chest."

I nodded as if I understood.

"I know it sounds corny," she went on, "but we were like two halves of a whole. It wasn't just some sleazy affair. He didn't make empty promises about leaving his wife; he put things into motion to do it."

"What do you mean, he put things into motion? He moved out? Filed for divorce?"

"He couldn't. He needed to protect himself first."

"Protect himself?"

"It wouldn't have been fair for his wife to get half of everything when he divorced her. Everything they had, they had because of Bob. But the guy who worked under him at the bank at the time, Bruce Mann, had talked to him about ways to fix it so he could come out of a divorce and not get the shaft. So Bob decided to take Bruce up on his offer, and they worked out a plan together."

"A plan."

"Little by little Bob pretended to invest in a print-shop—"

"That didn't exist?"

"Only on paper. Bob was really letting Bruce hold the money for him, and Bruce was making it look right."

"They must have been good friends for your—Bob to trust Bruce."

"No, they just worked together. But Bob was Bruce's boss, and he thought that was a safety net. If Bruce pulled anything funny, Bob could ruin his whole career."

"I wouldn't think that would be too reliable a safety net if there was enough money involved."

"It wasn't a fortune or anything. A little over fifty thousand dollars, I think—"

"But you don't know for sure?"

"It was just accumulating a little at a time so it would look legitimate, but I wasn't in on what was actually going on and never saw any kind of record of it or anything, so I don't know exactly what was there at the end. Bob just said that it would be enough to get us a new start in a new place. To let him open his own accounting firm the way he wanted to, the way his wife wouldn't let him."

"So what happened?"

"When everything had been funneled to Bruce, Bob told his wife the printshop was going under, that it had to be closed, that everything that had gone into it was just a loss they'd have to take. We waited another month after that, all the while he was letting her know how broke they were. Then he asked her for a divorce. As soon as the divorce was final, we were going to get married and go away and start over. Bob and me and my Mikey."

"Your Mikey?"

She closed her eyes tight and sat that way for a few minutes. When she opened them, she said, "I had an illegitimate son when I was thirteen. He's not right . . . retarded. And there are deformities. . . . He doesn't have arms . . . his feet are twisted. . . . He has to be in a special home."

I wasn't sure what to say to that, and with her frayed collar staring me in the face, all I could think of was "That must be pretty expensive."

"It is. I won't have him in a place that's not nice or doesn't take good care of him. There's state aid, but it doesn't go far enough for all he needs, and I have to make up the difference."

Not easy on a doughnut shop manager's or a vet's receptionist's wage.

"Bob was the only man who could accept Mikey. Always before—and since—whenever a man finds out about him, he runs the other way. But Bob wasn't like that. He was going to let Mikey go with us to our fresh start. He said we'd put Mikey in the best home we could find. For the first time since I knew I was pregnant all those years ago as a girl I was not going to have to work or worry about money or how to take care of Mikey. I had a good man who loved me. I was going to have a real home of my own. A life like other people have."

Her hunger for that was raw even now. Gone was the ever-cheery Janine. She was just a middle-aged woman who felt life had dealt her a bad hand on purpose. I didn't know if it had been on purpose, but it had definitely been a bad hand.

"What happened?" I repeated.

"When Bob told his wife he wanted out of the marriage, she did everything to try to hang on to him: She begged him to stay with her, pretended to have a nervous breakdown; they even had to put her in the hospital for a while. She just wouldn't let go. Not that she loved him or anything; she just couldn't seem to accept that he was divorcing her. She was a fanatical Catholic, always telling him she wished she hadn't married him in the first place, that she should have become a nun the way her mother wanted her to, the way her sister had. But since they were married in the church, they couldn't be divorced. It was so stupid. People get divorced all the time. So what if she was Catholic? Audrey is Catholic, and she runs a divorce group, doesn't she? It isn't like the fifties or something, when it would have been a scandal or socially unacceptable. This woman just went crazy over it."

Janine's voice caught, and I realized she was on the verge of tears as fresh as if she were recounting something that had happened last week. She seemed to fight the emotions, but the tears won and fell down her cheeks.

I searched my purse for a Kleenex and handed it to her. "Did he stay with his wife?"

Janine let out a mirthless laugh, clutching the Kleenex in a fist. "No. He moved out anyway. But she kept coming after him and coming after him." She closed her eyes again, and the look on her face was one of horror. Without opening them, she whispered, "She killed my Bob. She took one of his guns from his gun collection and shot him. In one minute she took away the only good thing that had ever happened to me. The only hope I had for the future."

Janine dabbed at her face, and I waited until she'd done that, blown her nose, and looked at me again. Then I said, "And the money Bruce had been holding?"

She took a jerky breath and blew it out. "He disappeared, and so did it. I'd barely come out of the shock of finding out Bob was dead and Bruce was already gone."

The impromptu move to Chicago?

I didn't say anything. I just let Janine go on.

"I went to his house. It was completely cleared out and up for sale. I went to the bank. But all anybody would tell me was that he'd moved away. That they couldn't give out information about where. I would have hired somebody to find him, but I couldn't afford that. I sent letters to his old address so the post office would forward them, but he never answered. Not a single one. I even pretended to be interested in buying his house so maybe I could get the real estate agent to put me in touch with him, but nothing worked."

"And then he came back."

"It's funny—isn't it?—how we find things out. One morning two months ago I was putting papers down for some new puppies at the office, not even paying attention to the articles or anything. But it was the business section, and all of a sudden I laid out a page, and there was Bruce's name. It just jumped right out at me, from an article about how the bank was doing some sort of reorganization that had started with bringing him back as head of the department a little over a year ago. Bob's old job."

"So what did you do?"

"I wasn't sure what to do. It wasn't like I had anything that proved the money should be mine or anything. And he didn't even know my name; Bob wanted to keep me a secret so no one would get suspicious. I didn't think I could just go up to Bruce, introduce myself, and demand the money back after all this time. He would have thought I was out of my mind. So I started to sort of follow him around whenever I wasn't working. I felt like I needed to keep an eye on him while I thought about it. One night I followed him to that church in Wheat Ridge and saw the sign for the Hunter group. I thought, Why not join that with him, get closer to him, maybe figure out something from there?"

"And since you've never been married, you just made up stories for the group?"

"I didn't have to make them up," she said very somberly. "Losing Bob was worse than any divorce could be. I've just talked about how it made me feel."

Pain still sharp after all this time. I'd worked so hard to get rid of mine. I wondered how much feeding and grooming it had taken to keep hers so fresh.

"Did you get around to telling Bruce who you were and asking for the money before he was killed?"

"Yes. By the third meeting I'd decided to convince him with the details of the printshop that only he and I—and Bob if he were still alive—would know."

"And how did Bruce respond to it?"

Janine's mouth got so tight that a white line appeared around it. "He laughed in my face. He claimed he didn't know what I was talking about. That he hadn't taken anybody's money, and he wasn't giving me anything. It wasn't as if he needed my money. He had plenty of his own, and he knew how things are for me because I told him about Mikey. But he kept telling me to leave him alone. That he had enough on his mind with his wife divorcing him and *her* trying to squeeze him for every penny, that I wasn't getting anything out of him."

"That must have been hard to hear."

She shook her head as if to say I'd never know how hard. "Bruce deserved to die. I just wish whoever killed him had waited until *after* he paid me my money."

"But there was still Melanie," I said.

"That young thing with those two healthy children and all his money and mine too. She should give it back to me even if he wouldn't."

"So you started to call her about it."

"I had to try, Jimi. It was my only chance with Bruce gone." Janine pushed away her barely eaten lunch and looked at me the way the Persian cat had looked up at her. "Since you're friends with her, do you think you might be able to persuade her to give me back the money?"

That put me on the spot. Served me right. "Oh, I don't know about that, Janine."

The white line reappeared around her mouth. "Oh, I get it. You can stick your nose in where it doesn't belong when it suits you but not when it might do somebody some good."

I took the jab. I had it coming. "You might try explaining all this to Melanie. Maybe she'd look at the situation differently." Although I wasn't altogether sure that a mistress who had been in on the scam to cheat Mrs. Humberger had the most rightful claim to the money. Even if she did need it more than anyone.

But I didn't say that.

Instead, the waitress showed up at our table to ask if we needed doggie bags, and I was glad for the interruption and the opportunity to wrap up this whole lunch in more ways than one.

Chapter Twenty-five

WHEN I LEFT Broomfield, I ran the errands I'd planned to do to keep myself out of the house for Audrey's visit, ending up a little after four at the drive-through branch of the bank I use. I needed to transfer money from the savings to the checking to pay some moving bills.

Chloe worked there as a peak-time teller—three o'clock to six weekdays. She greeted me with a "Hi, Mom" through the intercom when I pulled up to the island at the farthest end of the ten, but she sounded more begrudging than glad to see me.

I "Hi, Chloe"'d back to her.

"Did you get my message on your machine?" she asked then, none too pleasantly.

"No, I've been gone all day. I'm on my way home now."

"Is it okay if I'm not there for dinner tonight? I

want to go to the library to study. I'll just get McDonald's or something."

"You can't avoid Gramma forever, Chloe," I said, making an educated guess about why she wouldn't come home, eat, and change clothes before hitting the library the way she always did when we lived in the old house.

"I don't want to see her right now."

"We live with her. You'll have to see her whether you hide at the library for a few hours or not."

"I know." But there was hedging in her voice.

Dollars to doughnuts she was figuring this way she'd pop in after Gramma was in bed. The other way she'd have to sit down to a whole meal with her. I wondered if she had plans for every day from now until she moved out on her own.

"I really have a lot to do at the library," she went on, "and this way will give me more time."

The fallback excuse. I knew it for what it was: No parent forces her kid *not* to do schoolwork.

"There are cars lining up behind you, Mom. Can I just do this tonight the way I need to and not talk about Gramma right now?" Disgusted.

Apparently I wasn't being understanding enough. Or maybe I should have tried more reassurances this morning after all.

I put my forms into the tube and sent it in. I was hoping that Audrey would have made some headway with my grandmother and I could reassure Chloe that things would be different from here on. But until I knew that, I decided to give in on this. "What time will you be home, then?"

"Whenever the library closes."

And not a minute earlier. "Be careful."

Another teller did my transaction, and that was the last I heard from my daughter.

After making a quick stop at the grocery store, I drove out the back exit to avoid traffic. There's only a small service road in the rear separating the store from an apartment complex for senior citizens, but it leads to a street I can use to wind through the neighborhood to Gramma's house. Our house. And I use it often.

The three-story tan-brick apartment buildings behind the store are set around a canopy that looks like the entrance to a four-star hotel. Steve Kraner rented one of the apartments for his mother, so I'd been in one of them with Linda, and they really were nice. Expensive too. Especially to pay year-round the way Steve did even though his mother spent winters in Arizona and a good portion of the summer traveling to visit with relatives. This year she'd left the place vacant so much that Steve had moved himself and Nan Arnot into it.

By Linda's account, his mother's neighbors were not happy to have the ungeriatric Steve and his nubile young girlfriend keeping house right under their noses. There'd been some complaints.

As I turned onto the service road, I wondered if Steve was still staying in the apartment since Nan's death or if the neighbors were finally rid of him. I didn't have long to wonder. As I neared the far end of the complex, I spotted Linda's minivan in the parking lot beside Steve's white BMW. The BMW was empty, but Linda was sitting behind the wheel of the van. She didn't appear to be doing anything. Just sitting there. Watching the place. Looking like the wax statue from this morning, except that she'd changed her clothes.

I knew Steve wouldn't have the kids on a Tuesday, and I couldn't think of any other reason for her to be there. Besides, I didn't like the way she looked. So I made a quick turn into the parking lot to ask her if she was okay.

I thought she glanced directly at me, but as I pulled into the spot on the other side of her, she started the engine, backed out, and drove away. Just like that. Without so much as a wave.

I felt like an idiot. What was going on with her? Why hadn't she at least rolled down her window, said she couldn't talk, and *then* driven off?

Maybe she was mad because I'd called Audrey to take over where I'd left off that morning. It looked as if Chloe's shit list wasn't the only one I was on.

I put my car in reverse, debating about going after Linda. But just then I glanced in my rearview mirror and saw not an oncoming car in the way of my backing out but Steve Kraner himself.

I put the gearshift in park and rolled down the window, thinking all over again as he approached that he was an unlikely candidate to have two women hot for him. He was wearing those jeans that are cut like slacks, a blue shirt, and an argyle sweater vest that didn't quite reach the waistband of his pants, which hid below his stomach, leaving a stripe of shirt to peek out.

He was scowling like crazy, not increasing his appeal. But it did make his nose turn red.

"What the hell is going on out here?" he demanded when he'd reached my open window and slapped both hands on the doorframe to brace himself as he lunged partway in.

"Hello, Steve. Nice to see you."

He ignored my greeting. Guess he didn't respond well to sarcasm.

"Am I being stalked by the two of you?"

I glanced in my backseat to see if I'd picked up a passenger I didn't know about. There was only me. "What do you mean, are you being stalked by the two of us?"

"Don't play dumb with me, Jimi. First I look out my window and see Linda sitting here, and now you. What are you running? Shifts? Am I being watched or what?"

Defensive little devil. "Or what, I guess. I'm not watching you. I just left the store and saw Linda sitting here. I was going to ask if she was okay, but she drove off before I could. I thought maybe she'd just been with you and didn't want to talk."

"No, she wasn't with me!" he shouted. "She was just sitting in the van staring at the building like some kind of lunatic for the last hour. But then, that's what she is now, isn't it? A goddamned lunatic who can't get it through her thick head that the marriage is over."

I reminded myself that he was grieving the loss of Nan Arnot and maybe that left him with a short fuse. Or maybe he didn't want anybody to see his grief, and anger at Linda was a good camouflage. A really good one because if I hadn't known he'd found his lover dead only a few days before, I'd sure never have guessed.

"Linda's going through a really rough time right now," I said.

"Oh, and I'm not."

"I didn't say that. But what you're going through is different."

"Yeah, it's worse. But I'm not doing it in somebody else's parking lot."

"As far as I could tell, she wasn't bothering anything. She was just sitting here. Maybe she's trying to come to grips with things and needed to do that for some reason."

"What good would lurking around like a lunatic do? The manager said more than one of the ladies around here have noticed her and called him about it. Everyone is spooked after Nan's being murdered. The last thing anybody needs is some nutcase sitting in a van out here staring at the place. Hell, for all I know, maybe she was revisiting the scene of her crime, and the old battle-axes have reason to be afraid."

His accusations didn't sound serious, just nasty.

I can do nasty with the best of them, but I didn't. Even though some really low remarks about Nan Arnot's death serving as much of a purpose for him as for Linda came to mind, not to mention the one about his own motives for Bruce Mann's death too. But no, I behaved myself. Sort of.

"Guess it didn't count as lurking when you dropped in on her Sunday night, huh?"

"I was visiting my kids," he snapped.

"And bending Linda's ear in the process."

"She practically dragged me in. And then called me at three in the morning. She's the one who wanted to talk. Hell, she couldn't wait to start that let's-try-again crap. Nan wasn't even cold yet, and there she was, telling me she forgives me and we could work things out. She wanted to go with me to make funeral arrangements, for chrissake, and then move some of my things back afterward."

"If you were so against it all, why did you ask her out for coffee last night?"

"I didn't ask her out anywhere. She showed up here and tried to seduce me."

"And you hadn't invited her?"

"Hell, no. I tried to tell her on Sunday that there

was no hope for us even with Nan gone, but she wouldn't listen to me. Then she went and started the whole thing all over again last night. Only this time, when I put my foot down, she threatened me."

"Threatened you how? With what?"

"Oh, Christ. What am I talking to you for?" he said all of a sudden, pushing away from the car door. "You think she's some kind of saint when she's really a fucking lunatic. Just get out of here!"

That was what he did, storming off the way he'd come.

I watched him through my rearview mirror until he disappeared into the building, wondering what Linda had threatened him with. It must have been pretty bad. After all, he seemed more upset by her sitting in his parking lot than he was over the loss of the woman he was supposedly starting a new life with.

Gramma was already setting the table for dinner when I got home, and the house was redolent of her chicken cacciatore. I'm not big on chicken, and since I'd had it for lunch, even my grandmother's spicy tomato and pepper sauce didn't make more of it seem appealing. Not that I was going to say that at the same time I told her Chloe wouldn't be joining us for the meal.

I left my purse near the stairs, took the food I'd picked up for Lucy, and joined Gramma in the kitchen.

"Jimi. Where've you been all day?" was how she greeted me. "You had company."

"I did? Who?" Pretty smooth, I thought.

"Sister Audrey. She dropped by a little while ago. I didn't know where to tell her you were, but I asked her to wait in case you'd come home, and you never did."

"I'm sorry. I went to see Linda and then ran into

another woman from the Hunter group and had lunch with her. Then I did some errands." I picked up one of the place settings. That left only three. Apparently Danny wasn't making it home for dinner again tonight either.

"Chloe's going straight from work to the library to study," I explained as I put away the dish and silverware.

Gramma did a slow-motion nod that lifted her chin high and then set it back down knowingly. I didn't want to make a big deal out of Chloe's taking refuge elsewhere, so I went back to our other subject. "I hope entertaining Audrey didn't tie you up and keep you away from something you needed to do."

"I was glad for the company. We had a good talk."

"About what?"

"A lot of things. Your friend Linda. She's in a bad way."

"Things are rough for her now."

"I think your Sister Audrey is a good friend for her to have, though. She understands."

I took the lid off the Crock-Pot and sniffed the cacciatore. "You're right, she is understanding. I guess that's what makes her good at the divorce seminars."

"She understands about things around here too."

"You talked about that?"

"About how Chloe is mad at me for spouting off."

I turned from the Crock-Pot and leaned back against the counter as my grandmother tore lettuce for a salad. "Well, I was just at the bank, and I think Chloe's pretty mad at me too, so you're not alone. We'll just have to watch ourselves around her when it comes to Uncle Dad."

I thought I was doing pretty well at appearing to take this in my stride and getting my message across, as if I hadn't set the whole thing up and weren't dying to know if it had worked.

"I don't think the sister came to see you at all," Gramma said then.

"No?"

"I think she came to talk about us and tell me in a nice way to keep my mouth shut. I think maybe you asked her to talk to me."

"I didn't ask her, no."

"But you told her about me and Chloe."

"I told her about how things were going over dinner last night, yes."

"And she said she'd come here and see what she could do with me."

Looked as if I were on three shit lists today. Four if you counted Janine Cummings. A new record.

"Actually," I said, "Audrey pointed out to me how hard this all is for you and wanted to commiserate with you."

"So you hid someplace today, and she played like she was coming to see you to get to me."

No sliding anything past my grandmother. I should have known better.

"I was afraid you wouldn't talk to her if I just came right out and suggested it."

"A family should take care of its own problems. In private."

"Sometimes it helps for someone outside the family to put in their two cents' worth."

Gramma made a noise that sounded like "puh," and I knew I was still high up on that shit list.

"You mad at me?" I asked what she'd asked me before.

"You don't want me to talk to those girls, I won't talk to those girls."

"Why would I not want you to talk to the girls? Talking to you is the best part of our being here."

She did the "puh" again. Then she said, "You just don't want me to talk about that bastard father of theirs."

"To me, anytime you want. But no, not to Chloe or Shannon."

"Well, I can't make any promises. I'll pray, but sometimes . . . aay, I can't keep quiet."

"I know, Gram. It's hard. It isn't any easier for me. I see what Uncle Dad does and have to pretend I don't want to cut his liver out with a butter knife too. So, like I told you before, I'll come and scream to you, and you scream to me, and we'll both get it out of our systems without the girls knowing."

"And you'll go to church with me on Sunday?"

Ah, she was going to make me pay for my sins. Guess I owed her one for setting up Audrey's visit. Among a hundred other things I owed her. "And I'll go to church with you on Sunday," I said. Reluctantly.

"Okay, then."

Gramma put the salad bowl in the refrigerator, wiped her hands on her apron, and went outside to take some wash off the line.

I put Lucy's food away in the cupboard.

And wondered if I was being naive to hope that things would be better.

Chapter Twenty-six

I HADN'T BEEN to anything that wasn't a wedding or a funeral mass in more years than I could count. But bright and early Sunday morning that's where I was. Me, Gramma, and Danny. Danny never missed a Sunday or a holy day, and not just to take my grandmother.

By the time I was thirteen the Catholic Church and I had gone our separate ways. I'd encountered some lousy people who were big deals in the Church, and my adolescent idealism couldn't reconcile that with what I'd been taught about non-Catholics—good and bad—going to hell for eating hot dogs on Fridays.

If the lousy big deals were going to heaven, I figured I'd just as soon go to hell with the nicer ones. And eat hot dogs on Fridays.

But Danny, who'd seen worse than I ever would of people—Catholic and not—and society in general, was as devout as they came. I guess what it boiled down to was that he had faith. And I didn't.

Sometimes I envied him his.

After mass there were doughnuts and coffee in the church basement, and apparently that was part of the Sunday ritual for my grandmother and Danny because without discussing it, they herded me downstairs.

Gramma hooked up with a group of women her age and wandered off, but Danny got us two cups of coffee and led the way to the end of one of a dozen long school lunchroom tables. He set the paper coffee cups down and repositioned two folding chairs so his back was to a corner and I was facing him directly in front, nearly knees to knees.

I wondered if he did this chair thing in the interrogation room. Or if he was giving a silent message to the other parishioners to leave us to ourselves.

He reached for the coffee cups, handed me one as we both sat down, and then took a drink of his as if he really needed it.

"You do this every Sunday?" I asked, glancing around the rapidly filling basement to let him know that was what I meant.

"Usually. Nellie likes to socialize a little after mass."

"What about you? Am I keeping you from talking to friends here?"

"I don't do that much. Too many traffic tickets and teenagers in trouble that somebody wants me to get them out of. Mostly I sit here until Nellie's done."

So I was right about the silent message to stay away. "You can leave every week right after mass if you want. I'll come pick Gramma up, so you don't have to stay for this."

He grinned at me. "You mean today isn't the beginning of you coming with us all the time?"

"I'm not sure what I'm in for, but I hope not."

He kept grinning as if he knew something I didn't. I thought it was a good time to change the topic.

"You haven't been home much lately. Is living in a houseful of women getting on your nerves?"

"Nah. Murder cases keep you busy. Ask my ex-wives."

"Bruce and Nan still?"

He nodded and took a drink of his coffee.

"Are you close to arresting anybody?"

"You sure you want to know?"

"Sure."

"We don't have warrants yet, but some things are falling into place."

"Like?"

"Like I'd like it if you'd put some distance between you and Linda Kraner."

I rolled my eyes. "If Linda is the best you've got, you're in trouble." It occurred to me that maybe because I was right in the middle of this thing, he was using Linda as a decoy to distract me. Keep me defending someone he didn't seriously believe was the killer, and he could go about the business of looking into the real suspects without my butting in or nosing around where it really mattered.

"Did you know she's threatened Steve Kraner?" Danny asked.

"He mentioned it. But he wouldn't tell me what she'd threatened."

"To kill him."

"Right. Like she said, 'I could kill you,' when they were fighting over something. We all say things like that sometimes."

"No, it was more of an 'if you love that Nan person so much, maybe you should be where she is now.' "

"Same difference. Anger and frustration speaking. An empty threat."

Danny raised an eyebrow. "Did you know she took a household repair class about a year ago?"

"Oh, my God, lock her up right now. What have you been waiting for? A household repair class? That's criminal, isn't it?"

"Electrical wiring was part of the course," he said, raising his other eyebrow to join the first. "Complete with an easy-to-read handout about what not to do. Reverse it, and she could have fried Bruce Mann."

"Could have but didn't."

"We also have a check she wrote to the Safeway across from Steve Kraner and Nan Arnot's apartment on the same day as the murder there."

Okay, so she'd told me she hadn't been to the grocery store that day and that was why she was serving macaroni and cheese for dinner that night. She was in a bad way. She might have forgotten. Or meant that she hadn't done her big grocery shopping even though she'd run in to pick up a thing or two to tide them over.

"Linda always shops at that Safeway. Are you figuring she committed murder before stopping for milk and eggs or after?"

"She's also been hanging around that apartment complex this week."

Not just on Tuesday, when I'd spotted her? "How do you know?"

"Steve Kraner and the manager have called the cops a couple of times to report it. Plus Steve Kraner has hired a bodyguard, an off-duty officer who's logging all the time she spends sitting in her car outside Kraner's apartment, outside restaurants he's in, outside the houses of friends he visits, outside the funeral home and the cemetery the day they buried Nan Arnot. Outside nearly every place Steve Kraner goes, there's Linda Kraner. He thinks she's stalking him. He could be right."

"Or mooning over him." So that's where Linda had been since Tuesday. I didn't think it meant she was a murderer stalking her next victim, but it still didn't sound good. And it surprised me.

I'd asked her about driving out of the apartment parking lot when I'd pulled up that day, and she'd claimed she hadn't seen me. I thought it was a lie, but hey, everybody's entitled not to talk to someone if she doesn't feel like it now and then. She hadn't said why she was there in the first place, but since she'd seemed to be more like her old self the rest of the week, I'd forgotten about it.

I'd just been glad to see that she was back to her usual running-around schedule, which was where she said she was when I didn't find her at home so many of the times I stopped by or called to see how she was doing. Running around or at one of the three sessions a week she was having with Audrey now too.

I'd thought Linda was finally just getting her act together. She'd talked about looking for a job. Her personal hygiene was impeccable again. She even seemed to have more energy than she had in a long time.

Only now it seemed that what she'd really been doing part of that time was tailing Steve.

"*Mooning over* someone, *stalking* someone—maybe they're the same thing," Danny said into my mind wanderings.

"People behave strangely while they're trying to get themselves through divorce, Danny. She may need this as some kind of closure to convince herself he really has gone on with his life without her. But I'm telling you, she's better than she was. She's coming to it slowly, but she seems to be taking some baby steps ahead with her own life. She isn't planning to kill Steve, for crying out loud."

"What *you* see as her being better *I* see as maybe cold, hard intent. Premeditation. Could be she's made up her mind about offing her third victim, choosing her moment, and this time we're getting to watch."

Again I rolled my eyes, feeling more convinced that Danny didn't mean a word of what he was saying. "Look, if you don't want to talk to me about this, just say so. Don't go casting aspersions on somebody to throw me off the track and keep me out of your hair. There are other subjects, you know. The weather or Gramma or the girls or your love life."

"Is that what I'm doing? Throwing you off the track with false aspersions?"

"Aren't you?"

My grandmother came up to us right then, in a hurry to get home to her own bathroom all of a sudden.

I never did get an answer.

A tentative peace had settled over the home front by Sunday night. To the point where, over dessert in the living room, my grandmother even became the topic of an interview Chloe had to do for her cultural diversity class.

I kept an eye on them from where I sat at the old rolltop desk in one corner writing checks to pay bills. I appreciated the sight and sound and fact that we seemed to have risen above the most recent rift.

Then Shannon yelled down the stairs from the second floor to tell Chloe that Uncle Dad was on the phone and everything tensed up again.

Great timing.

Chloe left the room without making eye contact with either me or Gramma.

When she returned, she announced, "Well, everybody can relax again. I'm not going to Las Vegas for Christmas."

Uncle Dad was getting quicker with the letdowns. He usually dragged these things out longer. "How come?" I asked.

"Now he and his girlfriend are talking about going to California to spend it with her family, and he said I shouldn't plan on coming after all. Maybe over New Year's, he said. But you know how that goes."

Gramma was praying so fast and furiously that her lips were moving. But she didn't say a word or even glance up from stabbing toothpicks into the cake and tenting plastic wrap over them so as not to disturb the cream cheese frosting.

"I'm sorry, Chloe," I said.

"Sure," she answered, turning on her heel and going back into the living room to snatch up her school papers.

Still, my grandmother prayed and worked while I spied to make sure Chloe had gone upstairs before I said, "You made it."

My grandmother said, "That dirty bastard."

"Happens every time, Gram."

"Why do those girls keep believing him? Why don't they just tell him to go to hell? Why do they let him hurt them like that?"

"Because he's very convincing. Probably because he's convinced himself when he says it. He just doesn't see why it's any big deal if he doesn't come through. And every time the girls—Chloe at least—still hope he will."

"And she'd leave you, who does everything for her, on Christmas, if he would? Aay, I don't understand it. Chloe should spit in his eye. I thought she was a smarter girl than that, but look at her falling for—"

Gramma and I both saw Chloe standing in the kitchen doorway right about then.

It seemed she'd inherited her father's timing.

"I'm sorry you think I'm so stupid," she said to Gramma. "Excuse me for wanting to see my father for Christmas one time when I've spent every other holiday with *this* side of the family."

"That's enough, Chloe," I said.

She ignored me. "I didn't know it was a crime to want to see my own father. But then, everything to do with Dad is. Around this house anyway, isn't it?"

"Stop it, Chloe!" I said.

"You're no better than *she* is." She turned the fury on me. "You think just because you don't say it that we don't know? You're wrong. You think I'm as dumb as *she* thinks I am. You're glad Christmas with Dad didn't work out just so you can be right about him. Again. Well, good for you. You're right, he's a jerk who never keeps his word, and I'm a stupid ass for believing for even a minute that he would. Fine!"

She did that upward slice of the air with both hands the way my grandmother does with one, turned around, and pounded through the living room to the stairs again.

So much for peace on the home front.

I closed my eyes and wished for patience, wondering if the road to all of us living together was ever going to smooth out for real.

Or if I'd just made a colossal mistake in moving here.

Chapter Twenty-seven

IT WAS MY turn to bring paper plates, napkins, and coffee cups to Monday night's Hunter group. I bought some with Salvador Dali's limp-clocked *Persistence of Memory* pictured on them. Seemed appropriate. Besides, they were bright and on sale. Apparently Dali on dishes hadn't been a hit.

The meeting was at Beverly Runyan's place, an apartment near the University of Colorado's Medical Center on Colorado Boulevard. The apartment was in an old gray stone building with a security door that didn't lock, on the third floor of five.

Beverly's apartment door was open an inch or so when I found it, and I could hear voices coming from inside, so I knocked once and then pushed it open. Most of the group was inside, in a living room furnished with green sectionals of irregular shapes and contours and black coffee end tables, all circa 1950. The Dali paper dinnerware fitted right in.

I said hello to everyone. Beverly was sitting on an ottoman that had been repaired on one side near the bottom with duct tape. She pointed toward a doorway a few feet down the wall to my left.

"Kitchen" was all she said, like a drill sergeant giving an order that didn't need more elaboration.

I got the idea and went to set my paper goods down.

The kitchen was surprisingly large, with three walls of white metal cupboards, a cat's litter box where a table and chairs should have been, a butcher block in the center with a single tall stool beside it, and a vintage refrigerator that probably still worked better than the new models even though it wasn't much younger than I am.

I left the Dali gang on the butcher block alongside a bag of chocolate chip cookies and headed for the living room.

"You know what tonight is, don't you, Jimi?" Audrey teased me as I sank down onto the floor with my back against a wallpaper mural of deer in the woods.

I knew all right. And she knew this was not my favorite of the Hunter seminars.

Linda arrived before I was able to come up with a clever quip, and greeting her saved me.

Earlier she'd said she had some things to do on her way here, so we should each take our own cars. I'd offered to go along on whatever it was she had to do, but she did a song and dance about not knowing how long she'd be, if she'd be late for the meeting, not wanting to hold me up, and general hedging that let me know she didn't want company and didn't want to say why.

Of course I wondered if she was coming straight from trailing Steve somewhere, but you couldn't ask a thing like that.

Since she was the last of us to arrive, we got down to business.

"Tonight's seminar is our ego booster," Audrey announced, going on to lecture about the blow divorce often delivers in that area.

In my first go-round with these groups I'd been surprised to learn that even a lot of the dumpers suffered feelings of failure and doubts about themselves and whether they could be successful at future relationships. I'd pictured all dumpers as having big egos that left them sure they were too good to stick with their mates. My situation again. But not necessarily the way of them all.

The evening's exercise was designed to give that sluggish self-esteem some help. Unfortunately it always made me uncomfortable. I'd suggested long ago that as a volunteer I didn't need to be included in it. Audrey had laughed, said we all need a few strokes, and wouldn't let me out of it, so I was stuck.

She passed out three-inch-by-three-inch squares of paper—a stack to everyone—and then explained that we would each take a turn at center stage, at which time everyone in the group would write a comment about us and anyone who wanted to could speak up and share his or her appreciation of us with the rest of the group. It didn't matter what was said or written so long as it was positive. Something they'd found they liked, be it appearance or pleasant disposition or a good deed we might have done. Then we'd all get our stack of compliments to go through for a mini ego boost.

I didn't mind writing the comments, but it embarrassed me to death to stand up in the middle of a bunch of people, have them look me over, say or write even nice things. I'm a corner sitter, so for me this was more like sitting on the hot seat than basking in the limelight. It made me squirm.

"Let's do Jimi first and let her get it over with. This part of the seminar always makes her uncomfortable, and we wouldn't want to give her the chance to slip out on us when we aren't looking."

She knew me too well.

I stood and went into the middle of the room, taking a bow.

"First off," Audrey said, "I want to thank Jimi for being generous enough with her time to be our volunteer."

Everyone clapped, and I took another bow. Guess I shouldn't have jumped the gun.

Then she went on to say she found me to be a very observant person with a gift for insight, objectivity, and fairness.

I felt my face flush, wished someone would open a window to cool the place off, and hoped for a quick end to this.

It wasn't quick—at least it didn't seem to be—as nearly everyone added something to Audrey's list. Ron complimented me as a caring and understanding person. Linda announced that I was a good friend, neighbor, and baker. Gail seconded the understanding and caring stuff and added that she appreciated my sense of humor and pragmatic outlook.

Then we got to Beverly, Janine, and Clifford, and the tide seemed to change slightly.

Janine pointedly commented on my ability to be helpful . . . when I chose to be. Clifford put in a vote for discretion, and Beverly called me nosy—well, not in so many words. She said I was the most curious person she had ever known. But the note with which she hit *curious* was super snide, and then, under her breath, she muttered, "Let's hope curiosity doesn't always kill the cat."

So much for my ego getting a boost.

When they finished with me, I got to sit back against the mural. Then we moved on to our hostess.

Beverly didn't seem any more comfortable with the whole process than I was. She stood in the middle of the room in an "I dare you" stance that looked more as if she were about to take on all comers than to be complimented.

I had as much trouble coming up with something positive to say about her as she'd had with me. What stuck in my mind about her was her claim to have had a sex-without-emotions relationship with Bruce Mann and the sly way she'd let it be known she wasn't the only one in the group to have been involved with him.

I couldn't come up with anything nice to say about that.

Then there was her in-your-face personality and her impatience with the seminars, any sentimentality, everyone else's pain and suffering, and all of us in general.

No material there either.

Luckily Audrey didn't wait for anyone else to start. But then, she never did with group members who weren't apt to inspire a lot of fondness. She jumped right in with "Ah, our Beverly. Who's shown us how to be resilient in the face of hard times and a hard life. I think we've all learned from you."

Gail Frankin picked up the ball then. "I'd like to thank Beverly for recommending a doctor who's trying new treatments for people suffering the same disease my former husband is. I've passed the name on to him, and he has an appointment next week. But we'd never have even heard about him if it hadn't been for Beverly."

That about did it for her. A few minutes of silence passed while the rest of us wrote on the notepaper and she got to sit back on her ottoman.

Next up was Gail herself. There was no shortage of comments other group members wanted to make. She was lauded for her kindness, her sweetness, her softspokenness, her honesty, her looks.

I didn't say anything. I never did during this portion because I always felt bad for those members like Beverly who were hard pressed to have one or two comments voiced in comparison to those like Gail for whom the accolades seemed to go on and on.

But I didn't have any problems finding something positive in Gail to comment on in writing. Especially not when I thought about her outrage on Linda's behalf for what Bruce, Steve, and Nan had cooked up to cheat her or the fact that Gail had risked disharmony in her own family to swipe that file of Bruce's and give it to Linda to prevent it.

I wrote that I was impressed with her initiative, sense of justice, and strength in her convictions.

She sat back down where she'd been before, beside Ron on what should have been a corner piece of sofa if the sections had been fitted together, because it was triangular—wide at the back and nearly coming to a point in front. It made for awkward seating, leaving them with their upper halves against the back but their knees out at opposite angles over the sides so as not to touch. I was glad I was sitting on the floor instead of like that.

"Come on, Ron. You're up next," Audrey urged.

He gave an embarrassed shrug and went to stand before us all.

I was glad to see he'd stuck with the group even after Nan's death. He'd been staying close to Gail at the meetings since then, so I thought she had something to do with that. Another of her good deeds.

I liked Ron. He reminded me of some of the boys Chloe and Shannon brought around in spite of all his displays of toughness. Those displays had softened too, and it was heartening to see him finally smile, even shyly. If something good came out of everything bad, then I had to think that Nan's death seemed to have taken a monkey off his back and given him something he could deal with better than he could deal with her adultery.

It worried me a little that it also might have kept him from learning how to handle the emotions should another relationship in his future not work out, but I had to hope some of what we'd talked about in the seminars would stick.

Audrey must have been concerned about his reception, because she went first again. "I've enjoyed seeing you grow as a person, Ron," she said. "I think it's made you get in touch with your feelings."

He probably wouldn't have taken that from anyone but her. As it was, he turned red and ducked as if water had suddenly dripped down from the ceiling on the side of his neck.

No one else said anything, and this time I felt I had to. "I've been glad to see you showing up week after week even when I know it isn't what you've really wanted to be doing. That takes courage," I said.

"You got that right," he muttered. "The part about that I didn' wanna be doin' it."

Then he sat back down without waiting for the notes to be finished about him.

Janine's turn came next, and she slipped into place as if she were slinking out of hiding. I was surprised to see her here at all after our lunch. I'd thought that my knowing she'd come to the group under false pretenses might have kept her home.

As it was, she glanced at me from that center position as if she thought I'd shoot her down then and there and tell her secret.

I didn't have any intention of doing that and gave her a little smile to convey it. I didn't see where squealing would do anything but harm all the way around. Besides, her loss may not have been recent or through divorce, but it was still real and very powerful to her, so it wasn't as if she'd made a mockery of anything we'd done in the meetings.

"I think Janine is the hardest worker of us all," Audrey offered, setting off more remarks similar to that. Nothing as effusive as Gail's praises, yet Janine basked in what was said as if she craved it so much that any crumb was a feast. I felt bad for a hunger that great, so I wrote more than I'd intended about respecting her ability to ride through hard times so cheerfully and appreciating her upbeat attitude.

Yet even as I did, I couldn't help wondering if she was still trying to get her old lover's money from Melanie Mann. I was torn about that. If Melanie wouldn't miss the money, Janine could certainly use it. And I supposed that between the two of them, Janine had somewhat more of a right to it. But still it was an odd situation.

Then again, maybe something would work out for her with Clifford Silver, I thought as he launched into a pretty flattering commentary about her.

". . . a kind, tender person. Someone who'll come at a minute's notice when a call for help goes out . . ."

I hadn't realized he admired her so much and wondered if her flirting had won him over.

But then he explained that she'd helped him with his sick cat over the weekend.

I felt bad for her again and added a comment to my note about how nice she always looked.

"Your turn, Clifford," Audrey said when Janine took her seat again.

He marched up with an unusual bit of flair and gave us all a parade wave.

Janine started off the comments with her admiration of his devotion to his cat, and as I thought about what to write, I realized his whole mood had improved. He was making jokes about the proceedings and seemed more relaxed and upbeat than he had been since the start of the group.

I wondered if Bruce's picture of him had surfaced in a way that freed him somehow because he definitely had that kind of air about him, as if a big weight had been lifted from his shoulders.

I hoped that meant something good and fought an urge to write that he didn't look bad in leather. Instead, I noted my admiration of him as a conscientious and caring father who bent over backward to support his kids and spend time with them. Even if he was up to things he wouldn't want them to know about when he wasn't with them, but I didn't write that.

When we were finished, he mimicked my bow and nearly dived for his chair, turning the floor over to Linda.

She was easy for me. I echoed some of what she'd said about me: good friend, good neighbor, good person, good mother, good legs—I threw that in because I knew she was proud of them, and I thought I'd reinforce it.

But while I wrote the good things without having to put much thought into them, I wondered what was really going on with her to be following Steve around.

Was I right and was she just in the throes of some bizarre form of closure? What did she do when she followed him? Did she try to have contact with him? Was she trying to talk to him, to get him to go back to her? Was she getting all dolled up and hoping she'd be attractive enough to him that he'd get interested again?

Or was she maybe just protecting her own interests, watching him so he wouldn't get any more wise ideas about cheating her out of her share of what he'd now get back from Nan's estate? If that was the case, maybe it wasn't such odd behavior after all.

I also began to wonder if I could tell what her reason was if I followed her and watched the way she was watching him.

I could just hear what Danny would have to say about that when Steve's bodyguard reported it, but if I came away with some validation for what she was doing, I'd have a defense for myself and a logical, unsinister purpose for her actions.

The more I thought about it, the more I liked the notion. Okay, so I was dying of curiosity myself, and that might be soothed too. But I was nearly finished with the Kiwanis newsletter because I'd worked all weekend, so I figured I'd earned a day off anyway. And a reward of my own choosing.

I was thinking so much about the idea that I nearly missed Audrey taking center stage, the last of us.

She played it up, made jokes, and had us all laughing. Compliments shot from most everyone in the group. I didn't add anything but had no problem writing about how much I enjoyed her friendship, how grateful I was for her willingness to help whenever times got tough, and how much I appreciated the lessons I continued to learn from her.

When the other comments ebbed, she held her hands up in the air and clapped. "Let's give ourselves a round of applause," she said like an MC, and then we broke for coffee and cookies.

After that the rest of the meeting was spent reading through our papers and discussing how the exercise had made us feel.

But by then my thoughts were ditching this particular seminar I wanted out of anyway and I was planning my moves to spend the next day tailing Linda.

Chapter Twenty-eight

I WAS UP at 5:00 A.M. Tuesday. And after I dropped Shannon off at school, I headed out to the elementary school, which was Linda's last drop-off point of the morning.

I'd borrowed one of the two cars that sat unused in my grandmother's garage, a gold Nova my grandfather had driven when he hadn't used his copper and white '57 Chevy. The Nova was unobtrusive, and when I got to the grade school, I parked it on a side street across from the single-level redbrick building with its monkey bars, swing sets, and big oak trees all around.

Keeping an eye out for Linda's minivan, I hoped the pewter sky and thirty-three-degree temperature that were announcing winter would make sure she didn't have her youngest walk to school. It might not have mattered when she was in the staying-in-bed phase of her divorce adjustment, but as far as I could tell, she was back to doing routine things and being a conscientious parent again now that she was in this new one, so I thought it was a pretty good bet she'd show up.

While I was on the lookout for her, I also watched the procession of mothers and a few fathers depositing their children for the day. It made me feel slightly nostalgic for the time in my own life when the kids were easier, the problems smaller, and I'd thought I had my whole life mapped out and on course.

As I sat on the sidelines, I wondered how many of the mothers, especially, thought the same thing and had as rude an awakening as I'd had waiting somewhere down the road for them.

Nostalgia or not, when I thought about that and the difference in the person I was then and the person I am now, I realized that if I could have put my life into reverse and gone back, I wouldn't have.

That bit of reverie was cut short when I spotted Linda pulling into the parking lot from the side road she used. She waited her turn behind a half dozen other cars like a ride at Disneyland, not letting her eight-year-old out until she was in the unloading position at the front of the school.

I could tell even from the distance that she was put together for the day. Her hair was combed, and she had on a white turtleneck sweater that I recognized as her best cashmere. That put a point in the column for hoping Steve would notice her and fall back in love with her.

When her second-grader was out of the van, she didn't wait for him to walk all the way to his classroom, where the other kids were milling around with a disheartening lack of enthusiasm. She broke drop-off protocol, pulled out of line, and made a run for the parking lot exit.

Looked as if she was in as much of a hurry to get out of there as I'd been to get there.

I'd left the Nova's motor idling, so I just had to put it in gear and slip out of my cross street to get behind her on Oak Street. There was a car between us, and I stayed far enough back to see the big silver minivan without being so far that any more cars could come between us or running too much of a risk of losing her. I'd never followed anybody before, but what I was doing seemed logical. And hey, I watch TV. I'd seen it done.

As we approached the light and intersection of Oak Street and Fifty-eighth, I wondered if she'd turn left and head for Steve's apartment. When she got in the right lane and on came that blinker, I followed suit, glad to see the other car did too, so I wasn't right behind her at the stop.

Trouble was, she made a right on red and the guy in front to me pulled up, stopped, and stayed. And there I was: stuck.

"Dammit."

I considered honking at the guy up ahead to get out of my way. I considered pulling up onto the sidewalk and trying to get around him. I knew neither was logical or possible or would work. I just had to sit tight.

It seemed to take forever, but the light finally changed. I went like a bat out of hell, veered around the car in front of me as soon as I could, and made my tires screech.

I wasn't in too bad shape because Linda was only a few blocks away. This time when I caught up to her I didn't leave enough space for anyone to be between us and just hoped she wouldn't recognized the Nova.

I didn't really think she would. She'd probably seen it only once. As for me, I'd borrowed a baseball cap from Shannon—something I never wear—tucked my hair up under it, and kept the bill low enough to shadow my face. It may not have been much of a disguise, but then, from what I could glimpse of Linda in her side mirror she was intent on what she was doing and seemed oblivious of anything else going on around her anyway. Lucky for me.

She kept going west on Fifty-eighth to Ward Road, then turned right again and drove into 7-Eleven's parking lot.

I followed suit, only at an earlier entrance the minute I saw her turn. Synchronized driving. I parked on the side of the video rental store at the opposite end of the shopette.

I'd never been to a convenience store at seven fifty-seven in the morning. I didn't know it was such a hub of activity. Apparently a lot of people made it their first stop on their way to work, because the place was doing a roadhouse business of men and women in business suits of various shapes, sizes, and hues.

Linda jockeyed for a space near the door, left the van running, and dashed in as if she had somewhere she needed to be sooner than anyone else needed to be at work.

The 7-Eleven must have had a bang-up crew at that hour, because she was back again in five minutes flat, carrying a small plastic sack and a huge red and green paper cup with "Big Gulp" printed diagonally all around it.

The thing was enormous, filled no doubt with Coke, Linda's beverage of choice. It made my teeth hurt to think of drinking it at all, let alone so early and so much of it. If she did, I was probably going to follow her to more bathrooms than anywhere interesting.

Still, when she pulled out of the parking lot, I went

with her. Back out onto Fifty-eighth, going east this time. No surprise when we ended up at Steve's apartment complex.

Linda pulled into a space at the end of the two-lane lot that was directly in front of the buildings and angled against a curve in the sidewalk in such a way that she was staring head-on at Steve's BMW nosed in farther down at the curb.

I went past to Safeway, rounded the store, and drove into another section of carported spots across the service road from the complex. That lot belonged to the retirement community too. The Nova fitted right in with the other cars under the strip of awning, all sensible sedans or small economy models, with only a few fancy jobs of the Cadillac variety peppered among them.

I turned off the engine this time because Linda had. From my position I could see her pretty well, so I knew she was still in the van, that she hadn't gone up to the building in the time I'd driven around Safeway.

From the looks of how she was settling in, she didn't intend to. She just sat back, sipped her Big Gulp, and munched on something. Probably potato chips or pretzels she'd bought at 7-Eleven. I'd have chosen Cheez Doodles myself, but Linda wasn't fond of them.

We stayed that way for a long time. Long enough for it to occur to me that I should have brought something to do. A magazine, a book, a printout of the Kiwanis newsletter to edit, something. On TV these stakeouts don't seem so boring. I exhausted the contents of the glove compartment in about five minutes, leaving myself with nothing to do but look around.

I refocused on Linda. She was staring at the building, specifically at Steve's ground-floor apartment on the end. Maybe she could see inside the sliding glass door from her vantage point, but from where I was I could see only shadowed glass, so I counted the poles that held the carport up.

At about nine forty-five the loud roar of a motorcycle drew my attention. A helmeted man steered the thing into the closer lot and parked next to Steve's BMW. He turned the cycle off and dismounted, all the while glancing with regularity at Linda the way you look at an unleashed dog you aren't sure about but don't want to provoke with a stare.

She seemed to notice him but after a single glance went back to watching the apartment.

He took off the helmet and tucked it under his arm. He couldn't have been more than thirty, with pale brown hair and an oval face with a nose that was too short and turned up to look good. Still watching Linda, he headed for the building.

Steve's bodyguard or somebody's grandson? I wondered.

If he was somebody's grandson, the somebody was probably one of the complainers about Linda's being there, because he was definitely interested in her.

He disappeared into the lobby and reappeared about ten minutes later with Steve.

The bodyguard.

The two of them went to the BMW. On the way Steve saw Linda too.

"Fucking lunatic! Get the hell out of here!" I heard him shout as he got in the passenger side and left the driving to the bodyguard.

Linda didn't respond. She just started her engine, waited for the BMW to pull out, and pulled out right behind.

We were going to be a parade.

And all for Steve to have a haircut. For Steve to go to the dentist. For Steve to stop in at his defunct furniture store with its Closed for Business sign in the window. For Steve and his bodyguard to have lunch at a submarine sandwich shop. For Steve to go back home.

The bodyguard parked in the spot the BMW had been in before. Linda pulled into one a few spaces down, and that's where they were when I moseyed up to a place under the carport again, far enough behind that Steve and the bodyguard were going into the building by the time I got there.

Linda was staring at the apartment again. Zombie-like.

Maybe she *was* crazy.

But I didn't really believe that. In fact, as I sat there watching her, I started to think that the only method to her madness was to intimidate Steve. To knock him off his pins. To just plain give him a hard time. And I liked that.

Okay, so maybe it was a kind of weird way to get back at him. So what? He had it coming in a much bigger way than this.

But was she stalking him with intent to kill? If Danny had seen what I'd seen, surely he wouldn't think so. That whole notion seemed even sillier now than it had before.

I started to consider walking up to the minivan, getting in, and just asking her straight out if what she had up her sleeve was to give Steve a taste of what it was like to wake up every morning and wonder what she was going to do to him for a change.

That was when I heard her engine start again. Just for the heck of it I thought I'd see this through to the end. In for a penny, in for a pound.

I fired up the Nova, looking for signs of Steve and

the bodyguard coming out again. But they were nowhere in sight. Despite that, Linda pulled out of the parking place again and headed in the direction of Safeway. Maybe she was as hungry as I was and as sorry she hadn't packed a lunch.

But instead of her stopping at the store, from my distance behind her I watched her pass it up, go out to the light, and make a left turn onto Ralston Road.

We were on the move again.

I followed her to Wadsworth, where she turned right. About a mile south of the turn it occurred to me that we could be headed for Audrey's apartment, that Linda could very well have a session with her. I'd get my lunch break after all if that were the case.

It was. I trailed Linda all the way to the courtyard apartments and watched her until she was inside. Then, thinking about Steve and his bodyguard eating sub sandwiches, I found a place on Wadsworth and ordered a six-incher with ham, turkey, three cheeses, onion, olives, vinegar, and mayo. Drinks were self-serve, so I filled a tall glass with ice, added a lemon wedge and then water.

I ate sitting at a corner table by myself, used the facilities, and felt much better.

On my way out I got a refill on my water and took it with me back to playing tailgater.

I'd taken only thirty-five of the fifty minutes and was actually kind of looking forward to getting back to watching my old friend stick it to her creep of a husband a little while longer. I was also feeling pretty good about accomplishing this. Linda hadn't spotted me. I hadn't lost her—except for a few minutes at the start—and there I was, headed back for the second shift, fed, watered, and comfortable again. Maybe I should hire out for this.

I was still congratulating myself when I turned onto Audrey's street and realized Linda's minivan wasn't in front of the apartment anymore. It was gone. So, I assumed, was Linda.

Thinking it was a good bet that she'd gone back to watching Steve, I headed for his place, keeping an eye out for signs of the silver minivan along the way. I never spotted it. It wasn't at the seniors' apartment complex behind Safeway either.

I buzzed by the kids' schools, her usual hangouts, her house. Zilch. I didn't have any idea where Linda had gone.

By the time I admitted that to myself I needed to pick up Shannon, and I decided to call it a day.

So much for quitting my job as a technical writer to tail people.

Chapter Twenty-nine

I DECIDED TO edit the Kiwanis newsletter Tuesday night partly, I suppose, to punish myself for having wasted a whole day following Linda and then trying unsuccessfully to find her again. Besides, I needed to feel good about something, and finishing the newsletter now—when it wasn't due until Friday—might do that. A little anyway, I hoped.

So right after a too-quiet dinner with only Gramma, Shannon, and me in attendance, all of us with the pall of Chloe's continued absence hanging over us, I holed up in the attic with my computer.

I was glad to see that all the distractions that had gone on while I'd been writing the newsletter hadn't done too much damage. It was actually pretty clean. Maybe I write better when I'm not thinking about it. But the edit went pretty quickly, and by nine-thirty I was printing the finished material, when I heard a knock on my outside door.

"Who is it?" I called.

"Me."

Danny.

I wasn't sure why the sound of his voice seemed ominous. Maybe it was just my own mood.

I got up, unlocked the door, and let him in. He seemed down in the mouth, and I thought the ominous sound in his voice might not have been in my imagination after all.

He looked good otherwise, though. Dapper, in a tweed suit, cream shirt, and cocoa-colored tie still Windsor-knotted at his throat. But there were lines of strain radiating from the corners of his eyes and mouth.

"All the lights off downstairs again?" I asked, assuming that was the only reason he'd used the outside door.

"No. But it's late."

Good enough. None of us wanted him to come across one of the girls walking around in her underwear.

"Sit down," I said while I turned off the printer and closed out the computer for the night.

He propped a thigh over the arm of the love seat, and perched.

"Want a drink? A cup of tea? You bumming chocolate?"

"Shit, I really don't want to tell you this."

I sat on the arm of the chair across from him, my curiosity—and a little alarm—piqued. "Go ahead. What's the matter?"

He shook his head again, this time staring at the floor and worrying his forehead with his fingertips while he did. "It's about your friend Linda."

"You arrested her? Danny, you are wrong about her. I followed her around for a while today, and I don't think she's doing anything but dogging Steve to make him worry about what she's doing. But she isn't *doing* anything to him."

His expression went from reluctant to grim, and once more he shook his head. "I haven't arrested her, Jimi. She's dead."

There was a moment when I almost thought he was joking. Then a chill ran across the surface of my skin. "Dead?"

"The husband has the kids for the mid-week visitation. Kids kept calling to say goodnight. No answer. She wasn't lurking outside the apartment, hadn't been since this afternoon. Husband called in to the cops, afraid she was up to no good if she was out of sight. Somewhere in here my name came up, and I got notified, asked if I knew where she might be. I didn't. Cops sent a car around to the apartment. Couldn't find her. Went to the house. All the lights on. Patrolman could see her lying on the kitchen floor. Figured it was a heart attack or stroke because of her weight. But I just got the coroner's preliminary before I left to come home; he says it looks like an allergic reaction."

"Nuts."

He looked at me as if he couldn't believe I'd made such a flip remark.

"She's allergic to nuts. Big time, seriously, deathly allergic."

"Ah. Then maybe that's what she got into. There were some chocolate cupcakes on the counter. I'll have them checked out."

My turn to shake my head, even though it seemed tough to do in the thick fog I felt like I was in, too thick to cry, too thick to feel anything but dazed. "Linda was vigilant about staying away from nuts. She had to be. If she hadn't prepared the food herself, she didn't so much as take a bite without asking first if there were nuts in it in any way, shape, or form. If there was any doubt, she didn't eat it."

"So maybe this was suicide."

"Oh, God." I hadn't considered that.

"Is it possible?" Danny asked.

I shrugged once more. Linda had been in the pits. There was no denying it. I'd been worried about her offing herself. Until the past week.

"You okay, Jimi?"

No, I wasn't okay. But what difference did it make? I was more okay than Linda. "You're sure she wasn't murdered?" I heard myself say as if it were someone else.

"There's no sign of foul play. No reason to think she was."

"Did she leave a note?"

"Not that anyone found."

"Not even to her kids?" Her kids. God.

"No."

"I don't believe this." Or more to the point, I just couldn't grasp it. Linda was dead.

"Why don't we go for a walk? Or get a cup of coffee around the corner?" Danny suggested.

For some reason I was suddenly so exhausted I could hardly think. All I wanted to do was crawl into my bed and pull the covers over my head. "Thanks, but I don't . . . I'm not up for that. I just need to be by myself if that's okay."

He didn't budge. "I'm sorry, Jimi," he repeated, clearly not knowing what else to say.

"Me too. Linda was kind of wigged out lately, but she was a good person, a good mother, a good friend."

I was reciting the compliment I'd written to her the night before. Guess I didn't know what to say either.

"Why don't I sit up here with you for a while? Talk or watch some TV or a movie if you want?"

"I can't, Danny. I can't. But thanks." Surely he knew me well enough to realize that when I said I needed to be alone, I meant it.

"Okay." He stood. "But you know I'm right downstairs. You want company—even in the middle of the night—you come get me."

I nodded, and he headed for the outside door.

"Danny? Are the kids okay?"

"They're with their father. He might have been a cheating creep of a husband, but he seems to do pretty well by them."

"And what about Steve? Does he even care that Linda is dead?"

Danny did the shrug. "No tears."

Chapter Thirty

When Danny left, I'd gone straight to bed. But that urge to escape into sleep hadn't panned out. Sleep was the last thing I could do. Cry, pace, worry, rehash, feel guilty, angry, and guilty again by turns—those I could do. Sleep I couldn't.

I knew Audrey was an early riser, so at seven I called her. I wondered if anyone knew the right way to break news like this. I didn't. There she was on the other end of the phone, glad to hear from me, and I had to tell her Linda was dead.

When I did, there was silence on her end. I could see her in my mind, making the sign of the cross, saying whatever prayer it was she'd said when we'd found Bruce.

After a few minutes she spoke again, her spirit dampened. "What happened?"

"Danny says it was an allergic reaction."

"To nuts? Did the police know she was allergic to them?"

"No. The coroner said it looked like an allergic reaction to something. I told Danny about her sensitivity to nuts. When I did, he started to think she committed suicide. Do you think that's possible? I thought she'd been feeling better."

"She didn't seem as down this week as she was last. But sometimes if people are really determined to take their own lives, they put effort into looking as if it's the farthest thing from their minds to throw everybody off and buy themselves the space and freedom from being watched to actually do it."

"Did you have any hint that she was suicidal now?"

"You know how she's been. I've had trouble getting her to talk about herself at all. Steve is the only thing she's wanted to discuss, and she hasn't been happy with me trying to refocus her. She's even gotten furious with me when I try. In fact, yesterday she just up and walked out on our session. She said she had to get across town, was wasting her time with me, and out she went."

I didn't let on that I knew the session had been short, because then I would have had to explain my harebrained notion about following Linda and doing some good if I could figure out what she was up to.

"What did Linda need to do across town?"

"She forgot her purse at Beverly's apartment the night before and was going back for it. I even offered to ride along so we could talk on the way if she wanted, but she was just peeved at me. She said I didn't understand, that I couldn't understand what was going on with her. Maybe she was right. I must have failed her somewhere along the way."

"The person who failed her was her husband," I said.

We both lapsed into silence for a minute after that. I probably shouldn't have said it, but that was how I felt. It was one thing for a marriage to go bad. Another for one of the people to do wrong by the other, by the kids, when it did.

"The rest of the group should be told," Audrey said then. "But I'm in a bind, Jimi. I have to be in a church meeting most of this morning—in fact, you caught me on my way out the door—and then I have sessions back to back all day. Would it be too much to ask you to call everyone?"

There weren't many things I wanted to do less. But what could I say? "Sure. You're right, it wouldn't be good for them just to see it in the paper tomorrow. I'll make the calls now; maybe I can get hold of everybody before they leave for work." And get it over with myself.

"I can't tell you how much I appreciate it. I'm going to owe you another dinner for this."

"No big deal," I lied.

When we said good-bye and hung up, I dug out the list for this particular Hunter group, took that and the phone with me to the overstuffed chair, and sat down.

Since the list was alphabetized, Ron Arnot was first on it. I thought about Linda's having befriended him when Steve and Nan had moved in together and didn't relish telling him, of all the members, about her death. Linda had been a sort of surrogate mother to him. And on top of his just suffering the loss of Nan, I really didn't want to make that call.

I decided to start at the bottom of the list instead of the top.

Clifford Silver.

I dialed his number before I could think of a reason not to. When I told him about Linda, he was more upset than I'd expected him to be. I really knocked him for a loop.

"Oh, no. Oh, my God. No. Oh, no. What happened?"

I explained.

"Oh, God, no. She was . . . God . . . She'd just done me such a favor."

"She had?"

"She didn't tell you? I thought you knew. She didn't even tell *you*?"

"I don't know what you're talking about, Clifford."

"The picture, Jimi. She found the picture. And the negative."

"Linda did? Where did she find them?"

"Nan Arnot had them."

It took me a minute to digest that. "How did Linda get them?"

"She said she was at her ex-husband's place looking for something else and she'd found them. She looked at the picture—I wish she hadn't—but when she did, she realized it was probably not something I wanted out of my possession, and she took it and the negative and gave them to me. I owed her one for that. I really did."

"Linda was at Steve and Nan's apartment looking for something? For what? And when?"

"I don't know. I only know that she was standing at my car Monday when I came out of school and she gave me an envelope with everything in it. And now she's dead. God."

I heard his doorbell ring.

"Oh, Jimi, that's my ride. God. I just can't believe this."

"You'd better go. If you need anything, even just to talk, give me a call."

"Thanks. You too."

I hung up, hating what I was thinking about Linda and when she might have been in that apartment going through things. Before Nan's death? Since?

Maybe the day of it?

I shied away from the very idea of that, moved up the list to Beverly Runyan's name, and dialed her number.

She let me know the minute I identified myself that she'd just come in off an all-night shift, was headed to bed, and didn't want to be bothered with me.

"I won't keep you. I'm just calling the members of the group to let you all know before it comes out in the paper: Linda Kraner was found dead last night."

"Jesus, another one? What the crap is going on? First Bruce, then that Nan he was screwing, now Linda, who he was also boinking. Maybe I better lock my doors better."

I hadn't looked at it that way. And I didn't want to now.

"Linda's death seems to have been from an allergic reaction."

"To nuts? I know she was allergic to them. She never shut up about it. How'd that happen when she wouldn't come within ten feet of the things?"

"The police think maybe it was suicide."

"Then she wasn't offed by somebody else? Well, that's better."

For whom? Linda was still dead.

"No, the police don't think she was murdered," I said.

"Well, thanks for calling. I have to get to bed."

I didn't see the need but felt obligated to say, "If you want to talk later or when you wake up—"

"When I wake up, I go back on duty."

"I guess I'll see you at next Monday's meeting, then."

"Not me. I can't make it. I'm going out of town."

"You are? Business or pleasure?"

"Look, I'm really tired."

Hard to be polite to this woman. I just told her to have a nice trip and hung up, none too sorry to end the call.

Next on the list was Bruce Mann. Then Linda.

I skipped past them to Gail Frankin's number, dialed it, and woke her up. I could tell from the sleepy sound of her voice. But she assured me it was okay when I apologized. "My alarm was set to go off in ten minutes anyway."

Good thing she wasn't one of my kids.

"I'm also sorry to say that I'm calling with bad news."

"Oh. What now?"

I told her about Linda, including that the authorities believed her to be a suicide, and waited for the outpouring of sorrow I expected.

It didn't come. Instead, very quietly, she said, "Do you think she had a guilty conscience over Nan?"

I really wasn't up to this. "No, because I don't think Linda had anything to do with Nan's death," I said, hearing a new hedging in my own voice as I wondered again just when Linda had been in Nan's apartment looking for something.

"She had Nan's watch, you know," Gail said as if she hated to tell me.

"The silver antique with the opals?" I explained that it had been Linda's anniversary gift before it had belonged to Nan and that Steve had given it back to her.

"No, he didn't, Jimi. I overheard him at the funeral asking her where she got it. She said one of the kids had found it in Nan's things, recognized it, and brought it back to her."

A reasonable enough explanation. If it were true, why hadn't that been what Linda had told Audrey and me?

God, I hated where my thoughts kept going. All I could say was "I don't know, Gail. I know only that Linda is dead now too."

Silence.

Then: "I'm sorry. I know she was your friend. You must feel awful."

I said, "I'll let you go now. I still have to call Janine and Ron to tell them."

There was another pause before she said, "You don't have to call Ron. I'll tell him."

A muffled voice in the background said, "Tell me what?"

Then, in a slightly higher decibel level, Gail said, "I'll call him right away."

"Good" was all I said, as if I hadn't heard anything else even though my eyebrows were probably going to have to be pried out of my hairline. I got on with the good-byes so I could back out of this call the way I would have backed out of the room had I walked in on her and Ron, which was the way it felt.

Gail and Ron in bed together? When had that started?

I didn't have the oomph to try figuring it out and instead just counted my blessings. At least I wouldn't have to be the one to tell him about Linda.

That left me with Janine Cummings. Last but not least.

I was eager to have this chore over with, so I didn't waste any time before I dialed her number.

"This group has the kiss of death on it, doesn't it?" she said once I'd relayed the news. She sounded more weary than I'd ever heard her.

"I'd hate to think of it that way."

"It's true, though. Two members and the ex-wife of a third one all dead. What would you call it?"

Good question.

When I didn't answer it, she said, "Linda is probably better off anyway. She'd probably have ended up like me: no money, no life, no nothing. With Bruce Mann's hand in things, that's what happens to women like us. I know I'd have been better off dead. Your friend Melanie won't give me back my money, you know? Even telling her the truth didn't help."

"I'm sorry," I said, concerned over the depressed sound of this usually overly cheery woman.

"I asked Linda to help with that, but—"

"You asked Linda to help with what?"

"With convincing your friend about the kinds of things Bruce did to people. I just wanted her to back me up because she knew firsthand about Bruce's tricks. You know, like what he did with Linda's husband and Ron's wife?"

"How did you know about that?"

"Linda told me. One of the times I had to make a touch-base call to her. She'd just found out what Bruce had done, and she started talking about it and told me the whole thing. I didn't tell her what he'd done to me before, but after I talked to you and called Melanie Mann again and still didn't get anywhere with her, I remembered Linda and thought maybe she could back me up."

"Did she?"

"No. She said she was too busy with her own problems. But really it was that she thought she was too good for me. When I told her how things happened seven years ago with Bruce and my Bob and me, she said I was like Nan Arnot—the other woman—and she didn't see how I figured the money was mine. But I've been thinking, and maybe if you'd—"

Not a subject I wanted to get into.

Still, something else crossed my mind, something that had occurred to me after I'd heard her story the first time. "I've been thinking too," I said, cutting her off. "If Melanie were going to return that money to anyone, shouldn't it be to the man's wife? I mean, by rights, it was taken from her."

"She's dead!" Janine said in no uncertain terms. "She died when she killed him."

"Murder-suicide?"

"I guess you could say that."

"What about their kids? Were there any of those left behind?"

"The money is mine!" Janine insisted so defensively I was reasonably sure there had been a kid or kids orphaned by that incident. I was also sure I wasn't going to get Janine to admit it. So rather than prolong this conversation I said, "I'd better let you go so you can get ready for work."

I apparently said it with enough force to get my point across, because Janine dropped the subject.

"I suppose the arrangements will be in the papers?" she asked, her tone as cutting as it had been at the end of our lunch.

"I'm sure they will be. Probably tomorrow."

"I'll look for them."

"Good."

I was ashamed of myself as the group's volunteer and the shoulder I was suppose to offer for them to cry on, but I didn't tell her to call me if she wanted to talk. I was too afraid she'd feel more free to call about Melanie and that money. Instead, I just said good-bye and hung up yet again.

I closed my eyes for a few minutes, feeling the sting of the sleepless night I'd just spent and considered climbing into my bed for a little belated rest.

Seemed pretty appealing.

But it was too late now. I had to take Shannon to school. I had to get on with the day.

And I still had one call I needed to make.

Chapter Thirty-one

I SPOKE TO Steve Kraner briefly. If Linda had killed herself and had any thoughts that it might bring him to his senses about what he'd lost, or make him feel the kind of sadness or regret she'd been feeling, she was wrong.

He didn't even want to be bothered talking about her. Mostly he was miffed that it had fallen to him to attend to the details of her funeral.

What a drag for the poor dear.

She deserved better than that, and I told him so. Surprisingly he calmed down, changed his tune, and even rejected my offer to make all the arrangements so he wouldn't have to be bothered.

He did request that I go to the house to pick out something for her to be buried in and make sure there weren't any signs of her death that might freak out the kids when he took them home that afternoon.

So for the second day I made sure I was dressed and ready for public display by the time I took Shannon to school. She was unusually quiet. But then, I was too. Linda's death had affected all of us.

I went to her house after dropping off Shannon, but I sat in my car in the driveway once I got there. Tough to go inside knowing she wasn't there. And where she actually was.

We'd been walking into each other's houses uninvited for a lot of years, but this would be the last walk-in either of us did. Once Steve was back in residence with the kids that afternoon I'd turn over my key, and that would be the end of it. I might not even have reason to drive down this block again when the funeral was over.

I felt the tears well up in my eyes the way they had all night, but I was sick of crying. That wasn't what I'd come to do. So I tried to set my mind on automatic pilot, got out of the car, and went up to the house.

No knock, no "It's just me." I unlocked the door and went in.

God, it was quiet and still inside.

"Damn you, Linda."

I closed the door behind me. It was a toss-up as to which I wanted to do less: go through her things for burial clothes or check out the site of her death for any evidence of it. The stairs were right there in front of me, so I opted for that chore first.

On the upper level I passed the kids' rooms and glanced in as I did. All three of them were as neat as kids' rooms get. Their beds were made; the curtains were open; intermittent spots of carpet were showing among toys and discarded clothes.

For some reason I couldn't go by without straightening up a little. Maybe because it might be a long time before a mother did that for them again.

Then I made it to Linda's room. It was neat as a pin. Her bed was made too, and her window was even open a crack to let in a touch of clear, crisp autumn air.

It struck me as I stood in the doorway that if I were Linda, I'd have done the deed here rather than down in the kitchen. I'd have taken a bag of nuts—macadamia, because she said they were the worst—up to bed with me, munched a few lying down, and called it quits that way. At the very least I would have sat in a chair or on the couch downstairs. I wouldn't have eaten my last snack standing in the kitchen, where I'd fall to the floor when it kicked in.

But then, maybe I wasn't a good judge of what went through a person's mind when she killed herself.

Not wanting to spend any more time than I needed to at this, I went to the closet for her favorite dress, a teal sheath with a matching jacket that she was particularly fond of because she said it made her look thin.

I didn't know how extensive an outfit the mortuary would want but gathered nylons, underpants, a bra, shoes, the whole works just in case.

As I folded them all, I remembered the little homemade sack of charms my grandmother had sent Linda. I hated the thought of Steve's coming across it and adding it to the already long list of things he believed proved she was a lunatic, so I decided to see if I could find it.

I left the clothes on the bed and checked the nightstand drawer. Bruce Mann's file folder was gone, so it opened without a hitch. But Gramma's pouch wasn't there. It was in the second spot I tried, under Linda's pillow.

I don't know why, but the tears threatened again as

I held that silly thing in my palm. Guess even Gramma's magic couldn't take away the evil eye that had been on Linda.

But I didn't want to bawl there any more than I'd wanted to sit in the car and do it, so I put the bag in my pocket and smoothed the bedcovers. Then I picked up the burial clothes, went downstairs, and set them on the bottom step.

As I did, I caught sight of the garage door, and another thing struck me as odd: Why had Linda spent the last day she intended to be alive trailing her ex-husband? In fact, why had she spent the last week of her life that way? Surely I'd been wrong and she hadn't just been enjoying putting him on edge as a payback. If she'd been enjoying something—anything—she wouldn't have killed herself. She also wouldn't have been keeping tabs on him as a way of keeping tabs on the money so he couldn't do anything underhanded with it again. Why would she care about the future if she was opting out of hers?

I supposed it was possible she'd been hoping that seeing him might rekindle something in him, and when it didn't, she'd decided to do herself in, but it just didn't feel right to me.

Another thing: If she was just going home to kill herself, why did she go all the way to Beverly's apartment on Colorado Boulevard to get her purse? She certainly didn't need it for the trip she was planning.

But maybe I was just reading too much into things. Lack of sleep could do that. What difference did it make, after all, how she'd spend her last day? She was still dead.

I went through the family room and around the breakfast bar to get my other chore over with. There wasn't glaring evidence of exactly where on the floor

Linda had been found. No chalk outline or anything. But there was a sign, a dull yellowish spot on the otherwise immaculate white linoleum that looked as if a pet had piddled.

Linda didn't have any pets.

For some reason I'd expected blood, not urine. I wished it had been blood. Somehow there would have been more dignity for her in leaving that behind.

I wanted to use something disposable to clean up, so I dampened the sponge Linda wiped off the countertops with, got down on my hands and knees, and scrubbed.

It was from there that I spotted what she referred to as her epi-pin, a syringe full of epinephrine. It had rolled under the overhang of the cupboards.

I'd known Linda long enough to have heard the description many times of what happened if she had a reaction to nuts. A few minutes after ingestion her tongue began to swell, her throat closed down, and she couldn't breathe. Without something to counteract it she suffocated. The epi-pin was the antidote that kept that from happening.

So why would someone committing suicide reach for the one thing that could save her? I didn't think she would.

But she would have gone for it if the reaction had come as a surprise.

So maybe Linda hadn't committed suicide. Maybe it really had been an accident the way Danny had initially believed. I guess that made more sense except that I just couldn't shake the thought that Linda was too careful to have an accident like that. She read every label; she asked every waitress, every friend, every hostess who ever served her anything if there were nuts in what she was about to eat. If she couldn't find out, she didn't touch the food. Period.

But what if someone had given her something and said there weren't nuts in it when there actually were?

I knew for a fact that it could be done, because I bake chocolate spritz cookies at Christmas and the recipe calls for walnuts to be ground as fine as flour. Unless I reveal that there are nuts in them, no one knows it.

But why would anyone give Linda something with nuts in it and let her think it was safe?

Unless setting off a reaction was the point. A reaction that had the potential to kill her.

It occurred to me then that I could well be on my hands and knees in the middle of crime scene number three. I got up, went to the phone, and dialed Danny's work number.

It was only after I'd convinced him to come over there that I went to throw away the pee-soaked sponge and found one of my Salvador Dali paper plates in Linda's trash.

Chapter Thirty-two

WITHIN A HALF HOUR Danny and two uniformed police officers arrived at Linda's house. Danny parked in the driveway on the other side of my station wagon. The marked patrol car stayed at the curb.

I knew the minute I looked out the living room window and saw that patrol car that Danny didn't believe Linda's death was a murder. If he had, he'd have brought the forensics unit. He was just humoring me.

I pretended not to notice and pointed out everything I'd found, told him what I thought and why.

"She didn't kill herself, and this wasn't an accident, Danny," I insisted when I was finished. "You have to get experts over here."

"Let's go out on the porch and talk," he replied, taking my elbow to make sure I complied while he told the uniforms to have a look around, see if they found any more of those particular paper dishes.

I waited until we were outside to tell him that I'd left the Dali plates at Beverly Runyan's apartment on Monday night. And that Linda had gone back there the afternoon before for her purse.

"So you think Beverly baked something with nuts hidden in it and served it up on a paper plate that could be traced back to her in a snap?"

Well, not when he put it like that.

"All I think is that *somebody* gave her nuts without telling her and she died from it. You take it from there."

"I will. But I think it's a waste of time. Your friend either committed suicide by cupcake or got sloppy about her allergy and died accidentally."

"What do you mean, suicide by cupcake?"

"Coroner's report on the stomach contents indicates she had eaten a lot of those chocolate cupcakes I told you we found on the counter. Looks like only one or two had nuts in them, finely ground. None of what were left on the counter did."

I interrupted him. "And you don't think that proves she was murdered?"

"I think she was the murder*er*, Jimi," he said quietly, as if to be kind in breaking the news to me.

I shook my head, partly in disgust, partly in denial.

It was enough to make him want to convince me.

"She was involved with Bruce Mann. She may have been sleeping with him from the night after your group met for the first time—*before* he was sleeping with anybody else from the group. It means that when he started up with the nurse and that male teacher, not to mention trying to seduce Gail Frankin, it would have been another body blow to Linda's ego. Plus I'm betting that close company allowed her to find out somehow about what Mann had done with her ex to cheat her out of her share of their money before Gail Frankin even gave her that file. Motive: revenge. Opportunity: She was there to sleep with him, could have had a key, could have gotten to that heating vent anytime. Means: I already told you we found that wiring information. And as for Nan Arnot? You know I've thought from the get-go that Linda was good for that one and why. I haven't found anything to make anybody else look better for it."

"But now it's Linda who's dead. Murdered. How do you figure that?"

"I don't figure she was murdered. I think she was planning on her ex's being her third victim to clear the slate of people who'd hurt her and to get the money in the process. Maybe her conscience finally kicked in. Maybe it struck her that the death count was getting too high, that she was going to get caught. Maybe that depression she's been in finally caught up with her, and she figured it just wasn't worth it."

"So she came home, ground up some nuts, baked cupcakes—most without the nuts—then played Russian roulette with herself, eating them to see how many she could down before she got one that would kill her?" I was being facetious.

"I've seen people do some strange things, Jimi. That wouldn't be the strangest. Yeah, maybe it was a kind of Russian roulette. Maybe she ground up the nuts so she wouldn't know she was getting them until it was too late."

"Then, when she did, why did she go for the epipin?"

"Sometimes right at the end the fear of actually dying takes over and a suicide will reach out for help. It was probably just too late."

I wondered if he honestly believed all this or if he

was just trying to make me think he did to get me out of the way. "I can't buy it, Danny. And I can't believe you do either."

"Maybe it was as simple as putting nuts in a cupcake or two for somebody who likes them that way and then losing track of which ones had the nuts. Then we'd be back to its being an accident. Does that sit better with you?"

He was patronizing me. I didn't appreciate it. "If she lost track, she wouldn't have eaten any. She wouldn't have risked it. That was how she handled the allergy."

"That was how she handled it when she was in her right mind. But she was emotionally distraught now. She wasn't in her right mind. People don't do things the same way then, Jimi. They don't behave like themselves at all."

Just then one of the uniformed officers opened the front door and announced that they'd found a whole stack of the Dali dishes.

"Beverly must have given them to Linda to give back to you, and she used one to eat her cupcakes on," Danny said when the other cop had gone back in. Fait accompli.

"You just aren't talking about the Linda I knew, Danny."

"You said yourself she was wigged out lately."

"Not *that* wigged out. What about the dishwasher?"

"The dishwasher?"

"If she came home yesterday and baked cupcakes, there should be bowls and pans in the dishwasher."

Danny opened the front door and called in to the uniformed cops to take a look. One of them called back that the dishwasher was empty.

Danny turned to me again. "She must have run it, unloaded it, then had her cupcakes—part of a suicide's putting things in order before she did it."

I felt as if I were fighting a losing battle. "You aren't going to treat this like a murder, are you?"

"I'm not closing the books on it yet, Jimi. I'm just telling you what I think happened here."

"Linda killed Bruce Mann and Nan Arnot, then herself." In a nutshell.

He tightened his lips and did a double shrug—shoulders and eyebrows. "That's where the evidence points. Linda is the thread that runs through it all. I'm sorry."

"Steve runs through it too," I said. "He could have killed all three of them."

"Except that his alibi for the time of Nan Arnot's death holds up—he has a sales receipt with the time of death on it—and he's steered as clear of Linda as possible in the last week because he's been afraid of her. And he has the bodyguard to back him up."

I didn't know what else to say to convince Danny that he was wrong. Maybe he wasn't. After all, he'd had a night's sleep. I hadn't. Maybe his way would look better when I did.

We stood there in silence for a few minutes. Then he said, "Look, why don't you go get your car washed or something? God knows it could use it. Just keep yourself busy and leave this to me, huh?"

In other words, get lost.

"If I leave, will you go inside, really look around, and at least consider that I might be right and someone killed Linda the same way they killed Bruce and Nan Arnot?"

"She didn't die the same way. They were electrocuted. But I'm here to search the place, Jimi. To give it a going-over and see if I missed something."

I looked at him, reminding myself that he was a good cop. That he knew what he was doing. That he wasn't the kind of guy to take the easy way out. I had to trust that somewhere along the line I'd raised a doubt or two, enough that he really would take a closer look. But that was all I could do now.

"Okay. I'll leave. But I'll be near a phone all day—either my cellular or at home—so call me if—"

"Anything comes up or I have a question I think you can answer for me about Linda, I will. Now go. Do something to take your mind off this."

There must have been a hundred times when the girls were small that I'd said, "Now go play with your toys." That's just what Danny's words to me sounded like. I fought the urge to stick my tongue out at him.

He was right about one thing, though, I realized as I glanced in the direction of my car: It really was a mess. The trip to Bruce's house with Gramma and the one to see if Melanie had moved back and missing the road both times so I had to turn around at Red Rocks had the wagon pretty coated with dust. I thought of driving to my meticulous friend's funeral in it and knew she wouldn't have liked that.

"Call me," I ordered by way of saying good-bye, and I left Danny standing on Linda's porch, watching me go. Probably to make sure I actually went.

Once I was in my car he finally turned and disappeared into the house. I started the engine but didn't pull out right away. First I put in a call to Steve Kraner, telling him what was going on, not to bring the kids home until he checked first to make sure the police were gone, and that I'd drop off Linda's clothes later on.

Then I took all my frustrations and went to the car wash like a good girl.

Chapter Thirty-three

APPARENTLY WASHING CARS is a newly booming business because places are springing up all over town that specialize in it. Not just the drive-through, mechanized kind, but car beauty shops where you hand your baby over to attendants who give it the personal touch.

I hadn't used one before. They aren't cheap, and I am. But in Linda's honor I took the diaper wagon to one of those.

They weren't busy on a Wednesday morning. In fact, I was the only customer, so they took the wagon right in and pointed me to the waiting room, complete with coffee and tea and a wall of windows so I could witness the procedure. In case I was nervous about it, I guess.

I was getting more tired by the minute and was afraid if I sat down, I'd fall asleep, so I made myself a cup of strong tea and went to stand at the window to watch.

It was not fascinating.

One young guy and a much older man, both dressed in matching white polo shirts and marine-blue chino shorts, started inside with rags and spray bottles in hand, vacuum at the ready.

About the third squirt on the inside of my windshield my mind wandered.

I consider Danny my best friend, and I know there isn't a better cop anywhere. But I really believed he was wrong about Linda's death.

To me, it just didn't fit that she had killed herself, and I didn't believe her death was an accident either. I knew Linda. I knew how careful she was about that allergy.

Besides, if two other people had been murdered, I didn't find it unlikely that so had my friend. And Linda as the killer of those other two people? It didn't add up to me the way it did to Danny.

I had the same feeling I get when one of my kids tells me something that just doesn't feel right. I've learned to follow that instinct. To listen carefully to every detail, to look for the holes. Generally the girls are sliding the untruths in among the truths, and I have to figure out which is which.

So which was which here?

I knew for a fact that Bruce Mann had not been a nice guy. He'd cheated his first wife out of her share of their marital assets, reduced her to driving an old wreck that had ultimately cost her her life. I knew he'd helped at least two other people do the same thing: his boss of years ago and Steve Kraner.

I knew that he'd kept all the marbles from the deal with his boss and that Janine resented it because she'd been the boss's lover and had planned on that money to cushion her future. I also knew Linda had refused to back up Janine's story to convince Melanie to give her the money back.

I knew Beverly Runyan had been involved with Bruce. And she knew all about everything else he'd been doing with Linda and with Clifford.

I knew Bruce had shaken Clifford's self-image and then blackmailed him with that picture on top of it. I knew Linda had found that picture and looked at it, so she knew where to return it. I knew Nan Arnot had had the picture before her.

I knew Ron Arnot had found out that Nan had moved on to Bruce in her affairs of the heart. I knew he was a lot less torn up about Nan's death than he had been about her leaving him. I knew he'd been the one who had made the police suspicious of Linda in the first place. I knew he was sleeping with Gail Frankin.

I knew Gail Frankin had disliked Bruce immensely. Enough to steal his file and blow the whistle on his part in stealing from Linda. I knew she hadn't liked her cousin Nan. I knew she wanted me to believe she was convinced Linda had killed Nan.

I knew that Steve Kraner was being cheated on by Nan Arnot and that Nan Arnot had plans to leave him for Bruce and keep the money he'd swindled Linda out of. I knew that with Bruce Mann, Nan Arnot, and Linda all dead, Steve got to keep everything for himself.

I knew that Linda had told two different stories about how she'd gotten her watch back. I knew her having found Clifford's picture punched holes in her story about Steve's returning the watch. I knew that more than wanting her half of their assets back from Nan, she'd wanted Steve back from Nan.

I knew a whole lot of stuff that still didn't amount to enough to stop the niggling at the back of my mind that I was missing something.

Was it because I was trying not to believe what everyone else seemed to about Linda? That she'd killed Nan Arnot?

Maybe.

But even if she had, there was no way I could believe she'd killed Bruce too. I didn't want to, but I could see her being so desperate, so angry that she tossed a toaster oven into Nan's bathtub. But that was a lot different from the way Bruce had been killed even if they both were electrocuted.

Danny had said it himself right after Nan's death: "The killer was right there, at the time of death face-to-face, to watch it happen. Not nearly as neat or clean or patient . . ."

But Linda's death was neat and clean and had given the killer that same distance. And the same element of a crapshoot.

No one knew how long Bruce's heating vent had been rigged before everything happened just right to kill him. What if the rewiring of the vent had been discovered before that? He might never have been killed at all.

And what about Linda? What if there had been nuts in only one of the cupcakes? If she had eaten her fill without ever touching the one with nuts in it, she wouldn't be dead now either.

I'd only been facetious when I'd said Linda was playing Russian roulette with herself, but was it possible someone else was playing it with her? And with Bruce?

My mind balked at the thought that people could

be being killed as a game, and I focused on my car again to escape for a minute.

The work was moving from the inside to the outside of the car. This particular place advertised a hand washing, so while one attendant gathered sponges and chamois cloths, the other unrolled a hose and began to rinse the dust off.

I watched, but I couldn't keep my thoughts clear of the murders for long.

What if the murders really had been some kind of game devised in some kind of sick mind? Anyone else could be at risk. There might be a booby trap waiting anywhere for anybody.

That idea scared me. I considered calling Danny and telling him. But I could just hear his calm, rational voice in my mind, talking about evidence, about likelihoods, about killer profiles, about his evidence against Linda. He'd think I'd gone around the bend.

Maybe I had. Maybe I just needed sleep, and the lack of it was taking its toll, making my imagination run wild. A crazed serial killer playing Russian roulette? Come on, Jimi, get real.

I forced my attention back to the car wash that was costing me more than a steak dinner in a four-star restaurant. I figured when it was finished, I'd go home, try to get a little sleep. Maybe some rest would make everything look different. I'd be able to think more clearly. Not go off on ridiculous tangents. Maybe see things Danny's way.

I checked the clock on the wall above the windows, then glanced out into the garage again, wondering how much longer this would take.

The attendants were pretty efficient. As soon as the guy with the hose had one end rinsed, the guy with the sponge started to soap up after him. Water was pooling around the tires, burnt umber shaded from the dust and then soapy white mixed in to make a nice shade the color of Halloween pumpkins. It was hypnotizing to watch. Snowy suds swirling with rusty red, around and around . . .

All of a sudden I remembered something. Something from a while ago that really didn't fit.

In fact, it didn't fit so much that I knew it was important.

Chapter Thirty-four

MAYBE I WAS wrong. That was what I kept telling myself as I sat in my car outside the apartment. What I was feeling was: *How could I be right?*

It was twelve-fifteen, and I knew the signal: If the curtains were drawn on the front window, that meant Audrey had a session in progress and no knock on the door would be answered. She'd said she had back-to-back sessions, and I was hoping to catch her between two. But in the meantime all I could do was wait. And wonder what I was going to say when I got in there.

Just before one the apartment door opened, and out came Audrey with an elderly woman whose face was blotchy and swollen from crying. Audrey patted her arm, comforted her.

The woman smiled in a way that said she felt slightly less miserable. They talked a little more, and then the woman got into her car.

And I got out of mine two spaces down.

"Jimi! I didn't see you there," Audrey said when I called to her.

"Do you have a few minutes?"

"Longer than that. My one o'clock canceled, so I get a lunch hour after all. Come in and have a sandwich with me." She met me halfway, linked her arm through mine, and turned back to the apartment.

"Thanks, but I'm not hungry. You go ahead, though, and eat while we talk so you don't miss your lunch on my account."

She leaned her shoulder into my arm, moved her head closer to mine, and said in an aside, "Trouble at home, or are you feeling as bad as I am about Linda?"

"Both." It was true. Even if the way I felt was not what I'd come to talk about.

"How is Gramma since I saw her? Did I do any good?"

"You did. I think you did anyway. But she saw through our setup."

"Oh-oh. I don't suppose she liked that."

"No, she didn't. But that's okay. She appreciated how much you understood her point of view."

We were in the kitchen by then. Audrey pointed to the chair at the back of the U-shaped space her small table occupied, told me to sit, and asked again if I wouldn't have a sandwich with her.

When I assured her I couldn't eat if I tried, she took out bread and lunch meat and made herself a sandwich standing at the end of the counter that formed the third side of that U.

"Tea, at least? You'll have tea, won't you?"

"Sure," I lied.

That corner hadn't bothered me the night we'd had dinner here, but sitting at the back of it now made me feel claustrophobic. I fought it and said, "It really helped Gramma to know that you hated what happened to your sister and your niece all those years ago as much as she hates what goes on with Uncle Dad now."

Audrey was setting the kettle on to heat, and I saw her pause slightly before she did, her bushy salt-and-pepper eyebrows taking a small dip toward each other. "What happened to my sister and my niece all those years ago," she repeated as if she might not know what I was talking about.

"The Humbergers, weren't they? Bob Humberger was your brother-in-law. He was Bruce Mann's boss. And Janine's lover. Your sister was a devout Catholic who regretted not becoming a nun like you had. And who couldn't accept the idea of a divorce."

Audrey's chin rose high with a nod as she brought her lunch to the spot across from me and sat down.

"Bob Humberger and your sister didn't die in a car accident, did they?"

"Oh, but they did."

I shook my head in denial. "Your sister shot her husband."

Audrey took a bite of her sandwich, chewed very slowly, and stared at me while she did.

It made me uncomfortable, so I went on with what I'd pieced together while I'd been waiting outside. "Your sister went off the deep end the way Linda did, had a nervous breakdown, even had to be hospitalized."

"Sometimes I wonder if the church doesn't put too much burden on its people by not accepting divorce."

"And there was the added burden of Bruce Mann having helped her husband cheat her out of everything the same way he did Linda's husband."

Audrey nodded again, slowly, studying me, gauging just how much I knew, I thought. Then she seemed to come to some conclusion.

"Money was what Marie and Bob were arguing about in the car that day," Audrey said, seeming to get into the swing of my story. Then she said, "You didn't come here today to talk about your own problems, did you, Jimi?"

Right then *she* was my biggest problem. I liked the woman. I'd respected her. I'd trusted her. I didn't want to think what I was thinking.

"Did you know Janine was the other woman in your sister's divorce?"

"No, I didn't." And her surprise was too genuine to be staged. "Bob kept very quiet about that. I never knew whom he was involved with. I don't think even Marie did. I certainly would never have guessed it was Janine. Or anybody else I'd ever run into. How do you know?"

"Bruce Mann's widow worked with my mother years ago. We reconnected after his funeral. Janine approached her about getting back the money Bruce had kept when he helped your brother-in-law hide it to cheat your sister."

The eyebrows registered more surprise just as the teakettle whistled.

The sound startled me and made me aware of just how tense I was. And of how fast my heart had been beating even before that. Faster still now that I'd laid my cards on the table and let her know I knew about her family's connection to Bruce. About her connection to Bruce.

"You've been busy," Audrey said.

"So have you."

She made two cups of tea and brought them back to

the table. I never took my eyes off her, afraid I might end up with mine toxically laced or with that scalding water in the face or something.

I didn't. She just set the mugs on the table and sat down again. But I was beginning to realize I didn't have the best seat in the house. Had she wanted to scald me, being stuck in that corner made me as vulnerable as a bird in a cage. But vulnerable or not, I had to go through with this now that I'd started it. I had to know.

"You understand so well what's going on with my grandmother because you've been carrying around the same kinds of feelings for a long time, haven't you?"

Audrey smiled a small, secret smile. "God didn't put only good people on this earth, Jimi."

"And Bruce Mann was one of the bad ones."

"Along with my brother-in-law—people who aren't honest or fair. People who lie, cheat, steal. Hurt other people for their own gain."

"Hurt other people like your sister."

"Like my sister. Marie was a gem. A kind heart. Gentle. A good person. Not exciting, maybe. Or adventurous. Just a plain, decent, caring woman. But like your ex, Jimi, that wasn't enough for my brother-in-law after a while. He wanted more. He wanted out, and he got out."

"And he took everything with him."

"Not only the money. Marie's dignity too. He shook the foundations of her life. He shook her faith."

"And Bruce Mann helped him do it."

"Helped. Encouraged. Abetted."

"Then kept the money that rightfully belonged to your sister and your niece."

"Just my niece. There really was a car accident, and my sister died that day too. Then Bruce disappeared with the money before I could do anything about it, before I could claim it for her."

Audrey sounded weary. Defeated. I tried to tell myself it was because she was tired of the struggle to stay ahead of the game, that maybe she was even relieved to have been found out.

So why didn't I feel any more relaxed?

"Did Bruce know you or who you were or that you were related to his old boss when he signed up for the seminars?"

"No, I'm sure he didn't. I don't know how he could have. He'd met Marie at company Christmas parties and picnics, things like that, but there was never an occasion for him and me to cross paths. I knew who he was, though. I knew the name. And I knew what he'd done."

"How did you find out?"

"Marie caught on to his and Bob's scheme, and she told me about it. You remind me of her, Jimi. Inquisitive. A tenacious puzzle-solver. When things didn't seem to make sense, she wouldn't give up until she found out why. Just like you."

Audrey picked up her sandwich as if she were going to take another bite, but she seemed to think twice about it and set it down without eating any more.

"Marie didn't have a car of her own, so when she was ready to confront Bob, she had me take her to his apartment. But he was in a big hurry to get somewhere. She said she'd ride along, that he wasn't getting away with this. I followed, so I could take her back home when they got where he was going.

"I could see them fighting. Shouting at each other. On the highway. Driving fast. Then I saw the gun. I didn't even know she'd taken one with her. She wasn't thinking straight, I knew that, and if I'd known that she went to see him with any intention but to talk to him . . . well, I wouldn't have taken her."

"She shot him while he was driving?"

"I never knew if she pulled the trigger accidentally or wasn't thinking clearly enough to realize what would happen or if she intended it as a murder-suicide. But yes, she shot him. The car veered into the cement wall. Spun. I couldn't avoid hitting them."

That surprised me. "You were in the accident too?"

She didn't answer me right away. She just stared through me, lost, I thought, in an old memory that had to be one of the ugliest she carried around.

Finally, very quietly, she said, "I hit them. Broadside. My sister's side. Then another car hit me, and a different one hit them and—"

"Weren't you hurt?"

"Yes. But I killed my sister." Another pause. "In no small part because of Bruce Mann."

She pushed her plate away as if she couldn't stomach the sandwich on it now and stood. "I need sugar for my tea. Do you?"

"No." I wasn't drinking the tea. I wouldn't dare. Any more than I'd get near anything electrical in this place.

But Audrey didn't come back to the table with sugar. She came back with a gun.

At first I wasn't sure I was seeing what I was seeing. Then I wondered how I could have been so stupid. Poisoning, electrocution, I guess I hadn't thought her repertoire included anything as immediately threatening as a gun.

But there it was, a shiny silver revolver with a mother-of-pearl handle and a caliber I couldn't even guess at because to me a gun is a gun, nothing I ever want to be anywhere around. Certainly not sitting across the table from. It made my heart beat even faster than before, thudding in my chest, pounding in my ears. I felt sweat bead on my upper lip, pool under my arms, and that damn corner seemed to close in on me for real.

Audrey sat down, set the gun in front of her on the table, but didn't take her hand off it. "Do you want to hear the rest? Or do you already know it?"

I thought about making a run for it, but that was impossible to do from where I was sitting. There was less than two feet of space between the table and the cupboards and none at all between the table and the wall on the other side.

My brain took a dip into history and old thoughts of Audrey. We were friends. She was a nun. She wouldn't shoot me.

Then I reminded myself that mine wouldn't be the first murder she'd committed. That she wouldn't have taken out the gun at all if she hadn't meant to use it, and I stayed put. As stiff and still as a statue. Wondering what I was going to do.

She seemed to be ignoring the presence of the gun, so I did too. At least I tried to appear to.

"With your brother-in-law dead, Bruce Mann got to be the focus of the same kinds of feelings my grandmother has for Uncle Dad," I said in a hurry, hoping that I sounded sympathetic and understanding and that I might be able to find some way out of this if I kept her talking.

"Not only that, Jimi. But as my sessions with Linda went on and I started hearing more and more about her ex-husband not paying child support and claiming he didn't have any money after Linda had said they were pretty well off, after I heard about the way he was living, that raised red flags in me. Especially when I found out just how well Linda and her husband knew Bruce Mann."

"Was it pure coincidence that he ended up in the group?"

"I guess that depends on how you look at it. I didn't do anything to bring him in if that's what you're thinking."

"And you knew about electrical wiring from your time in Africa, helping modernize the living standards of the people there." Another of my guesses.

Audrey nodded.

"So you rigged Bruce Mann's heating vent."

"Is that what gave me away, telling you about Africa?"

"No. It was the dust that was being washed off your car when I took you to pick it up before going to Bruce's house that Monday night for the meeting. The night we found him dead. Your mechanic was washing your car, washing off the same red dust I had on mine from missing the road to Bruce's house and having to turn around at Red Rocks. I just remembered seeing it. And there was no reason you would have been to Bruce's house before that night we were all there together and he was already dead. After I remembered that, other things started to fall into place."

"Other things?"

"Janine told me Bob Humberger had been killed seven years ago, the same time your niece would have come to live with you. She'd also told me how upset Bob Humberger's wife was about the idea of divorce. And why. And that she had a sister who was a nun. Things like that."

Audrey smiled serenely. Not the smile of a killer or a crazy person. More like a loving parent, proud of my accomplishment in figuring this all out.

I wondered if that meant she wouldn't kill me.

I wasn't counting on it.

Keep her talking, I told myself.

"You'd been up to Bruce's house to rig the vent. Missed the road. Had to turn around at Red Rocks. That's how your car got dirty. But what I don't understand is why you did it that way. Why did you leave the element of chance? Why not just go up there and shoot him?"

She shook her head. "I'm God's servant, Jimi. I arranged the opportunity for Him to take Bruce before Bruce did any more harm to any more people. But it was up to God from there. If it wasn't God's will for Bruce to die, he wouldn't have."

It made a sick sort of sense. More sense than my serial killer theory.

"But what about Nan Arnot? Was it God's will for you to throw that toaster oven into her bathwater?"

Audrey shook her head again. "I didn't kill Nan Arnot."

My stomach did a half turn that made me feel slightly sick. I didn't want to know the answer, but I asked anyway. "Who did?"

"Linda."

My first thought was that Audrey was lying. I'd been defending Linda for so long, I had a hard time believing it. But then, I couldn't think of a reason Audrey would lie about it now, and I finally had to swallow the pill I'd been trying to hide under my tongue.

"Linda killed Nan Arnot?" I said.

"And it was my fault."

"How?"

"Bruce's death started her thinking about how much better off she'd be if Nan Arnot died. I didn't take it seriously enough, I guess. I didn't believe she would actually put the fantasy into motion. I thought she was more likely to hurt herself. But she was serious. She did it."

"She told you that? She confessed?"

"No. But in our sessions she kept going back to it, to Nan Arnot's death itself. She'd say more and more things that let me know she'd been there. Then she'd back away from it, talk about how Nan had died from electrocution the same way Bruce had, so the same person had to have killed them both. As if it would camouflage what she'd done."

"But you knew better."

"I also knew that for the first time since her husband had left her she was feeling as if she had some power again. She'd taken action and liked it. But then, when it didn't get Steve to come back to her, she started talking about him dying."

"Was that why she was following him? To kill him?" I asked, although I still couldn't absorb the truth of it.

"I think she was plotting it, yes. Looking for the right time. The strength to go through with it. She kept saying the death of a spouse was easier than divorce. A clean-cut, not a jagged, edge. That after a death the wound can heal, life can go on. But after a divorce the cut keeps being reopened and reopened, the kids had to be shared, finances would be impossible. . . . I knew she was planning something to save herself and her kids from that. She was going to kill him too."

"So you gave God the opportunity to stop her. You baked her some cupcakes. How many of them were laced with ground nuts? One? Two?"

"Only one."

"If she hadn't eaten that one, she'd still be alive. But

if her kids had gotten hold of that one, it wouldn't have done them any harm."

"I had to give God the opportunity, Jimi. Don't you see? Linda was disturbed. More disturbed than I could help her through. And it was what I'd done to Bruce that first started her thinking about taking things into her own hands. I hadn't stopped her from killing that young girl; I hadn't taken her seriously enough. I couldn't let her kill again without giving God the chance to stop her Himself."

"So you sent the cupcakes home with her yesterday. When she didn't stay for her whole session."

"I told her I'd baked them as a peace offering because she'd been so upset with me at our other sessions lately and insisted she take them with her even though she was leaving mad again."

"And you gave her the cupcakes on those plates I'd left with Beverly?" That part didn't fit. "Did Beverly give them to you because she wouldn't be at the next meeting to return them herself?"

Audrey shook her head, her expression confused. "I don't know what plates you're talking about."

Danny must have been right. Linda had gotten them from Beverly herself, used one to eat Audrey's cupcakes. They hadn't meant anything at all, and here I'd thought they were so important.

I looked at the gun again. I could feel my heart beating in my throat by then, and I was so antsy I might as well have just downed two pots of coffee. I had to fight not to squirm. "So what happens now?"

Her hand tightened around the handle, and she brought it up, pointing it directly at me. "We let God make another choice, Jimi."

Simple as that.

The black hole in the center of that barrel seemed

big enough to swallow me. It was a little late, but I was wishing I'd told Danny about the red dust, told him what I thought about Audrey as the killer, told him I was coming here. But I hadn't. I was on my own.

"How does God make the choice?" I asked.

"I've had this loaded with only one bullet since the day I rewired Bruce's heating vent. I decided then that if anyone figured out it was I who did it and came for me, it would be my way of giving God the opportunity with me too."

But the gun wasn't pointed at her. It was pointed at me.

"Now God can choose between us, Jimi." She spun the cylinder and raised the gun so it was aimed at the center of my face.

Maybe I should have been going to church all these years after all.

"What if I'm the one who gets the bullet? Then what?" I asked.

"I spend the rest of my life in Africa. I can hide there forever—if that's God's will. If it isn't, then maybe I'll get the bullet and you'll live to tell the story."

"How about we just let it be God's will about whether or not you can get away? Tie me up, take off, and you might get clear out of the country before anyone finds me."

"You're funny, Jimi." She meant it because she smiled. Serenely again.

It was no comfort that I amused her when that gun was still pointed at my head. No comfort as the sweat poured out of me and the walls of that corner closed in. I decided that if I was going to die in that kitchen, it wasn't going to be sitting there doing nothing. I lunged out of my chair.

But Audrey must have seen it coming. She jammed the edge of the table into my stomach. It slammed me back down and pinned me between the table and the wall behind me, knocking the wind out of me at the same time.

I doubted that she'd set this up beforehand, so I didn't think it was a good sign about whose side God was on.

"I'm sorry, Jimi."

Click.

It took me a second to realize she'd actually pulled the trigger while I'd been catching my breath. Another second to realize nothing had happened.

I pushed back on the table, but she had me wedged in tight and I couldn't get a good grip. She still had the advantage.

But now the gun was pointed at her face.

"Don't!"

Click.

Another empty round.

My turn again.

I'd only been kidding about the Russian roulette. How the hell had I ended up playing it?

Instead of pushing against the table with my hands I tried with my whole body. But still I couldn't budge it.

"Dammit, Audrey, you don't want to do this. You don't want my kids to be as abandoned as your niece was."

"If it's God's will, Jimi."

Click.

There was no relief when I heard the trigger strike against nothing again. In fact, with each click my anxiety went up another notch.

I tried sliding out of my chair, but Audrey shoved the edge of the table even harder into my gut, knocking the wind out of me once more and bending me over the tabletop, my nose nearly dipping into the tea.

The tea.

The gun was aimed at Audrey again. I grabbed my full cup and threw the liquid in her face. It caught her off guard more than it burned her by then, but surprise made her ease up on her side of the table. I finally pushed it in her direction and got out of that corner, but she shoved it back again with enough force to clip my hip and catch my foot on the leg, so I fell sideways into the edge of the counter so nearby.

Audrey was right there, at the end of my only escape route, blocking me from running, the gun pointed at my face once more.

"It's not my turn," I said with a nod at the gun, sounding like an idiot but under the circumstances figuring anything was worth it to buy me some time.

"You're right," she answered, swiveling the gun on herself.

I lunged again.

She pulled the trigger.

Only this time the gun didn't just click.

Chapter Thirty-five

When I got divorced, I nearly went crazy. It hit me that hard. And hurt that much. For years after the actual acts of filing papers and getting court dates and having decrees handed down I was in a long, dark tunnel. I'm not proud of how much time it took me to get through that tunnel, but along the way I'd had help.

I'd had Linda to hold my hand, to listen to me, to prop me up when I wasn't sure I could stay standing on my own. I'd had Linda to walk me through the corridors of the courthouse on the day my marriage ended; I don't remember much more about that day, but I remember her being there with me.

And I'd had Audrey, whom I'd met halfway down the tunnel and who'd showed me how to go the rest of the way through and come out in a better place than where I'd gone in.

I buried them both that week.

And almost as terrifying as facing Audrey's gun was knowing that I understood a good portion of what had driven her and Linda. That I'd been at those same drop-offs in the tunnel where the pain was too bad, the mad too big not to do something—anything—to ease it. Where the frustration, helplessness, and outrage at what someone else was doing and getting away with were grizzly demons that never let me rest.

I'd ridden past those drop-offs and left the demons in the tunnel. Linda hadn't. As for Audrey, family and people who love you get dragged through the tunnel too. Just as she'd been with her sister. And somewhere along the way she'd picked up the demons and taken them on as her own. But the thing was, I knew how they both had felt.

In fact, I felt a little of it on Sunday night, when I drove over to Linda's house to give Steve my key to the place. More still when the smug SOB asked if we could go out sometime.

But I settled for a scathing "Not on your life" and walked away. He wasn't worth any more than that. If only Linda had realized it, she'd have still been here.

The first snow of the season started to fall as I drove from Linda's house back to my new one after leaving my old block for the last time. Flakes fluttered down into my headlights, melted when they hit the windshield, dampened the ground that was still holding on to what it could of the heat.

The lights were on all over the first and second levels of Gramma's and my house as it stood waiting for me up the hill of the front yard when I got there. Danny's car was in the part of the driveway that runs alongside the place. Chloe's was on the street. I pulled into my spot, nosed the hood of the car as close as I could to the garage, turned off the engine, and got out to walk up the stairs to the porch, hoping I could make it all the way to the attic without any obstacles.

I unlocked the door and stepped into the embrace of furnace-generated heat and the sound of laughter coming from the kitchen.

Here? Now? Where somberness and the effects of family turmoil had been lingering an hour before?

I had to check it out in spite of myself.

The girls were sitting at the breakfast bar. My grandmother was standing on the other side of it like a lunch counter waitress, pouring mugs of hot Ovaltine just the way she used to for me when I was a kid. Danny was at the end of the counter, drinking a cup too, and they all turned my way as I joined them.

"Gramma and I had a talk. We made a pact," my older daughter announced once we'd all said hello.

"I'll keep my big mouth shut or pay a ten-dollar penalty," my grandmother told me gamely.

"And Gramma's going to get us wallpaper for our rooms and help us paint them any color we want. I want mine green—*dark* green," Shannon added.

The girls polished off their hot chocolate and headed upstairs then, leaving Danny, Gramma, and me alone.

"I know you don't like me bribing those girls, Jimi," my grandmother said the minute they were out of earshot. "But I'm who got us into these messes lately because I couldn't let up, and I needed to be who got us out of them."

"It's all right," I told her, just happy to have a happy home again.

My grandmother and Danny exchanged a look before Gramma said, "And I mean it too. I'm not saying anything about that dirty bastard. I'm not even going to think about him. From now on he's not even a fly on the wall in my book. No, sir, it's no good to let things like that eat at you and make you act the way you know you shouldn't. It won't happen here. Not anymore."

Not the way it had with Audrey, I thought. But it didn't need to be said.

"Uncle Dad backed out of the New Year's visit too," Danny said when my grandmother sipped her drink and he finally had the chance.

"Damn," I said. "He just can't ever come through, can he? Did Chloe take it hard?"

"Pretty hard. Same as always," Gramma said.

"But she doesn't know we know. Shannon told us," Danny said. "When she did, our Rose Nell here pretended she didn't know anything and went in with her deal to lift Chloe's spirits."

"And you did it without saying anything against Uncle Dad?" I asked.

It was Danny who answered. "Not a word. She just told Chloe how happy we are to have you all here with us and never mentioned her father."

"Aay, you see what we got over here with those girls? He's missing it, that jackass. He threw it away. And I got it. All my dollies here with me. The hell with him."

I had the thought then that maybe this living arrangement would work out after all. Maybe Gramma would be able to keep her resentment and feelings about Uncle Dad under control. A little anyway.

Because we'd all learned that the alternative was a lot worse. Whether it came in words that cut or acts that killed. We all were better off without them. Just the way Audrey had counseled but, in the end, hadn't been able to do herself.

"Well, guys, I think I'm going to call it a night," I said, still craving the solitude of my attic.

"Sure. You go get some rest, Jimi. Tomorrow I'll make you meatballs. You'll feel better."

I laughed at that, said goodnight, and made it as far as the door before Danny said, "You sure you're okay, Jimi?"

I didn't need to think about it. "More okay than I knew."

And so, maybe, would everything else be now.

At least for a little while.